Read what people are already saying about

MY HUSBAND'S SON

'A perfectly paced psychological thriller that sucks you in, sticks with you and **shakes your very core**'

Blooming Brilliant Books

'I would **HIGHLY RECOMMEND** this one to all psychological thriller/suspense lovers!'

The Suspense Is Thrilling Me

'Hauntingly realistic, disturbing and intriguing! . . . This is a **truly gripping**, psychological thriller that I guarantee you won't be able to put down'

What's Better Than Books

'A perfectly paced piece of psychological suspense**. A book that drives on unremittingly, dragging the reader along in its wake'

Cleopatra Loves Books

'I found *My Husband's Son* really easy to read, the author writes well and **keeps the intrigue going throughout** the book'

If I Could Only Read Faster

'There's danger, lies, twists and the ending is literally jaw dropping . . . I would put this **in my top ten reads of the year**'

Nicki's Life of Crime

Deborah O'Connor read English at Newnham College, Cambridge, before going on to become a television producer. Born and bred in the North-East of England, she now lives in East London with her husband and daughter.

MY HUSBAND'S SON

DEBORAH O'CONNOR

twenty7

First published in Great Britain in 2016

This paperback edition published in 2016 by

Twenty7 Books
80–81 Wimpole St, London W1G 9RE
www.twenty7books.com

A CIP catalogue record for this book is available from the British Library.

Paperback ISBN: 978-1-78576-195-9
Trade Paperback ISBN: 978-1-78576-194-2
Ebook ISBN: 978-1-78576-193-5
7 9 10 8 6
This book is typeset using Atomik ePublisher
Printed and bound by Clays Ltd, St Ives Plc

MIX
Paper from
responsible sources
FSC
www.fsc.org
FSC® C018072

Twenty7 Books is an imprint of Bonnier Zaffre,
a Bonnier Publishing company
www.bonnierzaffre.co.uk
www.bonnierpublishing.com

For Alan, my huckleberry friend.

Prologue

He appears from behind the door like a gift. He is alone, his stare daydream-soft.

She sees a chance, steps forward and puts a finger to her lips in warning. Keep quiet. His gaze narrows. But he is not scared, not yet.

She hesitates. Despite everything, he is not hers to take. Then he smiles. Gap-toothed and cresting a thick patch of blond hair. His eyes are a dark, almost black, brown. A beautiful child. She reaches for him.

'Let's go.'

He tilts on his heel, wary.

Her hand around his wrist, she leads him into the corridor. She decides against the lift and heads for the stairs. Before they descend, she checks to see if they have been followed.

Soon the boy is slowing, asking to go back. She tightens her grip and they take the steps two at a time, the red lights flashing in the soles of his trainers. Still he protests. Cajolery abandoned, she half pulls, half carries him until finally they reach the ground floor and find themselves funnelled into a car park. Sheltered from sight by a shallow overhang, she releases her hold and tries to think. What to do next? She stole him on impulse. There is no plan.

While he nurses his wrist, she scans the horizon. In the near distance she can see the neat incision of dual carriageway curving *its way down through the landscape, while to the right is a small clump of houses. She decides on the carriageway. It is the riskiest of the two – between here and there is nothing but open ground; they will be exposed, easy to spot – but if they can make it across they might be able to lose themselves in amongst the small peaks on the other side.*

She takes his wrist and urges him forward, through the grass. They make good progress, but the road is further than she thought. She increases the pace and soon the boy is stumbling, struggling to keep up. Each time she feels him about to lose his footing, she braces and yanks him into the air. He dangles from her hand and his feet lift off the ground. He rights himself, she drops him to the floor and they continue.

They're almost there. Ahead, the traffic roars. At the side of the road she stops to let him rest. There are tears on his face. She glances at the block from which they fled. They need to push on, but she does not move.

The boy senses an opportunity and asks gently to go back.

She considers the possibility. She could release him, let him retreat. He would be reunited with his family and although a small amount of confusion and distress would follow, it would be minimal, soon forgotten.

The boy realises polite negotiation is not working and starts to beg. He gulps down a sob and, for a second, his features contort into a familiar expression.

The arrangement of cheeks, brow, nose and chin is one she has seen before. It feels like finding a match, a key that fits. It seems to make his face shine extra bright.

She grabs his hand and assesses the flow of cars.

'Stay close.'

She waits for a lull in the traffic. As soon as a gap appears, she launches them both into the middle of the road. Then they are running, horns beeping, the air searing her lungs, as they try to make it across to the peaks on the other side, to safety.

1

The day I stumbled upon him was just like any other. I'd been out of town, at a sales presentation, and I was on my way home. I was tired and I wanted to get some wine to have with dinner and so, even though it wasn't the nicest of streets, I stopped at the first place I could: an off-licence.

The place had seemed normal from the outside, but inside was a different matter. A long, thin room, it was badly lit and only slightly wider than your average corridor. The shop was made stranger still by the fact that the till, alcohol, crisps, sweets and cigarettes were all securely displayed some distance from the door, behind a metal cage of brown wire squares.

I made my way to the opposite end of the room and I'd almost reached the counter when a man appeared behind the cage. He noticed me looking and gave it a rattle.

'It might not look pretty, but it works a treat. No shoplifting, no getting beaten up.'

He wore a sovereign ring on every finger and the curl of them through the cage made it look like he'd been blessed with an extra set of golden knuckles.

I laughed politely and peered through the holes, trying to see what was for sale, but then a movement behind the cage caught my eye. I peered closer.

Silhouetted by a single, weak, fluorescent light, I saw a small boy. He was in a shadowy corridor that led to the rear of the shop, rocking back and forwards on his heels. He leant forward, into the light, and I caught a glimpse of his face. And even though it was only a glimpse, my body responded instantly: my armpits blotting my shirt, my ribs fractious with air.

I steadied myself against the counter. I was seeing things. I must be.

I forced my attention back to the man.

'A bottle of . . .' But then I couldn't help myself and my eyes reached over his shoulder, to the boy.

My first instinct was to look for any signs of distress, but he seemed well cared for. Apple-cheeked, his jeans and T-shirt were smart, his blond hair clean and neatly shorn. I tried to work out how old he was. He seemed to be about eight, the same age Barney would've been by now. And then, as I always did whenever I calculated Barney's age, I immediately thought about what age Lauren would be if she were still around.

I realised that the man had followed my gaze to the now-empty doorway. I looked away as quickly as I could and was scrabbling to come up with something that would explain my interest in the back of his shop when he answered a question I hadn't asked.

'He's home sick with a cold.'

The off-licence's door-siren went and a woman wearing a fake Lacoste jumper pushed a pram up to the counter. Without asking what she wanted, the man hoisted himself off his stool and went to the vodka shelf, his hip jowls escaping from his too-tight Newcastle United shirt as he reached for her favoured brand. The woman placed her money in the metal drawer through which all cash and booze was exchanged and, as he pulled the drawer forward, it made a satisfying 'shunk-shunk' noise. The customer snugged her vodka next to the baby, lumpish in his blankets, and directed the pram back out onto the street.

'A bottle of rosé?' I said, pretending to scour the shelves. I was desperate for another look, but I wanted to reassure the man that I wasn't bothered, that the child wasn't on my radar.

'Rosé?' It was as though he'd never heard the word before. 'Not much call for that kind of thing round here.' He sniffed. 'I might have some out the back.' He headed off towards a small room to the right of the counter.

Feeling calmer, I watched as the boy tiptoed out of the corridor and over to the confectionery. Positioning himself directly beneath the Dairy Milks, he placed a foot on the first display shelf and pulled himself up to the rack. He almost had one of the bars in his grasp when he realised I was watching. He froze, his unsupported leg dangling in mid-air. I gave him a wink, letting him know he was OK. Still, he hesitated, not sure whether I was to be trusted.

'I knew we had some somewhere.'

It was the man, returning with a dusty bottle of pink Jacob's Creek.

The boy took his chance, snatched a chocolate bar away from the pile and got down from the shelf unseen. He began to retreat into the corridor, pressing himself flat against the wall. He was almost free and clear when he made the mistake of shoving the chocolate into his jean pocket. The crackle of the wrapper pricked the man's ears and he turned round, whiplash fast.

'What are you doing out here? Stealing sweets again?'

The boy shook his head.

'I don't believe you,' said the man. 'Empty your pockets.'

Slowly, the boy reached his hand towards the pocket containing the chocolate bar.

I didn't want him to get in trouble so I said the first thing that came into my head.

'Champagne. The other thing I need is a bottle of champagne.'

The man turned back to me, the boy's crime forgotten.

'Champagne?' He licked his lips. 'Pricey stuff that.'

I thought about our overdraft. I should change it to something cheaper, but I didn't want to draw any more attention to myself than necessary.

The boy peeped out from behind the man. His eyes were the same dark brown as Jason's, his two front teeth wonky with a large gap in the middle.

I tried to think rationally. Maybe the only reason he seemed familiar was because I was looking at him through the prism of the cage. Maybe it was because its pixelated version of the world mirrored those blocky computer mock-ups the forensic artist had done of Barney at various future ages.

Jason had a line of the mock-ups Blu-Tacked to the walls in the spare room, the fakery of the pictures growing more and more obvious as the distance widened between the last real photo of Barney and the forensic artist's increasingly diluted guesswork. The first image had him sporting a childish bowl-cut, the second a tracksuit top zipped to his chin, and then the 'oldest' had him in a white open-necked shirt, his hair cropped and stiff with gel. In all of the images his face wore the same half-smirk and dead eyes.

Was this him? Could it be?

It didn't matter what I thought. The one person who would know immediately was his father.

I looked through the cage and round to where the man had disappeared into the storeroom. I could hear the chink of bottles being moved as he hunted for champagne. Jason was teaching forty miles away, at a community college. If I called him now, he could make his excuses and be here within the hour. I was reaching for my phone when the man returned to the counter.

'Here you go,' he said, brandishing a bottle of Moët.

I placed the money in the metal drawer and tried for one last look. The boy was sat cross-legged on the floor, oblivious, tucking into his chocolate booty.

Grabbing the carrier of bottles, I backed towards the exit, unsteady in my heels, and tested behind for the door handle. Outside, in the daylight, I half-ran, half-walked to the car.

I tried to straighten my thoughts. My heart felt as fat and red with blood as if it had been my own daughter back there, but finding Barney so close to home after all this time was outlandish. I didn't want to bring Jason here on some wild goose chase, but my reaction to the child had been so immediate, so visceral. That could not, in good faith, be discounted. Still, I hesitated. Should I just call it in to the police?

In the car I dialled Jason's number, but his phone went through to voicemail. Of course. He kept it turned off in class. I started the engine. The man in the off-licence didn't seem to have realised that I'd recognised the boy, but I couldn't be sure. For all I knew, right this minute he might be bundling him out the back of the shop and into a van; already moving the child on to somewhere else, somewhere dark and secret that we'd never be able to find. There might not be much time.

I'd go to the college and talk to Jason in person. I'd persuade him to come back here with me now, before it was too late.

I barrelled down the college hallways, the tick of my heels loud on the herringbone parquet. I reached Jason's classroom and approached the door's small, square window. Inside he was writing on a blackboard, his students sitting around him in a semicircle. He'd just said something that had made them all laugh.

He looked up from his notes and, on reflex, I took a step back away from the window.

The drive had dampened my fervour.

I kept thinking about probabilities.

Ten days earlier there had been another setback in what was now a five-year search for my husband's son. A British family on holiday in Istanbul had seen a boy matching Barney's age-progression photo, begging with a street gang in Taksim Square. It had been a credible lead and everyone had got their hopes up, especially Jason. But within a few days the police were able to confirm the child's connection to a local Turkish family. Jason had been crushed.

After that, what was more likely? That I'd just happened to chance upon Barney? Or that, because of recent events, I'd wanted so badly for someone, anyone, to find him that I'd projected him onto the next child I'd come across?

Jason asked for a volunteer. A track-suited man in his mid-forties came forward and got down on the ground. Jason knelt beside him and, after lifting the man's knee into a right angle, he laid his arm out wide and gently tilted him into the recovery position.

Wearing a blue-and-grey-checked flannel shirt, grey jeans and white Converse low-tops, Jason wore his blond hair undercut with the top kept long and gelled back, away from his forehead. He had a habit of rubbing his hand against the short undercut when he was worried: the friction seemed to calm his nerves.

I tapped on the glass and he looked up. Maybe the last few weeks had skewed my judgement, but I couldn't ignore my gut. I needed a second opinion.

He gave me a questioning frown-smile, trying to work out what I was doing here. I beckoned him out to the corridor and, after setting the class an exercise to be going on with, he made his excuses.

'Everything OK?' he asked as he shut the door. He looked behind me, as though there might be someone there who could offer an explanation for my presence. 'Has something happened?'

'Everything is fine. Just fine. It's just – I was just –' I'd been holding my breath and the words sounded more hurried than I'd intended. 'I know this is going to sound weird. I was in this shop. There was a kid, behind the counter.' I forced myself to say it out loud. 'He looked like Barney.'

His eyes widened but then, within seconds, he recovered his composure.

'OK.' His voice was calm. Five years of countless disappointments had left him cautious.

'I want you to come and have a look. Now.'

'Now?' He looked back at the classroom.

'If we wait then there's no guarantee he'll be out in the open like this again.'

'You're really fired up.'

'I, of all people, wouldn't come to you like this unless I thought it was important. You know that.'

He took a breath and exhaled slowly.

'No stone unturned, right?'

I smiled. This was his favourite mantra.

'Exactly.'

'Let me finish up.' He checked the door window. The students were getting restless. 'I was nearly done anyway. Then I'm all yours.'

'Thank you.' We hugged, my embrace a combination of relief and gratitude, and he returned to the classroom.

It didn't take long for him to assign homework and gather his things and then we were on our way, towards the exit that led to the car park.

Outside, the day had finished with a scorch, the mid-September heat quilting itself over the town, the only sounds the bark-bark of a tetchy dog and the half-hearted wails of a distant siren.

I waited until Jason got into his Golf before walking over to where I'd parked.

Once inside my car, I looked back over to him, ready to coordinate our departure. The sun was shining directly onto his windscreen, a blinding white glare. He hadn't shaved in days and his stubble glittered in the light. I watched as he reached his hand up, ready to flip down the visor, but then he paused. Lifting his face towards the heat, he closed his eyes. It looked like he was offering himself up to the sky.

We reached the off-licence, parked and came together on the pavement. Jason took in the tramp asleep on a bench and the teenage boy trying to balance pushing a pram with keeping control of two unruly Staffordshire bull terriers. Swearing loudly, he was directing his curses evenly between the crying baby and the misbehaving dogs.

'What were you doing in this neck of the woods?'

'I had an area-manager meeting, in Gateshead.'

I took his hand and led him over to the entrance. An illuminated blue sign protruded over the width of the shop's scuffed façade, announcing the off-licence's name – Wine City – in a cartoonish red font. Wires looped and dangled to the right of the sign's edging, overspill from the electrics within.

'The lighting in there isn't great, but it's good enough.' I tried to sound reasonable. 'You'll need to direct your attention out back. There's a corridor.'

For a brief moment I considered the possibility that, if the boy was indeed Barney, his captor might recognise Jason. If that happened, then the man would know we were onto him. It was a risk, but one I decided was worth taking.

Jason pushed back his shoulders and lifted his chin. He didn't seem to harbour any real hope that the child inside was his son.

'Here goes.'

Once the door had swung shut, I took up a position to the left of the shop and waited, braced for the reaction I was sure would come.

Alone, I began to imagine how the rescue might play out if Jason was able to make a positive ID. How the police would force their way in through the front door with a battering ram, how they would disperse inside to secure the area, how Jason would follow behind and find Barney shivering and crying in the corner and how he would scoop him up into his arms and to safety.

But then it seemed like no sooner had Jason gone inside than the door was swinging open and he was back on the street, clutching a soft drink.

'Well?'

'Not Barney,' he said, holding his free palm out flat in apology.

He went to head back to his car and I grabbed his elbow.

'Wait. You don't think there's even a slight similarity?'

'He looks nothing like the mock-ups. The bone structure, his nose. It goes against everything the forensic artists have always said.'

'What about the bloke behind the counter?' I asked, unwilling to give up quite that easily. 'He seemed dodgy.'

'There was no bloke. It was a woman. Maybe he'd finished his shift?'

I felt a tightening at the base of my skull. The beginnings of a headache. I'd thought that once I'd had his verdict I'd be able to put my mind at rest, but now I found that wasn't the case.

'Jason, please,' I said, 'take another look.'

He studied my face, as though searching for an answer. Unable to find what he was looking for, he sighed and, apparently deciding to humour me all the same, returned inside.

Again I waited. I pictured his eyes roaming over the child's hair, build and facial features and held my breath, certain that this time, he would see it.

He seemed to be taking much longer. I let my heart race. Maybe he'd had a rethink. But as he exited the shop he shook his head.

The tightness at the base of my skull began to spread across the rest of my scalp.

'I'm so sorry.' I reached for him but he shrugged me away. 'I thought it was him, truly.'

'No harm done. You did the right thing.' His voice was soft but I could tell he was upset. 'And I know you meant well.' He set his gaze forward, towards where our cars were parked. 'But now I'm tired. Can we please go home?'

4

'Heidi, what are you doing?' shouted Jason from across the landing.

'I need to finish an email,' I said, 'then I'll be right there.'

There was a splosh and I heard the squeak of the hot tap being turned on.

'OK, but hurry up, the water's getting cold.'

I smiled and turned back to the laptop, relieved things were returning to normal. As soon as we'd got home from the off-licence, he'd suggested an early bath together. His way of letting me know that he'd already drawn a line under today. But while I'd been grateful for the gesture, in truth, when it came to the boy, I wasn't done.

While I knew that Jason must be right – if he couldn't recognise the kid as his son then no one could – I was unable to forget him. The way I'd reacted to the child continued to niggle. And so, before joining Jason in the tub, I'd decided to see what I could find on the man who ran the off-licence.

The company I worked for was called Bullingdon's. It supplied alcohol and soft drinks to pubs and restaurants. Bullingdon's had a sister company called Yellow Arrow that did business with smaller-scale retail outlets – vending machines, newsagents, off-licences. Every employee in both companies was required to register any meetings or sales calls in a huge shared database. This meant that if anyone from our sister company had ever had anything to do with the shop we'd been in today it would be recorded on the system. It was a long shot, but I figured that a little research on the bloke behind the counter wouldn't do any harm. If anything, it might serve to put my mind at rest.

Clicking on the *client database* icon, I typed in the name and location of the off-licence and pressed search. Nothing. Maybe I hadn't put the address in right. The database was notoriously sensitive. I cross-checked the details with Google Maps. Wine City, 119 Coatesworth Road, Gateshead. I'd spelt it correctly, but it was easy to see how someone might get the name of the road slightly wrong. I tweaked the address, this time making sure to drop the 'e' from Coatesworth, and once more pressed *search*. Before long, the database yielded a potential hit. It was a match. Filed by a rep named Sharon Hannah, it detailed a sales call she'd made back in June. I opened it up. Wine City traded mostly in super lagers, white ciders, tonic wine and other fortified beverages. Sharon reported that although she had left a variety of product samples on-site, there had been no take-up or further correspondence. Moving down to *client details* I saw that she'd recorded the leasehold of the shop as having been taken over in January of this year by a Mr Keith Veitch.

Veitch. That was a fairly unusual surname.

Opening a fresh window, I typed in his name and hit *search*. He'd only been at the shop for nine months. Where did he work before then? If I could trace this man back more than five years, I might be able to see where he was working around the time Barney was taken, and if he was based somewhere nearby then maybe I could connect him to his disappearance.

The computer finished its search. I looked at the screen, but there was nothing. It seemed that, prior to taking over the leasehold of the Wine City off-licence, the history of Mr Keith Veitch was a blank – for my company's sales records, anyway.

I went back to the name of the rep who had written the report: Sharon Hannah.

Scrolling through the company-wide address book, it didn't take long to find her email. 'Hi Sharon,' I typed. 'Wondering if you can assist me with a client query?' My fingers hovered over the keyboard while I worked out what to say. It would be too odd for me to ask her about the boy outright, but I needed to make sure that if she had noticed anything strange about the man running the off-licence, or the child in his care, she thought fit to mention it.

It was a stretch, but I decided my best bet would be to say I'd been in the shop on non-work-related business and had noticed one or two products for sale that looked like they might be fake. Head Office had recently sent out a series of memos urging us to be vigilant for signs of profit-damaging bootleg vodka and had promised mini-bonuses for anything that led to a successful prosecution. Explaining I didn't want to get the manager into unnecessary trouble, I told her that before I made out an official report I wanted to see if she had noticed anything during her last visit to set alarm bells ringing.

The message sent, I was about to close the laptop when a *new email* envelope popped up in the bottom right of the screen. I felt a tiny ripple of excitement. It was from Sharon Hannah. That was quick – maybe she had noticed something weird about the place and wanted to get back to me right away. But any hopes I had were dashed as soon as I opened the email. Nothing more than an automated out-of-office reply written in turquoise copperplate font, it informed me she was going on extended leave to get married and would respond to my query on her return from honeymoon at the end of October. I checked today's date – that was over a month from now. Shit. I closed the laptop. Enough. Jason would be wondering where I was.

After taking off my blouse I unzipped my skirt and rolled down my tights. Unhooking my bra, I stepped out of my knickers and was reaching for my dressing-gown when I caught sight of myself in the mirror on the back of the bedroom door. I startled, shocked even after all these years, at the sight of my de-robed body. Once upon a time my bra had rested against skin dense with fat. I'd been a size eighteen. All rolls and pudge. Now, instead, there was a neat pear of a ribcage, a flat expanse of muscle in place of the belly that used to stodge low over my knickers.

I pinched at the meagre layer of fat around my hips.

Everyone sees weight loss as a signal you've finally taken control of your desires and appetites. They assume you prefer this smaller, lean version of yourself. They never consider the opposite. That you might be thinner because you lost control, that you prefer your old self. That, if you could, you'd like to go back to how you were. Before.

I cleared the smudged mascara from under my eyes and pinned my fringe up off my face. I'd had my hair coloured its usual dark brown only a few weeks ago, but there was already a smattering of silver roots at the scalp. Twisting the rest of my hair up into a high bun, I reached across to my underwear drawer. Rifling beneath the knickers for the packet of folic acid I kept at the back, I popped a tablet out of the foil, chucked it to the back of my throat and dry swallowed as best I could. Although we had yet to discuss trying for a baby, I'd been taking the supplements for a while. I'd read an article saying new research had shown it was beneficial for women to take folic acid in the months prior to conception so that the body could build up the reserves it needed to create a healthy foetus. I'd seen no harm in starting the course of tablets immediately – I figured I needed all the help I could get.

As I crossed the threshold of the bathroom, I took off my dressing-gown and Jason wolf-whistled. I gave my bum a wiggle and he laughed.

'I thought you were going to leave me alone in here all night.' He held up his hands. 'I'm starting to prune.'

Caramel-skinned and with eyelashes so long they should have belonged to a girl, he had this tendency to dip his chin ever so slightly whenever he looked at me, as though he was shy and this was the first time we had met. A small movement, it was a mannerism reserved for me and me only, a physical tic that harked right back to when we first got together.

I stepped into the tub, my slender frame allowing me to position myself at the opposite end to Jason with room to spare. He'd added too much bubble bath and thick white foam covered the surface of the water.

'I'm worth the wait,' I said, scooping some of the foam onto my palm and blowing it at him. It disintegrated into a snowstorm of sausage and marble shapes and, as they lazed their way back down to earth, some of the shapes descended onto Jason's face and hair. Once they'd settled, he directed his lips at each of the blobs, dislodging them with exaggerated puffs of air.

I moved towards him and closed my eyes, ready for the kiss. As his mouth met mine I heard water slopping over the sides of the bath and onto the floor.

He pulled away, leant back and ducked his head. The moisture turned his blond hair an immediate sheeny black. Resurfacing, he smoothed it from his forehead and blinked the droplets from his lashes. He reached for a bottle of beer balanced on the linen basket. Taking a gulp, he wiped away the sweat on his forehead. I swivelled round so that I could lie back onto his chest. Following my lead, Jason slotted his thighs around my hips.

'A few weeks and it'll be our wedding anniversary.' Steam sheeted off his shins and up to the open window. 'Shall we have some people round? To celebrate.'

'We could have a barbecue? Make the most of this Indian summer.'

'Done.'

He paused, thinking.

'But then we should do something with just us. A meal?'

I imagined the evening to come. The awkward silences, the search for conversation.

'Sounds good.'

I loved being married to Jason. I loved our everyday life together. I did not love our anniversary.

Ask any couple what happens when they celebrate their special day and they tell the same story: at some point in the evening one or both of you will take great pleasure in reliving how you got together in minute detail. You will dwell, misty-eyed, on the first flirtation; retell the moment of your meeting to each other over and over again, with lots of 'and remember when's and 'then you said to me's and finishing of each other's sentences as you marvel at the Sliding Doors twist of fate that helped two become one.

But that never happened with us, and it never would.

Neither of us had ever spoken it out loud, but the only reason our paths crossed was because we had both attended the same conference. And the only reason we were at that conference was because we'd both lost our children. Coordinated by the NSPCC, its theme was child safety and its aim was to improve the communication and procedures between everyone from Interpol to the Scouts. It was held over three days at one of those hotels that are all stale pastries at breakfast, patterned carpets and overheated rooms. Jason and I had been invited, along with members of the police and social services – and other parents who, like us, had had their children stolen from them.

I'd seen Jason on the first morning. I'd just finished a seminar in which I and key personnel from the worlds of teaching and healthcare had spent an hour discussing the inadequacy of DBS criminal record and sex-offenders' register checks as a vetting tool for staff who work or come into contact with children. Afterwards, I'd wanted nothing more than a cup of tea and a seat in a quiet corner, but instead I'd been corralled into coming along to the next scheduled session by our seminar's moderator.

The session was on Megan's Law and Jason was part of a panel there to discuss its various pros and cons. He, along with the other speakers, was given a formal introduction at the start and I remember thinking how unnecessary that was in his case. Jason, along with his then wife Vicky, had endured so much press coverage in the months after Barney was taken that it had driven their relationship to its very public end. I and everyone else in the room had known who he was as soon as we set eyes on him.

Wearing an oversized suit borrowed from a friend, he'd kept rubbing at the shortest part of his buzz-cut hair, near the base of his scalp. With dark brown eyes, a gap-toothed smile and weathered, wind-burnt skin, he looked both older and younger than his twenty-seven years.

I spoke to him that afternoon. There'd been a coffee break and the only remaining free seats had been right next to each other. That night he came back to my hotel room and we'd talked until the early hours. The conversation was erratic. We flitted between funny potty-training anecdotes (it turned out both Barney and Lauren had had a thing for leaving stealth poos behind the living-room curtains) and shy confessionals (Jason revealed he had once been so desperate to talk to his son again that he had resorted to the services of mediums and psychics). Then, as dawn was breaking, we had talked about our new love-hate relationship with sleep. We admitted that we both now struggled with the lottery of what each night may bring. Sometimes we hoped to see our children in our dreams and sometimes we recoiled from the acute cruelty of our own unlimited imaginations. Jason understood that, which no one else could. Our dreams had the power to sustain us just as much as they had the power to destroy us.

Obsessing over our stories was like finally being allowed to pick at a scab on your knee you've wanted to attack for ages, a scab that everyone else has told you to leave alone.

Six months of a long-distance relationship later and Jason had asked me to come and live with him. I didn't hesitate. I packed up the flat in Rochester and moved north within the month.

Our anniversary plans dispensed with, Jason ran his finger through the bubbles and began to talk about a new qualification he wanted to go in for. Were he to pass, it would take him to the next level of first-aid instructor. I nodded enthusiastically, trying to show my support, but all the while my thoughts kept straying back to the boy in the shop.

I didn't want to raise the subject again, but I couldn't get his face out of my head.

'About that boy today –' I ventured, once he was done.

'We've talked about this,' he jumped in. 'You were only trying to help.'

I took a breath, steeling myself for what I was about to say.

'Maybe we should go back and take another look?'

There was a pause in which I was grateful not to be able to see his expression. If I couldn't see him then, for a few seconds, I could kid myself that he'd changed his mind.

'Heidi, no,' he said quietly. 'I asked you to leave it alone.'

'Please,' I said, twisting round to face him. 'What with that mesh cage and the awful lighting, maybe you didn't get a proper view? What harm could it do?'

He took another sip of beer. I decided to keep going.

'Or, if you don't want to go back then maybe we could call

Martin and ask the police to feed it into the investigation? They could do a background check?'

He finished the last of his drink and in one movement, tossed the bottle across the room, into the bin.

'Why are you doing this?' he asked, after a long pause. 'I know you mean well, but believe me when I tell you that that boy was not Barney.' His eyes were bloodshot. 'The forensic artists, they know what they're doing. They've talked me through every new picture, why the bone structure develops as it does, why they think his eyes will now look like they do, why his nose will seem bigger and his mouth smaller.' He propped his feet up on the sides. I looked at the exposed soles. Pocked with tough, yellow callouses and half-healed blisters, they charted his love affair with long-distance running. 'That kid, his face didn't match up to any of it. Not that I could see.'

He was right. Of course he was right.

He let out a breath and, taking my hand in his, used his thumb to start stroking the edge of my wrist.

'It's more than that. As soon as the midwife handed Barney to me I knew he was mine. Everything about him – his smell, the way he looked, the shape of his fingers and toes – all of it meant he was my son. He was only just born, but he knew it and I knew it.' He reached out his other hand and, cupping his palms together, cradled my hand inside them. 'Those stories you hear about babies being mixed up in the hospital and the parents not realising, that could never have happened to me. The connection we had, that bond, it was animal-like.' He released my hand and it dropped back under the water. 'It never went away, even as he got older.

That's why I'm certain the next time I lay eyes on him, I'll know. No matter how many years have passed. There'll be that connection. I've told the police – when the time comes, when they find him, I want the psychologists and social workers kept at bay. For the first while, anyway. I don't need our reunion to be supervised. I'll know him and he'll know me.'

I thought about the family reunions we sometimes liked to watch together on YouTube. The kidnapping back-stories were as varied as they were international. There was the Israeli boy, now man, taken by his father in order to override what he felt was an unsatisfactory custody arrangement; the Florida woman, stolen as a baby from the hospital where she had just been born; the South African girl, abducted aged four, only to be recognised two years later as her mother passed by her on the street.

Jason's particular favourite featured a family in Bogotá whose six-year-old son had been kidnapped and held by a drug cartel for four years. At the time the boy was taken, his father had been a government official responsible for delicate congress negotiations that, if successful, would have resulted in an extradition treaty extremely damaging to the cartel. The boy had been taken as a bargaining chip but then, confusingly, even after the legislation stalled, his captors had refused to release him.

The YouTube clip was made up of grainy, bleached-out news footage and narrated in Spanish. Shot from a distance, it showed the mother, father and three sisters waiting nervously by their car. Behind them were trees. I always thought it looked like they were standing by the edge of a forest. As the video begins, the family are holding hands, searching the horizon, watching and waiting.

Then, off camera, there is the sound of a car approaching. The family stiffen. As the camera pans right, we see a tall, thin boy wearing a football strip emerge from a blacked-out people carrier. As soon as the boy is despatched, the van accelerates back the way it came. The boy stands there bewildered for a few seconds and, almost before he has time to know what is happening, his family are rushing forward to embrace him.

The first few times we'd watched it I'd felt the same as Jason. It was life-affirming. It gave hope. But then I googled the story. It turned out there was a reason the cartel had not released the child, even though he was no longer useful. After he was kidnapped, the boy had been placed in the care of one of the cartel's captains and his wife. The couple were childless and, over time, had genuinely grown to love and care for the boy. They'd claimed that the child loved them too, and so it had been accepted that the child would stay with them for ever. But then, as is often the way in cartels, the captain and his wife were murdered over a territory disagreement. Without them around the boy was a burden and so the cartel had given him back. There had been no mention – in any of the articles I'd read – of how the boy felt about the situation. It was not clear whether he was happy to return to his family or whether he'd continued to yearn and grieve for the people he now thought of as his mother and father.

After that, whenever I watched the clip back, I noticed the split second just before his mother brings him into her arms, when he turns away, and takes a single step back, towards the disappearing people carrier. All I could see in the kid's expression as the vehicle pulled away was loss. His family, the family coming towards him, are now strangers.

* * *

Jason scanned my face, left to right, left to right, over and over, like he was reading a book.

'Look.' He softened. 'It goes without saying I've had a rough ride of it recently. But this is always a stressful time of year for you. You know that. It might be colouring your judgement more than you think.'

He paused, waiting for me to respond. When I refused to meet his eye, he sighed and took my hand. The ends of his fingers were smooth and nubbed. Before he was a first-aid teacher, Jason had been a welder, and the years he'd spent in the fabrication shop still showed themselves in various parts of his body.

'I admit there have been times when I've recognised Barney in every lad I see. But you have to respect me when I tell you that that kid we saw in the shop wasn't him.'

'The boy out in Istanbul,' I said, referring to the sighting a few weeks earlier. 'You only saw a photo of him and yet . . .'

It was like I'd slapped him.

'The police thought there was a genuine similarity,' he murmured. 'And so did I. The story seemed to fit.'

I looked at the part of his body that showed above the water. His loss of appetite these last few weeks was evident in the lean, drawn lines of his chest. I felt a surge of guilt.

'You're right, I'm sorry. I shouldn't have brought it up.' I moved forward and lay myself on top of him. The warm water was slippery between our skins. 'I won't mention it again.' I took his hand in mine and as we webbed our fingers together, I ran my lips over the prow of his collarbone.

He rested his head back against the edge of the bath and once he'd closed his eyes I moved up to his neck and the point at which his stubble tapered to clear, caramel skin. Then I kissed him there, softly. He smelt of sweat and lavender bath foam. Releasing my hand, I dipped it under the water and smoothed it across the neat curve of muscle that angled from his hip to his groin. He shivered. Opening his eyes, he reached for my hand and gently replaced it back onto my leg.

'It's been a long day.' He shuffled out from under me and got to his feet. 'I'm tired.' Water cascaded from his body.

He stepped out onto the mat and the resulting current shifted me into the recline he'd just abandoned. Without him for company the water level dropped considerably. My shoulders and chest were now totally exposed, my nipples pinking the surface.

He wrapped a towel around his waist. Smoothing back his hair, he went to leave. As he reached the door he turned back to look at me.

'Love you, wife.'

'Love you, husband,' I replied on cue.

He smiled. This was a favourite exchange. And with that he was gone.

I looked down at my body. The bubbles had all but disappeared. An oily grey scummed the surface. Hoisting myself to standing, I waited until the water had drained from my limbs and then, making sure to fit my feet exactly into the two damp imprints he'd left behind, I stepped onto the mat.

5

I arrived at my friend Carla's new flat to find her in the middle of unpacking.

'Perfect timing,' she puffed, pointing at a large cardboard box stranded in the middle of the hall. 'Give us a hand carrying that through to the kitchen.'

'And here was me thinking you'd asked me over for the pleasure of my company.'

I bent down and placed my hands underneath the corners of the box. Carla was about to grab the opposite side when she stopped and nodded at my feet.

'Are you going to be all right hefting this in those?' she asked, eyeing up my red patent wedges.

'These old things?' I said, swivelling my ankle to better show off the height of the heel. 'I could run marathons in these.'

'No wonder you've got a dodgy back.' She retook her position at the end of the box. 'OK. One, two, three, go.'

As we lifted it into the air, the pots and pans inside clanked and shifted in protest. We staggered down the corridor into the kitchen and, as soon as we'd deposited it onto the floor, Carla stood up and placed her hands on her hips, triumphant.

'Who needs men?' I said and pulled a bottle of Moët from my bag. I hadn't felt able to share it with Jason (too much of an unhappy prompt) and so it had been languishing in my car since that day at the off-licence. 'Time to claim our reward.'

I popped the cork and was looking for something to pour it into when I realised Carla had a strange grin on her face.

'Carla?'

'Now you come to mention it,' she blushed.

'Carla,' I said very quietly, so as to disguise my excitement. 'Are you seeing someone?'

'I don't know if "seeing" is exactly the way I'd describe it.' She looked to the floor, suddenly coy. 'You can't see much in the dark.'

'You dirty cow,' I said, abandoning my search for a glass in favour of drinking straight from the bottle. 'So who is he?' I asked, the fizz tickling the back of my throat. 'I want to know everything.'

'It's early days,' she said, unable to wipe the smile off her face, 'and he's . . .' She hesitated. 'He's a fair bit younger than me. But he's very mature,' she reassured me, 'and very good-looking.'

I offered her the bottle in a toast. 'To good friends and new beginnings.'

'And getting laid for the first time in two years,' added Carla, taking a glug. Wiping the overspill from her chin, she laughed, her black corkscrew curls bouncing around her face. I laughed, too, enjoying the blood tingle of the drink as it made its way down to my feet.

'Who lived here before you?' I asked, gesturing at the orangey pine cupboards. 'This place looks more like a sauna than a kitchen.'

'Grim, aren't they?' she said, ruffling some vegetable crisps onto a plate for us to snack on. 'Soon as I can afford it I'm going to rip them all out.'

I noticed that her ginger tom, Jasper, was snoozing on the sideboard, his tail scarfed snug around his body.

'The cat seems really traumatised by the move,' I said, rubbing his chin. Immediately, he started to purr.

'As you can see. Which reminds me.' She motioned to the kitchen counter and two shiny silver keys. 'I got you a set cut. That is, if you don't mind looking after him every now and again?'

'Course not, you know that.' I'd often gone over to her last place to feed and check on Jasper whenever she went away for weekends or conferences. Carla was an osteopath and often attended research seminars that might benefit her practice.

I stroked the cat's ears, smoothing them down against his head, and soon he was squinting in pleasure. I realised Carla was watching me carefully.

'How's Jason?' she broached. 'Sounds like he's had a pretty rough month?'

'He has,' I said, fixing my gaze on Jasper. 'But if anything it seems to have made him even more determined to carry on with the search. It's like the disappointment has given him this whole new injection of energy.'

I wanted to go on and tell her about the boy in the off-licence, but I'd promised Jason I'd leave the subject alone. Still, I hadn't been able to forget the effect he'd had on me. It would be a relief to get someone else's perspective, someone neutral.

'And,' – she came closer and placed her hand on my arm – 'how are you? I was looking at the calendar before you arrived and I couldn't help but notice the date.'

'Oh, you know,' I said, trying to keep the tremor out of my voice.

'Lauren would have been twelve?'

I felt my chest constrict and tried to breathe through it.

'That's right, almost a teenager.'

She scanned my face, trying to gauge how I was coping with the topic of conversation before she carried on.

'You're not going into work, are you? Tomorrow, I mean?'

'I am, actually. I want the distraction.' I kept my tone light. 'It'll be easier than moping around the house all day.'

Carla nodded. As always, she understood.

September 21st. My daughter Lauren's twelfth birthday.

The last birthday she had lived to celebrate was her fifth. I'd hired the soft-play at the leisure centre and Lauren and twenty of her friends had spent the afternoon jumping up and down on the giant, plastic-covered foam shapes and bouncy castle until their party dresses were dirty and ripped. During those two hours I'd sat back and watched the fickle world of the five-year-old in action. Allegiances had been won and lost, leaders of different soft-play fiefdoms had been created and usurped, jealousies nurtured and petty grievances cried over. I'd put Lauren's hair into a French plait and tied the bottom of it with a blue velvet ribbon, but after just half an hour in the soft-play, the plait had come loose and her fine brown curls had wisped in the clammy air.

I took another glug of champagne, my throat bulging uncomfortably in its bid to deal with such a large amount of liquid all at once.

'Steady on,' said Carla, taking the bottle from me. 'We've got all night.'

Carla. She was my closest friend in the North-East and, until I'd met her, I had to admit that I'd found forming bonds here to be a tricky business.

Back in Kent, my friends had all been people that I'd grown up and gone to school with. They'd been there when I'd become a single mum at an age when I should have known better and they'd been there when Lauren had first gone missing, staying by my side throughout all the days, weeks and months that followed. With them, there had never been any need to explain or recount or tell, they just knew. But then I met Jason. Everyone had encouraged me to move north to be with him, away from everything that had happened. So I did what they said. I moved. I started again. However, it didn't take me long to realise that adding friends to this new life was going to be more difficult than I'd bargained for.

What happened to my daughter now defines who I am. I'm not sorry about that. I wouldn't have it any other way. She was everything. But, because of this, whenever I meet someone who could be a potential friend, it's impossible to answer even the simplest questions about myself – what I do, who I'm married to, whether I have any kids – without also having to tell them my whole story at the same time.

At first, I would just blurt it all out. Be matter-of-fact about it right from the off. It didn't take long for me to realise that this was too much to expect someone to take in all at once. It was as though my situation required such an initial rush of intimacy – a bit like having an emotional one-night stand – that it was then impossible for the friendship to grow from there in the way that it normally would. And so, after a few unsuccessful attempts at making friends, I tried a different tack, deliberately not mentioning anything about Lauren until I'd got to know the person better. It felt like I was carrying a ticking bomb, but it seemed to work. Until

I finally came clean, that is. Then, they would always try to be sympathetic and nice, but it was obvious they felt like they'd been misled and, after a polite few weeks, they would stop returning my calls and emails.

With Carla though, it had been different.

I'd landed my job with Bullingdon's a month after I'd moved in with Jason and, although I'd done a lot of work in sales before, this was the first gig that had required me to spend most of my day at the wheel. A few weeks in and my shoulders had locked up so badly that I was unable to turn my head from side to side without whimpering in pain. I booked to see an osteopath and that osteopath turned out to be Carla. Divorced and in her early fifties, she was spindle-thin, six feet tall and had spiral black hair shot through with hot pink streaks (she changed the colour of her streaks on an almost monthly basis). With an uncanny ability to read people's bodies (her fingers could feel out the injury, strain or trauma stored deep within your muscle and sinew, no matter how well it might be hidden), she'd heard everything in that very first appointment and it hadn't phased her one bit. It was as though the whole doctor–patient thing somehow legitimised my telling her my entire medical and personal history straight off the bat, as though it had demanded it. And so, what began as a series of professional questions on an assessment form was able to develop into something more, something real. After six sessions on her table, I had a fixed back and a good friend.

I thought again about the boy from the off-licence. If there was anyone I could confide in about this whole crazy situation, it was Carla. I could trust her. She would tell me what I should do.

I pushed myself up onto the kitchen counter and let my legs dangle against the cupboards below.

'If you really want to know, the last week has been stressful in more ways than one.'

'Go on.'

I cleared my throat.

'What would you say if I told you that I thought I'd seen Barney?'

'What now?' She cocked her head. 'Seriously?'

I nodded.

She blinked hard and backed away from me slightly.

'I'd say you should call the police.'

'But what if it wasn't as simple as that?'

As I recounted what had happened and how Jason had been unable to recognise the child in the shop as his son, Carla's face grew serious.

'How did he seem? I mean, who was the boy with? If you think he's being hurt then, whoever this kid is, you need to do something.'

'He seemed OK. I couldn't really tell – it was all so quick.'

She absorbed this for a moment.

'How long ago was it that you saw him?'

'A little over a week.'

'And you still feel the same?'

'The way I reacted to this kid, Carla, honestly, I'm finding it hard to ignore.'

She went to interject, but I held out my hand, stopping her.

'I realise that when I saw him it was under very bizarre circumstances. We were still reeling from the Istanbul sighting. Maybe I saw what I wanted to see?'

Frustrated at being cut off, Carla had puffed out her cheeks, but now, as I acknowledged my doubts, she let them deflate.

'On top of all that,' I went on, 'how likely is it Barney would turn up less than fifty miles from where he first went missing?' I put my head in my hands. 'I keep going round in circles. I think I'm losing it.'

'And you can't ask the police for help? On the quiet, I mean.'

'Jason would be furious. I gave him my word.'

Taking the end of a purple curl between her fingers she pulled it away from her head until it was stretched to twice its usual length. Holding it taut for a few seconds, she let it spring back to shape and clapped her hands, her cheeks the high rouge they turned whenever she drank.

'This is the way I see it. Hearing you talk,' she gestured at how worked up I'd become, 'you simply trying to forget this kid is not going to happen. But I also get where Jason's coming from. Barney is his son and so even now you'd expect him to spot him in a crowd.' She went to reach for the bottle but thought better of it. 'That means the only thing you can do is go back to him with something concrete, something he can't ignore.'

I thought of the database search I'd carried out on the man and the off-licence. 'Like what?'

'I don't know. Maybe there's some connection between this man or this shop and Barney's disappearance. Jason created his own case files, didn't he?'

I nodded. I'd pored over them with him many times when we first got together.

'Why not go through his files again and see if there's anything in there, some detail that was overlooked at the time because it seemed meaningless.'

I could tell she was sceptical, but then so was I. I appreciated her advice all the more for it.

'You're right,' I said, tipping the last of the champagne down my throat. 'Something concrete. That's what I need.'

6

Carla spent the rest of the evening feeding me pitta bread and hummus and insisting I help her alphabetise three boxes' worth of yoga and Pilates DVDs. I made my excuses around ten and arrived home to discover Jason had gone out. He hadn't mentioned having plans. Figuring he'd nipped to the pub for an impromptu pint, I decided to use the time alone to my advantage and went up to the spare bedroom.

Requisitioned as a kind of 'Find Barney' HQ, as well as housing the computer on which Jason monitored various missing persons forums, the room also contained a filing cabinet full of Barney paperwork. Carla had confirmed what I already knew to be true: I needed to find something, no matter how small, that linked the off-licence, or the man that ran it, to Barney's disappearance. And if I couldn't, then perhaps my conscience could rest.

I'd only gone a few steps into the room when I became distracted by the line-up of 'future' Barney sketches Jason had permanently tacked to the wall. Designed to help the public identify Barney as he changed and grew, each time another year passed, the forensic artist would create a new version of what they thought he might now resemble. The police readily offered up these images for consumption, while at the same time being at pains to point out how much harder it was for their experts to produce an accurate projection of a child whose last 'real' photo available showed them at a very young age. Until they reach five, a child's facial features more closely resemble those of a baby; after that, their face gives much clearer indications of the adult they might one day become.

Stepping over Jason's old bag of welding tools, I moved in close to the most recent picture, a projection of an eight-year-old Barney. The artist had styled his fair, almost yellow, hair into a crew-cut and framed his eyes with thick blond lashes. I tried to marry up the picture with my memory of the boy from the off-licence. Jason had been right when he said they didn't match. The hair colour and eyes were the same, but the rest of his features were more doubtful.

I noticed that a corner of one of the early sketches had wilted forward onto itself, revealing a large dent in the plaster. I traced my thumb inside its hollow oval, remembering the day when, a little over a year ago, another sighting of Barney had come to nothing. On that occasion the collision of metal against wood, mirror and glass had been immediate. As soon as he'd got off the phone with the police, Jason had taken his welding tools to this and other parts of the house in a fit of rage that ended only once he'd exhausted himself.

It was always the same. Despite Jason's years of experience at dealing with disappointment, at some later point there was always a cost. Take the last few weeks. Since the false sighting in Istanbul, life had been business as usual. Jason was eating OK, sleeping OK, working OK. But then, little by little, I knew he'd resort to the coping strategies I'd seen so many times before: rising at dawn to go for punishing ten-mile runs, skipping teaching jobs so he could binge-read the files he'd put together on Barney's disappearance, paying heed to the internet trolls who taunted him with false claims of his son's whereabouts. It was like watching a lit fuse. Sometimes it might burn slowly, so slowly that you were lulled into thinking it had fizzled out. But then, just when you were least expecting it, there'd be that nitrate flash.

I withdrew my thumb from the hole in the wall and some plaster dust came away with it. Jason had remained subdued since this last setback. Still, I was under no illusions. Rubbing the pale pink powder between my fingertips, I reattached the picture and took a step back. My stomach noosed tight. Jason's disappointment would produce its normal fireworks, of that there was no doubt. It was merely a question of time.

Barney's five-year-old face stared out at me, his dark eyes wide and questioning. I wondered, as I often did, what Lauren might look like if she were still alive. How tall would she be now? What about her hair – would she have cut and coloured it into the latest teen fashion or would she have kept it long? I thought ahead, to her birthday tomorrow, and what the day might bring. I knew that Mum and Dad would phone at some point and that Mum would probably tell me about the flowers she had taken to her grave that morning. A sharp, small reprimand that I hadn't been there in Kent to go with her. Not that I'd ever wanted to visit Lauren's grave. I found the tiny headstone that marked where she lay to be too solid, too real. In the past, when I still lived down south, I'd preferred spending her birthday somewhere she had loved. For the first year without her I'd gone to the swimming baths and had floated around in the shallow end, remembering her fear and delight when she managed to swim without armbands. The following year, I'd whiled away the afternoon walking the circuit from her infant school to her friends' houses again and again, in a loop, until my feet blistered.

Her past few birthdays though, I found I functioned best if I kept busy. Last year I'd volunteered to attend a sales conference in Swindon and tomorrow I'd deliberately scheduled an entire day's worth of back-to-back client meetings.

I checked my watch. It was just after 10.15 p.m. Wherever Jason was, he'd probably be home soon. If I was going to go through his stuff I'd need to be quick. No longer sure if he used one or all of the drawers in the cabinet, I decided to start at the bottom and work my way up.

There had been a time when I'd have known exactly where to find what I was looking for. In the early days, when we'd first got together, the circumstances surrounding Barney and Lauren's disappearances were our favourite topic of conversation. We'd spent many an evening studying his files together, combing them for clues that might help the investigation. They'd been like those long chats that all couples have when they start seeing each other that go on for hours and hours. But, instead of stories about our school days or our dreams for the future, Jason and I had talked and talked about our lost children. We'd go out for dinner and get so engrossed that our food would go cold. The restaurant would empty around us and the lights would be turned on to try and make us leave. Then, unable and unwilling to stop, we'd go out into the night, blinking and jittery and walk home instead of getting a taxi so that we could keep talking for as long as possible.

As time had gone on though, those sessions with the files had happened less and less, until finally, they stopped completely. It might have been because Jason felt the sessions were no longer necessary (I was now so familiar with the details of Barney's case) or maybe it was something else. Either way, a kind of a Chinese wall had grown up between me and the files. It wasn't explicit. Jason hadn't forbidden me from reading them. However, at the same time, there was definitely the sense that to do so would be akin to looking at his private journal.

Getting down on my knees, I opened the first two drawers, only to discover they contained replacement printer cartridges and A4 paper blocks. Worried Jason might have moved the files without telling me, I gave the third drawer a tug. But it was stiff on its castors or had got stuck and, no matter how hard I yanked, it refused to budge. I needed more leverage. I got to my feet and this time I used both hands. That didn't work either. The drawer wasn't stuck; it was locked. Checking to see if the top one was the same I hooked my index finger around the metal handle and pulled. It slid open to reveal a row of five large lever-arch files. Relieved that Jason hadn't moved them somewhere else after all, I considered the locked drawer. Presumably it contained important papers: maybe the mortgage or insurance documents or Barney's birth certificate? Still, it was odd he hadn't thought to mention it. He must have forgotten. No matter, I could get at the Barney paperwork and that was all I was here for.

Coloured grey with a white spine, each of the files was filled to bursting. I lifted them out one by one, and once they were stacked on the desk I took a seat. Of course, the police had their own mountain of official material to which only they had access, but that hadn't stopped Jason from amassing his own records: one file for every year that Barney had been missing.

I looked at the cover of the folder sitting before me marked 2010 – the year Barney disappeared. The first thing in the file was an Ordnance Survey map folded into quarters. Jason had secured its place in the ring binder by hole-punching the sides. I'd seen it many times before but now, as I opened it out onto the desk, I tried to look upon it with fresh eyes. It contained an overview of the area in which Barney was last seen. Charting three square miles, the left side of the space was dominated by a rectangular block of council flats and adjacent car park and playground. I studied the map as best I could, not sure what I was looking for. Apart from the flats, the rest of the area was overlooked by the low peaks of the Eston Hills and grassland, bisected at one point by the A19. I thought for a moment. The A19 did lead north, towards the town in which the off-licence was situated, but, apart from that slim nugget, there was nothing else of remark.

I moved onto the next page. Printed onto shiny, bluey-coloured paper, it was an architect's drawing of the block of flats from the Ordnance Survey map, named Ashbrook House. The text at the side of the drawing revealed the structure was ten stories high and contained sixty different dwellings. Designed so that the front doors faced out onto the same side, each flat was accessed by open, half-walled walkways that ran lengthways across the stretch of the building.

Jason had marked flat 56 with a large red circle. Situated on the eighth floor, the front door to this particular flat was located directly next to the stairwell that led to the floors below.

Flat 56. The last place Barney had been seen before he vanished, apparently into thin air.

There were many theories about what might have happened to him, some more credible than others. Theories aside, the facts as I understood them from Jason were these:

Barney James Thursby had disappeared on an idle Wednesday afternoon in July 2010. That particular morning, Jason had described how Barney had been up with the lark, bouncing on his and Vicky's bed, blowing raspberries and begging them to come downstairs and play. Eventually, Jason said he had given in and gone down to the kitchen, where he made Barney his favourite breakfast of dippy egg and soldiers.

At the time, Jason had yet to retrain as a first-aid teacher and was still a jobbing welder, helping to construct the burners on a nearby power station. That morning, as he left for work he gave his son a kiss goodbye, got in his van and drove away without so much as a backward glance. From then on in, as per usual, Barney was in Vicky's care. A mobile hairdresser by trade, she often took Barney with her on jobs in order to save on expensive nursery fees. This particular Wednesday, her diary was jammed with back-to-back appointments, and at around 3 p.m. she had headed for her final client. Aged seventy-eight and suffering from mild dementia, Mrs McCallum got upset if Vicky didn't do her weekly shampoo and set on the same day at the same time every week.

As Vicky navigated Ashbrook House's endless flights of stairs with the weight of her hairdressing bag slung on her shoulder – she would do anything to avoid the building's urine-riddled lifts – Barney began to play up. Dawdling behind, he kept grabbing hold of the metal handrail and attempting to swing from it. Vicky would no sooner have climbed three steps than she would have to retreat four, extricate Barney's hands from the railing and direct him back up the stairs. By the time they reached the eighth floor, her patience was starting to wear thin.

The temperature inside Mrs McCallum's tiny flat didn't help. The air dense with the muggy crackle that precedes a storm, there'd been a distant rumble of thunder as the old lady shuffled down the hall to make tea. Barney, meanwhile, instead of following behind, had tried to make a cheeky diversion into the living room. Ever since Vicky had started bringing him here he'd been obsessed with the tantalising collection of clown figurines that Mrs McCallum kept on the hearth, and took any chance he could to get at them. Vicky knew his game, though, and managed to grab him just before he reached the fragile ornaments. Her hands around his waist, she scooped him up onto her hip and took him through to the kitchen, where she plonked him on the floor and gave him his bag of Matchbox cars.

So far that day she'd been just about able to cope with the heat but now, as she came back up to standing, she found she had to wipe the sweat from her face. Setting her hairdryer and brushes out on the kitchen table she asked if she might open the front door so as to let some air flow through to where she worked. Mrs McCallum agreed and soon Vicky was hard at work on the old lady's sparse curls while Barney brummed and beeped his toy cars around her feet.

Barney played nicely but, every now and again, he would whizz one of his cars a little too fast across the lino and, when it came into contact with the hall carpet, it would fly up and spiral off into the distance. The first few times this happened Vicky would stop what she was doing and watch while he went to retrieve the toy. The hall dog-legged its way to the front door and she didn't want him wandering out onto that high walkway. Before long, though, she became absorbed in her work and her attention waned.

Afterwards, Vicky had claimed she could never be sure how long it took her to realise that Barney was gone. It could have been two minutes; it could have been ten. Whatever the timings, initially, she put his silence down to those clown figurines. Marching into the living room, she'd expected to find him, headless clown in hand. But the room was empty. Still thinking he must be up to mischief, Vicky had searched the rest of the flat, peering under beds and behind sofas. That, too, proved fruitless. Starting to panic, it was then that she ventured outside and onto the walkway.

Terrified he'd climbed the barrier, she looked over the side; she'd told the police she had braced herself for the sight of his prone body on the ground, eight floors below. But again, there was nothing. Her subsequent relief was mixed with a growing confusion. Where was he?

While an increasingly befuddled Mrs McCallum looked on, half her scalp in rollers, Vicky had sprinted back and forwards across the walkway, checking the nearby lifts and stairwells. When there was no sign of him there, she lunged for the stairs, taking them three at a time. It was at that point the thunderstorm finally broke, the heavy rain saturating the dry ground.

'Somebody help me. I can't find my son. Please help me. My son is gone.' Although she wanted to scream this out loud, Vicky had tried not to let the words crystallise in her mouth. She felt as though if only she could keep those terrible sentences at bay she'd prevent what seemed to be happening from ever becoming a reality, ensuring this would all be nothing more than a horrible scare: that day where for a few awful minutes she thought she had lost her beautiful boy.

I looked at the thin black lines demarcating the car park on the architect's drawing and imagined Vicky standing there in the rain. Desperately trying to spot the red dash of Barney's T-shirt in amongst the wet cars and motorbikes, she would be praying that his face would suddenly appear and that, within minutes, she would be scolding and cuddling him for giving her such a fright.

The drawings contained floor plans for every storey of the building and Jason had written in the people thought to be living in each flat at the time. Where possible, he had also listed any other salient information pertaining to them. I did a quick scan of the names and details listed. I knew it was unlikely, but I wanted to make sure that a Mr Keith Veitch, the guy from the off-licence, hadn't been a resident. As I searched for his name I was struck, as always, by the insalubrious nature of Ashbrook House. There was no Keith Veitch, but among the 154 people Jason had noted, there were three prostitutes, one drug dealer and two registered sex-offenders. One of the flats was derelict and regularly used as a doss-house by local drunks and addicts.

The question of whether or not someone from the flats had been involved in Barney's disappearance was something Jason obsessed over endlessly. Since we'd got together, he must have talked through dozens of different potential scenarios. Had Barney wandered off and been taken on the spur of the moment by someone who wanted a child of their own? Had a nearby paedophile noticed Barney's regular visits to Mrs McCallum's flat and, when he'd appeared at the door that day, managed to lure him away to who knows where? Had he been taken, used and then killed? Or was he still alive, suffering God knows what kind of abuse?

Another possibility the police had considered was that someone who had been visiting the flats had taken Barney. The police thought it significant that he disappeared the same week the fair had been in town. The fair was based on the grassland a mile or so from Ashbrook House, and kids belonging to the fair families had been seen hanging out in the playground at the bottom of the flats on more than one occasion. The one thing no one could figure out was why, if Barney had been taken, he hadn't screamed or put up a fight, and an explanation for this was that he had gone with the children from the fair. In awe of any kid who was older or bigger, he would have happily followed them wherever. However, intense questioning of everyone involved revealed nothing, and they were soon allowed to travel onto their next pitch.

Mrs McCallum, meanwhile, had proved to be an unreliable witness. Often confused, she couldn't remember Barney being in her flat that day. This was not unusual. Her reality was a shifting one. As far as she was concerned, the Vicky that came to do her hair was the Vicky from five years previously, a lively young thing who had yet to have a child or a husband.

Once Mrs McCallum's inability to corroborate Vicky's statement got out, it added fuel to the conspiracy theory that Vicky, or Jason, had been involved in Barney's disappearance. Some in the press, along with an army of armchair internet detectives, liked to speculate that the reason Mrs McCallum was unable to remember Barney was not because of her dementia but because he was genuinely never there. In carefully worded articles and cruel, uncensored forum posts they posited scenarios in which Vicky had done something, accidentally or intentionally, to hurt Barney before she arrived at Ashbrook House and had then conjured the whole unlikely wandering-out-of-the-flat story as a way of exempting herself from blame.

I returned the architect's drawing to the file and flicked ahead. The next page in the folder was a plastic wallet containing four photo composites. These were the people reported as being seen in or near Ashbrook House in the days before Barney went missing. Individuals who, despite repeated appeals, the police had been unable to identify. I pulled them out and set them next to each other. The first showed a bald man with bulging cheeks and a mean line for a mouth. The other two, also men, looked to be in their forties and early twenties, respectively. The middle-aged guy had a long, thin face with a goatee beard while the younger one had a pierced eyebrow and hair shaved close to his head. The fourth photofit, meanwhile, was of a woman. Sporting a large mop of frizzy hair, she had small, round eyes that seemed to disappear into the depths of her face and a snub nose.

I tried to compare the three men against my memory of the manager from the off-licence but, apart from his sovereign rings and football shirt, he was a blur. I should have paid more attention, but at the time my focus had been on the boy.

I was about to move on to the next entry when I heard the front door click.

'Heidi?' panted Jason. 'Are you home?'

My stomach clenched. Shoving everything back into the files, I heard the jingle-clunk of him putting his keys on the hall table followed by the tile-patter that meant he was in the kitchen.

'Heidi?' he shouted again, out of breath.

I'd almost got everything put back in what I hoped was the order I'd found it when his trainers thumped up the stairs.

I was halfway across the room, about to make my escape, when I remembered the four suspect photofits. They could be useful. I ran back to the cabinet, got out the file, removed the sketches, folded them into quarters and shoved them into my jeans pocket. Replacing the file, I slid the metal drawer shut and was ready to go.

My ear against the door, I waited for Jason to clear the landing and slipped out of the spare room. Tip-toeing into the bathroom, I flushed the toilet and appeared drying my hands.

'There you are,' said Jason, re-emerging from the bedroom.

I was all ready to feed him some line about my having only just got back from Carla's when I realised his hair was dark with sweat. He'd been running, at this hour. Reaching his thumbs into the neck of his T-shirt, he hunched and hooked it over his head.

'How far?' I asked, trying to disguise my concern.

He got down on the floor, unlaced his trainers and removed his socks.

'Fifteen miles,' he said, wincing as he peeled the soaked fabric from his reddening toes. He held out his wrist and nodded at his watch. 'I did a personal best.'

I looked at the door to the spare room and the files contained inside. Finding something in there to connect Barney's disappearance with the off-licence was going to be a long-drawn-out process. I'd return to it soon but, in the meanwhile, the boy's face would continue to gnaw at me.

Jason stretched his arms and yawned.

'I need a shower.' He pulled down his shorts and stepped out of them, towards the bathroom. His body was lithe and strong. Clean lines of muscle pulled tight over caramel skin, it seemed to pulse with the after-effects of his run.

'Wait.' I took a step forward and cupped my hands around his face. 'How about some company?' I brought his mouth to mine. His lips were salty with dried sweat. He returned the kiss but then, seeming to think better of it, he pulled away. Reaching down to the floor for his abandoned shorts and T-shirt, he screwed them into a ball and held them in front of his chest.

'You go on and get into bed and I'll join you when I'm done.'

'Promise?'

'I promise,' he said, backing towards the shower, and with that he closed the door.

7

The next morning, I was up and dressed before first light. In the end, Jason had taken so long in the shower that I'd fallen asleep. I hadn't heard him come to bed. Now, while he slept on, his arms surrendered high above his head, I took the alarm clock from the bedside table, perched on the old nursing chair we kept by the window and pulled the curtain to one side. Leaning forward, I placed the clock on the sill and waited for it to reach 6.07 a.m.

6.07 a.m. The time twelve years ago that Lauren, vernix-waxed and mewling, had made her way into this world.

In my hand was an old silver pocket-compass. Lauren's compass.

A few boxes of books, clothes and pictures aside, as time had gone on I'd gradually come to part with most of her things. Everything except this compass. A small heavy weight at the bottom of my bag, I tended to carry it around with me always, its presence a comfort I couldn't do without.

While I waited for the minutes to pass, I popped the catch and ran my thumb over the disc's bevelled glass. Her favourite thing by far – none of her teddies, dolls or gadgets came even close – Lauren had acquired it on one of our weekends at Mum and Dad's caravan in Whitstable. Trailing us around the town's junk shops, that day she'd been pouty and restless, impatient to return to the arcades and bags of pink candyfloss that ballooned onto the streets. But then, mooching through a tray of old coins and mariner tat, she'd come across what she'd thought was a watch. Engraved with an elaborate thistle design, it had a flat back, smooth except for a miniscule indented hallmark, and was topped with a metal ring loop that, when spun, gave out an ear-piercing ratchet-and-pawl burr. Clicking open its pull-fit catch, she'd brought it over to show me, fascinated by the mother-of-pearl dial, elaborate wind-rose and triangular degree markings. After I'd explained how it worked and what it was for, she'd stalked off into the far corner of the shop and, pretending to be lost, had flipped it open, her eyes widening as the needle pivoted north.

When it came time to leave, I'd asked her to return the compass to its tray, but she'd refused. Clutching it to her chest, she had pleaded with me to buy it. It wasn't expensive, maybe £10 or so, but, careful not to give in to her every whim, I'd said no. Still she'd continued to beg. Getting down on her knees, hands clasped, she'd promised me her pocket money, her favourite teddy, the birthday bike she'd set her heart on, anything so long as she could leave the shop with this old compass in her possession. Lauren Maisie Brogden. Aged four and three-quarters, curly of hair, bruised of knee and now, with the compass I of course eventually agreed to purchase, amateur explorer extraordinaire. A child with a chuckle so throaty she sounded like an old man; a child who insisted she read *Father Christmas Needs a Wee* three times a night every night (regardless of the time of year), once with me, once with Grandma and once with Grandad. Lauren Maisie Brogden. Proud owner of a fish called Bob and awkward teller of jokes. 'What did the fish say when it hit the wall?' she'd ask, pointing to Bob shimmying around his tank. 'Damn.' And then, before the punchline had time to settle, 'Do you get it Mummy? Damn. The fish is swimming underwater and so it hits a dam, which is this thing that keeps water in one place. But when you say it out loud it's the same as the swear word. Do you see?'

I checked the alarm clock: 5.56 a.m. Not long now.

Lauren Maisie Brogden.

It had taken me some time to realise I was pregnant. My periods had always been a bit all over the place and so, at first, hidden by the extra three stone I carried then, Lauren had stayed like a secret inside me, growing and swimming and making herself at home for my entire first trimester before she'd decided to show herself. Five months later and hours into a feral labour, she'd made up for those meek beginnings in spectacular style. With Mum at my side, cheering me on as best she knew how, I'd spent the night in hospital mooing and growling until finally, just as dawn was breaking, I'd roared Lauren out of my battered body and onto the bed.

Whenever Jason saw pictures from that time he would struggle to recognise me. I was so much bigger. But then, with Lauren gone, food became like dust. Unnecessary, unpalatable, forgotten.

The weight loss changed my face in ways I could never have predicted. Suddenly my eyes seemed bigger, my chin pointed, my cheekbones pronounced. In the first year without Lauren I couldn't walk down the street without people stopping to offer their condolences. Nowadays, apart from the odd puzzled glance, I can go about my daily life in relative peace and for this I am grateful.

I looked out at the row of Victorian terraces opposite. Identical in every way to our side of the road, there were no front gardens.

Instead, a single stone step acted as the tiny boundary between house and pavement. We'd bought the house just before we got married and, although it and the surrounding area were nothing like the orchards, fields and coastline of my youth, I'd grown to think of it as home. Built on a hill, our house was situated at the very point where the incline began to steep down to the town below. A river town – 'the steel river' Jason said they called it – its communities had been raised and fed around its ability to forge, smelt and temper. Nowadays, the steel industry existed here only in small, tentative pockets, pockets that Jason used to work, just like his dad and his dad's dad before him.

I angled Lauren's compass up and tilted it into the silty morning light. The needle wobbled for a moment and then lodestoned north, towards the iron-gored Eston Hills and beyond. North to where, right now, the boy from the off-licence was probably fast asleep. I wondered if he had a bedroom to call his own or if he was being kept locked up somewhere dark and out of the way. I tried to remember how the shop had looked from the outside. Did it have an obvious cellar or a basement?

On the bed behind me I heard Jason stir, and for a brief, ridiculous, second I worried he was somehow able to listen in on my thoughts. There was another rustle of duvet and then the bed-frame gave a loud, telltale creak. He was getting up. Padding across the room to where I sat, he reached his arms around my shoulders and leant his head against mine. I breathed in his sour sleep smell and for a moment I let my eyes close. We stayed like that a while and then, as he came back up to standing, I felt him tense. He'd registered the time on the alarm clock. I worried he might say something. That, despite his better instincts, he might try and find the words. Instead he stretched across to the dressing table, picked up my round brush and set about slowly pulling its bristles through my hair. And then he did it again and again, so gently, over and over, the repetition like some silent morning prayer.

I looked at the alarm clock: 6.03 a.m.

Lauren had disappeared while playing on her bike outside Mum and Dad's caravan. I had chosen that precise moment, the wrong moment, to pop back inside and start preparing lunch. She was out of my sight for less than two minutes.

Where had the boy from the off-licence spent last night?

I realised that Jason had stopped brushing my hair and again I worried he could hear my thoughts. Then I saw the clock.

As the final digit changed from a six to a seven I made a decision.

I had to go back and check on the boy. I needed to get a second look. I needed to be sure. Next chance I got, I was going back.

8

I reached the incline at the bottom of the street and the car strained against the gradient. Changing down to first gear, I pressed on the accelerator and began the slow climb. Most people were home from work and the slope was dense with parked cars, every windscreen alight with the setting of the soft September sun.

As intended, since my morning ritual the day had vanished in a haze of meetings and calls. I planned to dispose of the rest of my waking hours with a light supper, hot bath and early bed. Jason wouldn't mind. He taught an evening class on Thursdays and wouldn't be back till late.

I reversed into the nearest space I could and was locking the car when I noticed Mum. Parked further up the hill on the other side of the street, she was sitting with her hands clamped to the steering wheel, her arms out straight as though braced against some impending collision. I crossed the road and knocked on the window.

'Mum?' She startled out of her reverie and opened the door.

She studied me for a second and then creased her mouth into a smile.

'Heidi, sweetheart.'

Wearing a green wax jacket over a cream polo neck, I realised that in the months since I'd last seen her she'd had her hair cut. Where before there had been a neat swing of brown caped low on her shoulders, there was now a short, sleek bob, parted in the middle. Tucked behind her ears, the new style exposed her delicate jawline and plump, diamond-studded earlobes. It suited her.

'What are you doing here?'

'I didn't mean for you to see me. I just wanted to check you were OK.' She put her key in the ignition. 'I'll go now.'

'You drove all the way from Kent to check on me?'

She gave me a look.

'Shall we talk about what happened last year?'

'That was a misunderstanding.'

'I called you five times this morning. Five.'

'I was at work. If you can't get hold of me and you feel worried, you should phone Jason.'

She blinked fast and reached up to fiddle with the diamond in her left ear.

'Do you want to come inside?' I removed my hand from the car door and saw that I'd left a smudge on its buffed black paintwork. 'Jason's teaching. I could make you something to eat.' At the mention of his name she looked down at her lap. 'Or there's a park at the top of the hill.' I gestured behind me. 'Stretch your legs?'

She took a few moments to consider and, after buttoning up her wax jacket, got out of the car.

We embraced briefly, Mum squinting at the houses to her left and then, across the road, to my front door.

'It doesn't bother you?'

'What?'

'Coming straight out onto the street like that. Just your hall, your door, the step and then the pavement?'

I made a start up the hill. Mum scurried to catch up and we walked the rest of the way in silence, the low sun pushing our shadows forward onto the path. I looked at the collection of spindly grey limbs forging ahead. Stretched out like this, my shadow seemed to be holding Mum's hand, our arms swinging in perfect time.

We reached the park and headed for a row of metal benches in the corner. A long, narrow scrub of grass overlooking a children's play area, the space was full of people throwing sticks for a variety of skittish, twirling dogs. We took a seat and almost instantly the cold began to seep through my skirt. As it hit the back of my thighs I shivered. Mum pulled her wax jacket close.

'We went to visit her grave first thing and then your dad spent the rest of the morning in the garden.' She pulled her jacket even closer and the fabric made a crumpling, cardboard sound. 'You know he's taken to finishing off the edges of the lawn with my nail scissors?' She clicked her tongue and I tried not to flinch. 'They're so clogged with grass, I think I'm going to have to buy a new pair.'

When I'd first realised Lauren was missing, I'd run into the caravan's small living room to raise the alarm with Mum and Dad. Clicking her tongue, Mum had dismissed my panic and instead had offered benign theories about where she might have gone. After asking neighbouring holidaymakers to help us search the park section by section, we'd walked around, calling Lauren's name; Mum, all the while, was certain that she'd wandered off in search of one of the collie dogs that belonged to the family in the van next to ours.

I wrapped my arms around my chest and looked at the children's play area, empty except for a gaggle of teenagers packed into a small, dark space underneath the slide. The dropping sun had spread a buttery glow over the swings, climbing frame and roundabout. The teenagers were smoking and talking in low, serious voices; the tips of their cigarettes pinpricking the gloam, orange against black.

'I never noticed before. There aren't many trees. Not like home. The orchards. Is that why you moved?'

'Orchards? What have orchards got to do with anything?'

'It is hard to imagine her in a place like this. Does that help?'

'Mum, can we talk about why you're here?'

'Twelve years old today.' She pulled a fingernail across the needle-cord on her jacket collar. The ridged material vibrated dully. 'You were awful at twelve. Answering back, kissing boys, shortening your skirts.' She nodded at the teenagers under the slide. 'Smoking out of your bedroom window.'

I did a double take. All these years and she'd not once let on she knew. When I was fourteen I'd gone through a phase of lighting up a sneaky fag every night before bed. I'd fancied myself as Madonna in *Desperately Seeking Susan* and used to blow the smoke out the side of my mouth, taking care not to inhale too deeply as it made me feel sick. We'd lived in a modernist, seventies bungalow, the same bungalow occupied to this day by Mum and Dad, and my bedroom window, facing out onto the back garden, had been perfectly positioned, or so I'd thought, for acting out my Madonna fantasies.

'Don't be so naïve,' said Mum, registering my surprise. 'You used to reek of fags. Thank God you grew out of it. Disgusting habit.'

I smiled at the memory. I used to hide the butts in a pencil case, depositing them in the rubbish bin at the end of our street on my way to school. That street. That bungalow. I'd spent more time living there then I cared to admit.

I'd moved back in when I was six months pregnant. It had seemed to make sense. People ask about Lauren's dad, but I only ever knew the bloke's first name: Shaun. Lost to the blurry memories of stand-up sex in a nightclub toilet – unsurprisingly, I never saw or heard from him again. And so, my meagre salary barely able to support myself, let alone a child, I'd jumped at the chance when Mum and Dad had suggested the idea. Still, after nearly a decade of renting with friends, living back with my parents had taken some getting used to. Lauren had spent her first few months in the Moses basket in my room, below the same window I used to smoke out of. Then, when she was old enough, she'd moved into a cot in the bungalow's third, smaller bedroom. Situated down the hall, it had once been earmarked by Mum and Dad for a sibling that never came. The day I claimed it for Lauren, Mum had been thrilled.

The last sliver of sun disappeared from sight. The park was cast into a thick, purply dusk. I looked at Mum. She was staring at the darkening sky, the nub of her chin tucked into the top of her polo neck.

'I like your hair.'

She reached up and, misjudging her new length, found herself grabbing at her jacket collar.

'I thought it more befitting a woman of my age.'

'Don't be silly. You looked great; you still look great,' I said, nudging her gently.

She smiled and nudged me back.

'I had the radio on during the drive up.' Her voice was bright, as though she'd sensed an opportunity and was glad to act on it. 'They were talking about how long women leave it to have a baby these days.'

I stiffened.

'They said once you get to forty your chance of getting pregnant in any given month is just five per cent.' She stopped and turned to face me. Her thoughts seemed to have jack-knifed in some other direction. 'Did you have to go into work today?'

'I don't want to talk about it.'

'When I couldn't get hold of you . . .' She tailed off. 'It was like last year all over again.'

'When are you going to stop obsessing about that? I was away, at a sales conference. You couldn't get hold of me because I was busy.'

'They had to break down the door.'

'I have a bad back. I took one too many painkillers on an empty stomach.' I slapped my chest. 'I'm fine. As fine as I can be. Just like you and Dad.'

She slunk a little lower into her polo neck.

'Look,' I said, dropping my voice an octave. 'It's been a hard few weeks and today is always difficult but Jason takes good care of me.' I searched for something I could use to reassure her. 'We're going on holiday soon.'

'Oh?'

'Gran Canaria. The hotel is lovely. It overlooks the beach. We'll be there out of season so it should be nice and quiet.' I imagined the blue seas and sand to come. I realised I wasn't just saying it to make Mum feel better. Jason and I needed this holiday. It would give us a chance to relax and get back on track.

I reached for her hand.

'Stay tonight. I don't want you driving all that way here and there in one day.' I squeezed it hard. 'Please.'

She screwed up her eyes and leant forward, towards the skyline.

'It really is quite odd. I keep looking and looking and still, I haven't been able to spot a single tree.'

I released her hand back into her lap and got to my feet.

'It's getting late. Come on. I'll walk you back to your car.'

9

I waved Mum off and continued down the hill to our front door. Inside, the house was dark. I was about to turn on the hall light when I heard the squeak of chair against floor tile.

'Jason?'

'Back here,' he shouted. 'In the kitchen.'

I made my way down the passage and found him sitting at the table.

'Has there been a power cut?'

'The electric's fine.' He got up, came round to where I stood and kissed me lightly on the mouth. Easing my bag off my shoulder, he unbuttoned my coat, slipped it away from my body and offered me a chair. I let myself sink down onto the wooden seat and sniffed. The central heating was on full and its warmth had mingled with something sweet and vaguely familiar. I took another sniff, deeper this time. The air was thick, syrupy almost.

Jason pulled up a chair opposite.

'I know you like to mark today in your own way but this year I wanted to do something for you.' He cleared his throat. 'And for her, for Lauren.'

He twisted round and reached towards the sideboard. Holding whatever it was with both hands, he brought it forward and placed it on the table in front of me. I squinted in the gloom.

'I had to order it special.' There was the rasp of a lighter being struck. 'It was tricky to track down, but then someone on the internet pointed me in the right direction.' The lighter's yellow flame bounced and once it had settled he held it next to a pink birthday candle. As the wick caught and flared, a weak disc of light spread out onto the table below. I looked down and saw that the candle was wedged into the middle of a small, triangular biscuit. The biscuit was golden brown and decorated with tiny strips of orange peel and granules of sugar that twinkled in the light.

I recognised it immediately.

'Infar-cake.'

Jason smiled and reached for my hand.

'Dreaming bread,' he said quietly.

I moved my face in close to the plate and breathed deep. I'd come across infar-cake only once before, on holiday on the Isle of Mull. Its salty-sweet tang was unique. I broke away a corner of biscuit and placed it in my mouth. Rolling the crumbs around on my tongue, I felt the sharp granules of sugar soften and dissolve.

'Is it OK?' asked Jason. 'I spoke to the lady on the phone. She told me this was the right type.'

I squeezed his hand.

'It's perfect.'

Lauren and I had gone to Mull with Mum and Dad when Lauren was three. Dad had always wanted to go and so one week in May we'd rented a cottage and set off for the Hebrides. A few days in, I'd suggested Lauren and I explore the rock pools on a nearby beach. We'd had a great morning looking at the tiny fish and crabs that populated each enclave of water and had got so into it that we'd walked from one end of the beach to the other. By then it was lunchtime and so, instead of returning to the cottage, I'd led us into a village in search of a café. We soon discovered that the village contained nothing but a few fishermen's houses and a small shop that sold basic groceries. We were both starving and so, instead of trekking all the way back to the cottage, I'd decided to improvise.

Inside the shop I grabbed some bread, cheese and crisps and as I waited to pay I noticed a plate of what looked like flat triangles of some kind of bread for sale on the counter next to the till. They resembled a more solid version of an Irish potato farl. The shopkeeper noted my curiosity and explained that it was homemade infar-cake, a kind of shortbread, and that it was a local specialty. I added two of the odd-looking biscuits to my basket, and while the shopkeeper bagged them up she winked at my empty ring finger and told me that some people called the biscuits dreaming bread and that it was tradition to break the cake over a bride's head on the threshold to her new home.

Outside the shop, sitting on a low wall overlooking the Atlantic, Lauren had surveyed the strange, crumbly biscuit with suspicion. But then her hunger had got the better of her and after tentatively nibbling a corner, she had devoured the whole thing in less than three bites. Licking her lips, she had pushed her fingers back inside the greasy paper bag in search of leftover crumbs and had declared it the most delicious thing she had ever tasted, more delicious even than Phish Food ice cream.

I'd told Jason about that meal when we'd first started seeing each other. He'd taken me away for the weekend to a tiny stone house in Windermere. The first night there, the weather had blustered at the windows the same way it had in Mull. I'd told him that, despite the rain and being stuck in a small cottage with Mum and Dad, it had been a great holiday. The best.

The pink candle wax had started to drip and harden onto the biscuit.

'Thank you.' I blew gently.

With the light gone I blinked, disorientated. Sitting on that park bench earlier had left every muscle packed tight against my bones but now I felt them start to loosen. I thought about telling Jason how Mum had been there waiting.

He seemed to sense the change in me. He got up, came round to where I sat, lifted my arm and put it around his neck. Then, placing his hands underneath my legs, he scooped me up off the chair and carried me out into the hall.

I let my head fall heavy on his shoulder. His flannel shirt was soft against my cheek, his chest beneath it warm and firm.

He reached the bottom of the stairs and slowly turned sideways on. Taking care not to bang my feet on the walls or banister, he began his ascent, hushing and soothing me with tiny words and noises that formed a language all our own and before we reached the top of the stairs my eyes were already closed, asleep.

10

The following week I had a window of free time before my last meeting of the day, and I took my chance. I drove to the off-licence, parked across the street and grabbed my bag. Inside were the photofits I'd taken from Jason's file. It had been five years, but I hoped that if the manager of the off-licence, this Keith Veitch, was one of the unidentified suspects seen in or near Ashbrook House when Barney disappeared, I'd be able to match him to a picture, no matter how much he'd changed in the meantime. More than that, I hoped to get another look at the boy. I needed to know if he would provoke the same reaction in me. I needed to know if I was imagining things that weren't there.

Putting the composite of the woman with frizzy hair to one side, I laid the images of the three men onto the passenger seat. The bald guy with the hamster cheeks seemed to be of a similar age. Trying and failing to remember whether or not Keith had hair, I moved on to the second man, the one with the goatee. He had a slim, almost gaunt face. I thought of Keith's hip jowls. Maybe he'd spent the intervening years gaining weight? It was possible. Finally, I studied the man with the shaved head and pierced eyebrow. He looked to be in his mid-twenties, whereas I remembered Keith as more around the forty or fifty mark.

Memorising their faces as best I could, I left the photofits in a pile, locked the car and was about to cross the road when a portly man holding a clipboard appeared in the off-licence doorway, a middle-aged couple in tow. I watched as the man with the clipboard pointed at the shop's exterior. He seemed to be showing the couple around. I lifted my gaze up, to the blue and red Wine City sign. There, fixed on the wall above it, was a large LEASEHOLD AVAILABLE board.

I felt a twist of anxiety. After only nine months in the job, Keith Veitch was moving on.

Still watching the estate agent, I stepped into the road. I didn't see the van.

I put out my hands to break my fall. As the road's gravel made contact with the soft, private skin of my palm I twisted and hit the floor side-on. When I looked up I could see something black, its surface grooved with zigzags. It was a tyre. The tyre of a parked car on the street. Beyond the tyre I saw the scattered contents of my handbag, my business cards flapping in the wind.

I must have been in pain, but all I could think was how spongy the van's bumper had felt against my thigh bone and how surprising that was.

The driver ran round to where I lay.

'She came out of nowhere,' he kept saying as people started to gather. 'I braked just in time.'

I became aware of someone kneeling over me.

'Don't move her. She might have hurt her back.'

There was a growing murmur of voices. I looked in their direction. Trainers, flip-flops and slip-on leather shoes filled my vision.

I knew I had to convince everyone I was OK, otherwise an

ambulance and the police would be called. They'd contact my next of kin, Jason. It wouldn't take him long to figure out why I'd been here, on this street.

'It was my fault. I wasn't looking where I was going.'

It hurt, but I forced myself to sit up.

'I think we should call someone.' This was the driver again. 'My insurance.'

'I'm OK, honestly.' I mustered a smile.

'Are you sure?' asked the man at my side. I looked at his face. He seemed genuinely concerned. In his fifties, with blue eyes, and cheeks crevassed with acne scars (most of which were hidden by a brown beard). His chest and shoulders were bull-solid, his arms thick with muscle.

'I don't want any fuss,' I said, wincing at the searing sensation in my hip.

He didn't seem convinced. Still, he nodded and stood up.

'I'll take care of her,' he said, addressing the driver and small crowd on the pavement. 'You can all go on your way.'

He began gathering the strewn contents of my handbag. I watched until I saw him retrieve Lauren's silver compass and then set about finding my shoes. Somewhere during my tumble, my stilettos had fallen off.

'How about something to warm you up?'

I looked at my arms. I was shivering.

'And maybe a plaster for that knee?'

I let him help me to my feet and into a café a few doors down from the off-licence.

'She's had a bit of a bang, that's all,' he declared to nobody in particular once we were inside. He sat me on one of the fixed red plastic two-seaters that furnished the place. 'Kimberley, can you bring a mug of tea?'

A chubby girl at the till responded with a nod.

The man crouched on his haunches and moved in close to look at my knee. Remembering myself, I tried to hitch down my skirt, but it was no good – from where he sat it was impossible for him not to see my underwear. He stroked the outer circle of the wound with the pad of his thumb. Beneath his greying forearm hair, I could see two tattoos. Too faint to be professional, the one on his right declared an allegiance to Celtic Football Club, the one on his left outlined a winged naked woman, a large anchor placed diagonally across the length of her body. They were the kind you do with a needle and ink from a biro. The kind you see on sailors. Or ex-cons.

I looked around to see who else was in the café. There was only one customer. An old man eating his full English and reading the racing pages. Every now and again the long multi-coloured ribbons that hung above the entrance would fly up and brush him lightly on the back and he would tut at them as if they were a naughty child. A blackboard spelt out the daily specials in chalk and a clear-fronted Coke fridge hummed in the corner, dust balls dancing around the air vents where its bottom met the floor.

'Is this place yours?'

'It's not mine, but I'm in charge here, if that's what you mean.' He wiped his fingers on his black-and-white-checked chef's trousers. 'I'm Tommy.' He squeezed my hand. 'Tommy Bibbings. Nice to meet you.'

'Heidi,' I said, not giving out my surname. I always did this. I didn't like to tell strangers anything that might help them recognise me in case they started offering their sympathies about Lauren or Barney or both.

'I was at the counter when I saw him hit you,' he explained. His accent sounded Glaswegian but had blurred around the edges, suggesting he hadn't lived there for some time.

I decided to go with a half-lie.

'I wanted a cold drink,' I said. 'I've been driving all afternoon. I'm a sales rep.'

'Got distracted?' he asked, staring at my knee.

'I suppose.'

He looked up, studying my face for a second before he spoke again. I wondered if he thought I might be concussed.

'After what just happened, I think you should call it a day on the sales front.' He sat back on his heels, his eyes now perfectly level with the gap in my skirt. He didn't even pretend not to look. 'You should get someone to come and pick you up.' He nodded at my wedding ring. 'Maybe your husband?'

I sipped my tea and tried to work out my next best move. The estate agent and leasehold sign were worrying. How long did I have before Keith and the boy disappeared, possibly never to be seen again? This afternoon was clearly a write-off and, although I'd come back another time soon, I didn't want today to go completely to waste. Maybe my rescuer knew something that would help?

'I stop at that shop quite often,' I said, trying to steer the conversation. 'The bloke in there is really friendly.'

'Keith? Yes, he's quite the chatterbox.'

He knew him. Good. Realising it would seem odd if I started quizzing him on Keith straightaway, for the moment I decided to change the subject.

'You don't sound like you're from round here?'

He paused before answering, smiling in a way that suggested we were both playing at some game.

'Neither do you.'

'I'm from down south originally. Kent. You?'

'Clydebank. Just outside of Glasgow.'

We were both quiet then. Like awkward teenagers.

'When did you move here?'

'Do you miss home?'

We spoke at the same time, our sentences colliding into each other.

I realised the girl behind the counter, Kimberley, was watching us. I caught her eye and she pretended to be engrossed in wiping down the work surface.

'I don't think it will scar.'

'What?'

'Your knee, the cut.'

'Oh, good. That's good.'

We seemed to have reached some kind of an impasse and, not sure what else to say, we stared at each other. Tommy was the first to look away.

'I'll get the first-aid kit.'

As he retreated towards a cupboard at the back of the kitchen my phone rang. It was my boss, Yvonne.

'Where are you?' she asked before I could say hello. 'The meeting is in five minutes.'

My final pitch of the day. Shit. My stomach lurched; a sudden, rollercoaster drop. In the chaos I'd forgotten all about it.

'I was about to call,' I lied. 'I'm not going to make it.'

I noticed Tommy half-turn towards me, trying to listen in. I cupped my hand over my mouth and lowered my voice.

'Upset stomach,' I said, offering the first excuse that came to mind. I didn't want Yvonne or, indeed, anyone to know where I was in case the information somehow found its way back to Jason. 'I ate one of those garage sandwiches at lunch. I'm in a public toilet now waiting for it to stop. Can you get him to reschedule?'

'He wants to see you. You're the one he has the relationship with.'

I held my silence.

'OK, I'll try,' said Yvonne eventually, not happy but unable to argue. In two years I'd called in sick all of once. 'I'll let you know how I get on. Feel better soon, Heidi.'

I used my thumbnail to worry at a whorl of dried ketchup on the table. I felt terrible about missing the meeting, but I'd make it right with the client. Take him out for dinner somewhere nice as an apology.

I turned back to see Tommy returning with a green plastic box, a white cross on its side.

'Everything OK?' he asked, clicking it open.

How much had he heard? What would he make of my lie?

'Work,' I said, shoving my phone into my bag.

As he dabbed at my knee with cotton wool, I picked up the plaster he'd set out. Decorated with a forlorn-looking Eeyore, a bandage over his right ear, it hailed from an Elastoplast multi-pack that included Pooh, Tigger and Piglet.

'How come you have these?' I asked. 'Do you have kids?'

'I don't,' he said, 'but we have lots of wee lads and lassies coming in the café and they like to put them on.' He chuckled. 'Whether they've hurt themselves or not.' An expression I couldn't quite get a handle on flickered across his face.

I was trying to come up with another question, something that would give me the information I needed, when he patted my leg. 'All done.'

I examined the Eeyore plaster now covering my knee.

'Thanks for your help. I appreciate it.'

He got to his feet and looked down at me, as though he wasn't sure how to respond.

'I better get back to my kitchen,' he said, eventually. 'Nice to meet you, Heidi.'

11

Back home, I dumped my handbag on the front step and rootled around in it for my keys. My hip was already throbbing and now, as I returned to standing, I blanched at the pain. Hoping it was nothing a few tablets and a night with my feet up couldn't sort, I was about to put the key in the lock when the door opened.

'Thank God,' said Jason, pulling me inside. 'There's already loads of people here.' He wiped his hands on the blue-checked apron tied around his waist.

I looked at him blankly.

'The barbecue.' He waited for me to respond. When I didn't, he shook his head. 'You forgot.'

'The barbecue, of course,' I said. We'd talked about it only this morning, but I'd been so focused on my plan to go back for another look at the boy that, as soon as I'd left the house, it had vanished from my mind.

Jason was about to return to the kitchen when the doorbell rang.

'More guests,' he sighed, squeezing past me.

'Carla!' He greeted her with an exaggerated bow.

My ears pricked up. This was an unexpected bonus. If there was anyone I could talk to about what I'd seen this afternoon, it was her.

'Jason, Heidi,' she said, giving me a wave hello.

Wearing red lipstick and hooped silver earrings that brushed against her neck, I saw her hair streaks had been re-dyed a vivid, electric blue. A young man stood next to her.

'This is Mark.' She squeezed the man's arm and beamed like he was a prize she had just won at the fair.

'Glad to meet you, Mark,' said Jason, pulling him close to shake hands so he could give Carla a secret thumbs up behind his back.

I smiled and widened my eyes to show her how impressed I was with her new catch. At least twenty years younger, I now understood the source of her giddiness. Wearing jeans, an open-necked shirt and navy suit jacket, he was even taller than Carla and had wavy black hair swept back from his forehead, green eyes and a rosebud pout.

'Hope you don't mind me gatecrashing?' he said and, without waiting for Jason to answer, followed Carla inside.

While Jason went to tend to the barbecue, I stowed my handbag on the sofa in the living room and headed through to the kitchen. Mark was still there, alone.

'Drink?' I asked, hobbling over to the fridge. I needed to take some ibuprofen and soon.

Distracted, he didn't respond.

I followed his gaze as it fell upon the portable defibrillator and two fire-blankets Jason had fixed to the wall, a list of printed instructions stuck up beside them. The defibrillator was the kind you normally only see at emergency points in train stations. Everything you needed to stop a fire or start someone's heart, all in one convenient mounted spot.

'Mark? Lager?' I asked in a diversionary swoop. I was now standing right in front of him. I didn't wait for a reply and put the can in his hand.

'Thanks,' he said, belatedly.

He still hadn't made eye contact with Jason or I. But then we were used to this. It often happened with new people. They felt that perhaps they should say something, some words of condolence or sympathy, and sometimes they did. Having to chat to people we'd only just met about how well we were or weren't coping with the loss of our children was always hard and, when I and Jason would talk about it in private, we would always snip at how, though well intentioned, most folk were thoughtless and needed to learn how to keep their mouths shut.

Carla had been in the garden but now she re-entered the kitchen, went over to Mark, whispered in his ear and giggled. Smiling benignly, he let her lead him outside and over to the bench we kept pushed up against the back wall. I watched through the window as she motioned for him to take a seat. Once he was settled, she arranged herself on his knees, wrapped her arms around his neck and nuzzled her cheek against his.

I could not stop thinking about what I'd seen earlier. That estate agent showing people around did not bode well. What if Keith were to move on before I was able to establish the child's identity? I looked at Carla and Mark. I was itching to talk to her, but I decided I'd be better off trying to get her on her own at some point later in the evening.

Placing a couple of painkillers on my tongue, I washed them down with a mouthful of cold rosé and wondered how I'd go about explaining my injuries to Jason. There was one very simple excuse I knew he'd buy without question: high heels. Regardless of the sometimes ankle-twisting consequences, they were the one wardrobe staple I couldn't be without. I wore them all the time: to work, to the supermarket, to long walks in the country. Most people assumed it was because I was so short and, while this was true to a certain extent (stilettos allowed me the dignity of being able to reach the higher shelves of the supermarket without asking for help), in reality, there was more to it.

It was hard to explain, even to myself, but by wearing heels – things that by their very nature made it difficult to walk – I found I could force myself to stay conscious of the act of putting one step in front of the other. Yes, they hurt and, yes, sometimes they made life more difficult but, for me, that was kind of the point. Wearing them meant I never switched off to the sensation of the ground striking my ball, sole and heel; wearing them meant I never grew complacent about going forward, onward, towards whatever the future might bring.

I considered the Eeyore plaster on my knee. It was conspicuous. Jason would ask where it had come from. I reached for the first-aid kit. It would be easy to replace it with something anonymous and flesh-coloured.

As the anti-inflammatories began to dull the ache in my hip, I emptied a tub of coleslaw into a serving bowl and looked out at the crowd already here. We didn't have a huge space, but it was enough to comfortably host about twenty people, roughly the amount that seemed to have turned up tonight. It had been a concreted wasteland when we moved in, and Jason had set about renovating it immediately. Fitting a small deck outside the kitchen door, he'd used a thin gravel path to divide the rest of the rectangular space into two, laying lawn on the left and a row of raised beds on the right. I looked towards the end of the garden and the gate that led out to the back alley. A small group of Jason's first-aid-instructor pals had segregated themselves there and were nursing cans of lager, their bodies turned into each other, in some kind of huddle. Tesh and Anth meanwhile, welders Jason used to work with, were busy tormenting him while he tried to tend to the barbecue. Taking turns to run up and steal the tongs he was using to dish out the sausages and burgers, they would strut around the garden, brandishing them in the air like castanets, briefly returning them to Jason's grasp, only to steal them again the second he wasn't looking.

In the early days, when we'd first got together, normal stuff like inviting our friends round for a barbecue had never felt right. We'd both agreed it felt like some kind of admission. That it was as though we were saying that we accepted what had happened. But, back then, participating in anything more than the bare essentials of breathing, eating and sleeping had felt wrong.

Lately though, I'd started to realise that remembering our children and carrying on with our lives didn't have to be mutually exclusive. That we didn't have to live in self-enforced purgatory. Still, despite that, I couldn't get away from the feeling that taking part in these ordinary things felt fake. Like we were playing dressing up with a cardboard sword and a curtain for a cape.

Jason had set up his iPod and speakers on the wall near the raised beds and I noticed someone squatting down in front of them, fiddling with the buttons. He was finding it difficult to balance, with his knees veering so far out to the side that he looked like he might topple to the floor at any moment. Even from behind

I recognised who it was instantly: Martin. Or, to use his proper title, DS Martin Gooder.

Jason and Vicky's family liaison officer (FLO) since the day Barney went missing, the detective had been the main point of contact between them, the investigation and the media. Supposed to remain objective and professional at all times, he'd inevitably become very close to them as the years had gone by. Protocols and guidelines aside, I knew that Jason now considered him a dear friend first and a police officer second. I imagined Vicky felt the same way.

Before long the music changed and, satisfied with his choice, Martin tried to stand up. He made it up to his knees but then he wobbled and staggered backwards. It looked as though he was going to fall over but then, pushing his upper body forward with a kind of awkward, Cossack-style jump, he managed to right himself. Retrieving his drink from the wall, he ran his hand through his reddish-brown hair. Clipped short and parted in the middle, it resembled the part of a donkey's mane that sprouts up between its ears.

I headed outside and made my way around the garden, greeting everyone I had yet to say hello to. I noticed that Carla had detached herself from Mark for the first time since she'd arrived. Sitting on the bench, she was watching him acquire another plate of sausages from the barbecue. Finally – my chance to talk to her about this afternoon. I was about to make my way over to where she sat when, out of the corner of my eye, I noticed Mark gesturing to the high fences that corralled our garden.

'What's with Fort Knox?' he asked Jason, laughing at his own joke. Hearing him talk, I realised his voice had a jolting, public-school cadence I hadn't noticed first time around.

I saw Carla shake her head and try to throw him a not very subtle warning look. But either Mark didn't notice or he didn't care.

'Fort Knox?' Jason put down his tongs. 'We got them because...'

It was like watching an actor trying to remember his lines. I sprinted over to him as quickly as I could and nooked my head in under his arm. He looked down at me with a grateful smile.

'They were quite low when we first moved in. Some might say they weren't even proper fences at all.' He nodded in my direction. 'It meant that, for modesty's sake, Heidi had to sunbathe in her swimming costume and Heidi doesn't like tan lines. Do you, love?'

On cue, I shook my head.

'One badly timed white stripe on the shoulder or bum can lead to A. Fashion. Disaster.' Jason spelt out the last three words in the air with his hand. 'Then one day I had this brilliant idea. Fences. Big massive fuck-off fences.' He put down the tongs he'd been holding. He'd really hit his stride now. 'Big tall fences mean Heidi can sunbathe naked, just as God made her.'

Everyone laughed and we relaxed, confident there would be no more questions about the fences, for this evening at least.

The truth of the matter was a little different. When the fences were low we could see over the sides to the neighbours' gardens and their kids' swing sets, slides and deflated footballs going mouldy in corners. And so, even though it meant that, when the sun moved round, it could get quite dark out there on the grass (so dark there was no way I would ever, ever get a tan), as soon as we could afford it we'd put ten-foot panels in and Jason had spent a day creosoting them.

An hour later and we were running low on glasses. I left Jason teasing Carla about Mark ('Where did you find him? Studs.com?') and went to get some more from the cupboard. I wasn't gone long but when I stepped back outside I was met by the thump and splinter of human hitting wood. It sounded like someone had collided with our garden fence. Looking around, I saw Jason standing over Mark, horizontal in the flower bed. Jason's fist was raised. Next to him was Carla, her face in her hands.

'Jason?' I looked around for help. 'What happened?'

But everyone apart from Martin, who was already making his way over, remained where they were. After placing one hand on his shoulder, the detective used his other hand to ease Jason's fist back to his side.

'I – he – I . . .' struggled Jason as Martin guided him away from the scene.

Mark went to stand up, but his navy suit jacket had caught on the bush prickles he'd fallen on and so he was left to scrabble around in the dirt alone. Martin returned and tried to help. Seeing this, Jason ran back to where Mark lay and leant in so close to Mark's face that, when he next spoke, he speckled it with spit.

'You sneaky lying fuck!' shouted Jason. 'How dare you lie your way into our house and start asking questions like that, saying things like that.' He turned to face the rest of us. 'He's a bloody journalist.'

Martin had been in the middle of helping Mark up to standing but, on hearing this revelation, he let go and Mark fell back into the shrubbery.

'Oh fuck,' said Carla. Grabbing a half-open bottle of vodka from the picnic table, she retreated to the bottom of the garden.

Jason, meanwhile, began to pace up and down the decking.

My first instinct was to go and comfort him but I knew that, before I could, I needed to get Mark out of the house, otherwise Jason was liable to take another swing at his face.

Taking one arm each, Martin and I lifted Mark up to standing. Upright, he smoothed back his black hair, unperturbed. I realised this probably wasn't the first time this had happened.

As we escorted him through the kitchen to the hall, he slowed down to look again at the pictures of Barney and Lauren on the walls.

'Don't you dare look at our children,' I said, opening the front door and pushing him over the threshold.

After telling Martin that I had it from here, I went to close the door, but Mark put out his hand, blocking the way.

'Do you believe them? Jason and Vicky. What they said happened that day?'

'Don't start with that rubbish.' I knew he was baiting me, but I couldn't help but respond. 'Of course I believe them.'

He pushed the front door back open a little wider.

'It's just certain things.' He paused. 'Certain details about that day and the days after. They don't add up.'

'I think it's time for you to leave.'

He wedged his foot in between the door and the doorframe.

'I want Jason to find Barney,' he said, trying a change of tack. He put his hand on his heart. 'I could help with that. If the pair of you were to give me an interview, something that shows the . . .' – he chose his next word carefully – 'unique nature of your marriage, then I could do a big piece, something that would make people sit up and take notice.'

I crossed my arms.

'You could?'

Mistaking my response for enthusiasm, Mark continued with his spiel.

'Absolutely, people are so interested in the unusual bond you two must have.'

I shook my head.

'Lying your way into our home aside, how could you do this to Carla?' He shrugged and pushed back his hair. 'What am I talking about? You don't have a conscience. Your sort never do.'

As I went to close the door, he reached into his jacket and produced a card.

'If you ever want to talk,' he said and slotted it into the small pocket at the front of my blouse.

He was lucky I didn't catch his fingers in the jamb.

12

I went into the kitchen and slumped against the wall.

'Are you OK?' asked Martin. 'Maybe you should have a sit-down?'

Unable to process what had just happened, I didn't respond, and soon I felt the detective's flat, heavy paws on my shoulders. Gently, he pulled me forward, back up to standing and led me through to the living room.

'Stay there,' he instructed once I was on the sofa. 'I'm just going to check on Jason.'

Grateful for a few minutes to compose myself, I sank back into the cushions. Fiddling with the edge of the plaster attached to my knee, I gave the living room a once-over, trying to see if there was anything out of place. I knew Mark would have seen the photos in the hall but hopefully he hadn't managed to snoop in here. Not that we had anything to hide. There were no shrines with candles and offerings or anything like that, nor did we have any more pictures of our respective children on display than any other mum or dad. Still, the thought of him staring at the private pictures, the ones we'd deliberately never released to the press, made my stomach turn.

The kids were different ages in the pictures. Some were snaps of them as tiny tots in the bath or paddling pool while others were posed, uniform-clad photos from when they first started at nursery or infant school. Lauren and Barney in their square pine frames, made brother and sister by their absence.

If Mark had made it as far as the living room then he would almost certainly have noticed Barney's fire engine in pride of place in the centre of the coffee table. Jason and Vicky had given the toy to Barney for his second Christmas and it had instantly become his favourite plaything. Made out of metal, its red paintwork was battered and the cab at the front where the miniature model drivers sat still had bits of old biscuit encrusted in the windows. Jason had told me how, when Barney disappeared, he and Vicky had slept with the toy between them every night, its sharp metal edges prodding them in the hips. He'd said that it had been losing access to the fire engine – far more than making sure he got his half of the house or the furniture – that was the thing that had worried him most. Vicky had felt the same way. Somehow, he explained, they had come to an agreement where they promised to share it between them until Barney was found. Every two weeks, one of them would take custody of the fire engine, jealously holding it in their possession until they had to give it back to the other person by 6 p.m. on the allotted Monday.

My gaze went back to the photos. We only had one wedding picture out. We'd placed it right in the centre of the windowsill. Taken in the gardens of the registry office, it showed us walking together, holding hands. The photographer had caught the moment at which Jason was about to reach round and give me a kiss, his right foot still in the air, about to step forward.

I thought back to what Mark had said about wanting to do an article on us. What was it that horrible website had said when they'd first found out Jason and I were in a relationship? Some horrible joke about where we must have met – the Dead Kid Club, the Dead Kid Dating Agency – something like that.

Martin appeared in the doorway.

'Jason's upstairs and your guests will soon be on their way.' He paused, weighing up whether or not to relay the next piece of information. 'Your friend's in a pretty bad state. I think she'd like to apologise.'

Before I had the chance to reply, Carla elbowed her way into the living room. At some point during the course of events she had removed her earrings. Holding them together, she was pushing her fingers against the edges of the silver hoops as though she was trying to crush the circles in on themselves.

'I'm so sorry,' she said, her voice shrill. 'I should have realised someone like that would never be interested in me.' She spoke without making eye contact. 'He was so keen to come tonight, I thought it was because he wanted to meet my friends. I thought it meant things were getting serious, that he wanted to become part of my life.' She shifted from foot to foot. 'I am such a fucking idiot.'

'It's not your fault.' My words came out as a shout and she jumped. 'It's just –' I tempered my tone. 'You brought him into our house, Carla.'

'I know.' Her eyes went to the pictures of the kids on the mantelpiece. She retreated towards the hall. 'I should probably go.'

With Carla gone, Martin came into the living room.

'How are you doing?' he asked and sat back on the sofa without looking, straight onto my handbag. 'Sorry,' he said, trying to stem the tide of purse, keys and make-up spilling out over the cushions.

I noticed a flash of silver about to disappear down the back of the sofa – Lauren's compass – and grabbed it quick.

'It's OK,' I said once I'd returned it to my bag. I picked up a lip gloss that had rolled onto the floor and offered it to him. 'Unless, of course, Candy Shine is your particular colour?'

We both laughed, relishing the light relief, but then as our laughter disintegrated we found ourselves in silence, Lauren and Barney staring out at us.

'That journalist,' I said after a few minutes had passed. 'He said people are starting to forget Barney. Do you think that's true?'

Martin turned to face me and, not for the first time, I was reminded of a schoolboy who had yet to adapt to his new, adult-size body.

'I can't speak for the general public, but I can tell you that I and the rest of the team have not forgotten and will not forget. We take every lead, no matter how small, very seriously; that is to say, I mean –' he said, going red in the face. 'What I'm trying to say is we follow them up as best we can with the resources we have available.'

'That's good to know,' I said, realising I was circling around what it was I actually wanted to talk to him about.

'When you say every lead' – I knew I'd promised not to mention anything to Martin about the boy, but after seeing that estate agent today, I was terrified that if I waited too long they'd disappear, leaving me unable to ever find them again – 'what exactly do you mean by that?'

He swallowed, his Adam's apple bobbing out over the top of his T-shirt.

'Some of the biggest cases in history were cracked because someone made sure to follow up on what was an apparently minor detail. Whether it was Peter Sutcliffe and his broken tail light or Dennis Nilsen and the blocked drains.'

'How easy is it for you to get the team to do a background check on someone? I mean, do they need just cause, or can they do them on whomever they like?' I fished.

'If you're asking me to check out that journalist from today then I can't help you.'

'Not the journalist.' I stopped, not sure whether to say any more.

'What is it Heidi? What's bothering you?' He pressed a hand down on his sprout of hair, flattening it against his skull. 'You know you can trust me.'

'Jason would kill me if he knew I was even talking to you.'

'Come on, spit it out,' he encouraged. He removed his hand and his hair sprang back up on end.

'I saw this kid the other day, a boy.' I stopped, trying to gauge his reaction. He was listening intently. Reassured, I decided to carry on. 'There's no other way to put it,' I said, 'except to say he looked like Barney.'

I waited for his eyes to narrow and readied for the polite yet sceptical response I was sure would follow.

'What does Jason think?' he asked quickly. I relaxed. He was taking me seriously. 'Has he seen the child?'

'This is it,' I explained. 'I was so sure, I took him there immediately. He's certain it wasn't him.' At this admission I saw a small shift in the detective's face, his excitement gone. 'I know it doesn't make sense,' I said, trying to maintain his credulity, 'but I can't get this kid out of my head and now it seems that he and the bloke I saw him with might be moving on.'

'What is it you want me to do?' he asked evenly.

'At the very least, I wondered if you could get the team to do a check on the guy looking after him? Find out his name and history, if he's on the sex-offenders' register, that kind of thing.'

He sat up straight and cleared his throat.

'If you think there is a genuine likeness then I have an obligation to report this to my senior investigating officer who in turn will have an obligation to investigate. If you want to do that then I can put the wheels in motion. I'll need you to make a formal statement and Jason will have to do the same.'

'Does Jason have to be involved? It can't be done on the quiet?'

'In order to begin the investigation we would need to get you both on record.' He was about to continue when something seemed to catch his eye.

'Get us both on record about what?'

I turned to see Jason standing on the threshold to the living room. His shoulders were slumped, his chest concave. He looked like a punctured balloon. The crackle that had surrounded him these last few weeks was gone. The journalist showing up today seemed to have broken the storm.

'Heidi was telling me about a child you saw the other day. Heidi thought he looked like Barney?'

Jason looked at me.

'I keep thinking about him,' I said, scrambling my defence. 'I was asking if they could look into it.'

'I thought we'd agreed. You were just . . .' He faltered and turned to Martin. 'Judgements were definitely clouded.' He turned back to me, his voice gentle. 'Investigating is a waste of time. It would divert manpower away from valid leads. We'd have to get Vicky involved. Think it through.'

On reflex, Martin looked at me. Embarrassed, even after all this time, to talk about the old wife in front of the new.

'Have you told Vicky?' asked Martin. 'Has she seen the child?' And there it was again; the apologetic eye flicker.

'Heidi?' Jason looked to me for a response.

I blushed.

'It does sound ridiculous.'

'So?' asked Martin. 'Do you want me to talk to my SIO?'

'That's up to Heidi.'

I met Jason's gaze. He smiled, as though some kind of an understanding had passed between us.

'I was seeing things I wanted to be there.' I bit my lip. 'I shouldn't have brought it up.'

'That's settled then.' Jason's smile broadened. 'Now, if we're all done here, I could do with some help sorting out the garden.'

'Of course.' Martin got to his feet. He put out his hand to stop me from doing the same. 'Don't worry, I've got it.'

Alone in the living room, I collapsed back into the cushions. The sound of footsteps in the hall soon made me sit back up. It was Martin.

'That kid,' he said, checking to make sure Jason wasn't loitering somewhere behind. 'What you said about following up every lead.' He hesitated. 'I shouldn't be doing this, but if you can get a photo then I might be able to pass it on to our forensic artist. It's not an exact science, but they could compare him with the age progression images they've already done.' He made a camera sign with his hands. 'It needs to be a good, clear picture of his face, otherwise it won't work.'

I bowed my head in thanks.

'I can't promise anything, but maybe we can find a way to put your mind at rest.' At this, he headed back outside, presumably before Jason could notice he was missing.

Feeling lighter than I had in days, I hugged myself and smiled. A picture, of course. All I needed was a picture.

13

Later, with the house to ourselves, we set about putting things straight. I focused on the kitchen while Jason kept to the garden. Every now and again our paths would cross. I'd place a rubbish sack next to the back door or Jason would transport a stack of stray plates to the sink. Each time it happened was a surprise. As though, until that moment, we had forgotten the other person was there. We didn't acknowledge each other or even make eye contact; instead we'd weave and dip, hands in the air, hips sucked back, locked in a deft, silent tango.

The first time I knocked into him was by accident. We were in front of the fridge, going in opposite directions, and my elbow caught him sharp in the ribs. I didn't apologise.

Ten minutes passed and I was busy veering a heavy saucepan onto a high shelf when he appeared with a clutch of dirty pint glasses. I made sure to lurch towards him, enough to make one of the glasses smash to the floor. We stared at the shattered fragments, glittering on the tile. I held my silence. He was the first to break away, in search of the dustpan and brush.

After that he left me to it and retreated upstairs. As soon as I finished tidying, I followed him. He was in the spare room. I hovered by the closed door for a moment, listening, and then went inside.

He was standing opposite the wall of Barney's age-progression photos. I looked down. Spread out on the floor was a collage of colour photographs. Family snaps of Barney at various ages. Seeing the images positioned next to each other like this, it was easy to grasp the dislocation between the real, historical pictures of Barney on the carpet and the imagined work of the forensic artist on the wall. I watched as Jason shifted his gaze from the wall to the floor. Up and down. Back and forwards. Over and over. I could only guess at the chasm that must exist between the two sets of images and the other, third version of Barney that Jason carried around in his head. Was that what he was trying to do now, close the gap?

I slipped my arms around his waist and rested a cheek against his back. I felt him relax. He pulled me forward and hugged me into his side. I looked at the scatter of glossy photos arranged at his feet and with a start I realised he had muddled two of my Lauren pics in with his Barney collage. We kept our respective photo collections in shoeboxes on the same shelf. Both boxes were always close to overflowing. Some of my photos must have got mixed in with his.

The first imposter was a close-up of Lauren as a baby, no more than six months old, swaddled in a lemon bath towel; the other was of her as a toddler. Shot from behind, it captured her mid-air on a swing. I wanted to scoop them up immediately, to put them back with the others, but I couldn't bring myself to point out his mistake.

He went to rest his head on my mine and as he turned I intercepted him halfway with a kiss. Close-lipped, he reciprocated, took my hand and led me out onto the landing, towards our bedroom.

I dug in and tried to keep kissing him on the landing where we stood. He pulled away.

'You don't want to?'

I pulled him against the wall and kissed him some more.

'Here?' He looked down the stairs, at the front door, worried someone might see us through the frosted glass.

I turned around and, pushing myself up against the wall, arranged his hands on my body: one at the beginnings of my skirt, the other on my breast. But no sooner had I placed them there than he tried to turn me around to face him. I resisted and pushed myself back into his groin. He laughed.

'OK, OK. But not here.'

Again he took my hand and, after kissing me gently, went to lead me away, towards our bedroom. This time I followed.

14

A few days later and an opportunity presented itself.

My diary was usually jammed with sales calls or meetings of one sort or another but, arriving at work, I discovered that two of the clients I'd scheduled for that afternoon had cancelled. That meant between 2.30 p.m. and an early client supper I had a window of free time. After much cajoling I'd managed to reschedule the meeting I'd missed with Mr McDonald from that day I was knocked over by the van. It was the perfect chance to return to the off-licence.

I knew Martin's offer to help was probably nothing more than misguided pity; still, that aside, I was keen for a second look at the boy. Whether I could get the forensic artist a photo or not, I needed to be sure for myself and, more importantly, I need to be sure for Jason that I wasn't seeing things that weren't there.

Walking down the high street, I breathed in the mild autumnal air, enjoying the snick of my heels on the pavement. The sky was a high wide blue, flecked with cloud and, despite the season, most people were out without a coat.

My plan was simple. I'd go inside the shop and if the boy was in clear sight I'd ask the man behind the counter for something from the storeroom. With him gone, I'd use my camera-phone to take a picture of the child.

I was almost at the off-licence when a group of boys appeared up ahead. Backpacks dangling from shoulders, they were all clad in the same grey trousers, black shoes and royal blue sweatshirts. School uniform. Primary school, by the looks of it. One of them was kicking a football. Dribbling it in and around his friends' ankles, he would snug the ball back under his foot and pretend to take it off to the right whenever they tried to challenge him for possession. Then, at the very last second, he would flick it in the totally opposite direction. The sleeves on his jumper were too long and he kept pushing them back up onto his elbows.

They drew closer.

I watched as the largest kid in the group launched a particularly aggressive tackle. Sweeping in low, he went for the boy's shins, trying to bully the ball away. He almost succeeded in knocking him off balance, but the boy was too quick. Folding the ball back up into the air behind him, he turned to meet it and then used his knee to guide it down to the ground and over to the safety of the kerb. He lifted his face in triumph and his features came into focus.

I felt my heart jump.

Blond hair, wonky front teeth with a gap in the middle and dark brown, almost black eyes. It was the boy from the off-licence. Barney?

This was the first time I'd seen him up close, without mesh between us, and the effect was dizzying.

Without thinking, I got out my phone and started taking pictures. I was moving in for a better shot when I realised I'd caught the attention of a few passers-by. An elderly lady on a mobility scooter changed route and began gliding towards me, her face a mixture of suspicion and concern. Suddenly aware of how dubious I must seem I put my phone away, sidestepped into a nearby bus stop and pretended to study the timetable. The lady on the scooter came to within a few feet of where I stood and stopped. She sat there watching me, apparently debating whether or not to say something, while I kept my eyes fixed on the timetable. A few seconds later and I heard the squeak-thump of her scooter starting up. I waited until its battery-powered wail had faded into the distance and then I turned back to the group of boys.

They'd started a kick-around on the pavement directly in front of the off-licence, Chinese take-away and launderette. Laughing and shouting, they were passing the ball to each other in quick little movements designed to keep everyone quite literally on their toes. The boy was now red-faced and breathless, the blond hair around his neck and ears dark with sweat.

Lauren had been a devoted football fan. Thanks to my dad, she'd inherited an evangelical love of our local, two-bit team, Sitting-bourne FC. The proud owner of both their red and black home strip and their yellow and black away colours, she had faithfully attended every match they played from the age of four. During football season you could guarantee she'd spend the preceding bath-times before a match perfecting the chants she and my dad were planning to bellow in the stands that weekend. I would have to cover my mouth with my hand, hiding my smile, as Dad amended the racier chants into something more PG (the team's arch rivals were referred to locally as the Lilywhites, a nickname that easily lent itself to a very sweary rhyme when they weren't playing up to scratch). Once she had the hang of a particular chant, Lauren would try singing along with Dad. Surrounded by bubbles, the bottom of her hair damp and curling against her shoulders, she would do her best to make her small voice boom as loud as his against the bathroom walls.

My football knowledge had been zero but still, she'd tried her best. Saturday teatimes after a game would see her forego her usual *Powerpuff Girls* or *Charlie and Lola* telly in place of that day's match-day programme. Printed on shiny A4 paper, stapled in the middle, it was presented to me like a precious gift. 'Mummy,' she would say in the bossy, officious tone she'd recently picked up from her Year 1 teacher, Miss Moorehouse, 'I would now like you to read out who played today and which position they held.' While her finger slid down the team line-up, I would dutifully read out each player and whether they were centre-half or left-back. Her lips would move in sync with mine, silently mouthing the names of her heroes.

Dad still made sure to buy her a new Sittingbourne scarf every year without fail. But now he took it to tie around her headstone. He said the black and red stripes looked nice against the grey marble and green grass.

The kids had got a steady rhythm going. As the ball picked up speed, the large boy fumbled a pass. He panicked and kicked the ball with too much force. It ricocheted off the shoulder of another boy and flew into the air, straight towards the window of the take-away. They all flinched as it impacted hard against the glass. Within seconds a small Chinese woman wearing a purple velour tracksuit had appeared.

'No football!' she shouted from the doorway. Her accent was full-blown Geordie. 'There's a park less than two minutes away. Go play there.'

Anticipating her ire, some of the kids had already collected their backpacks and were skulking away down the street. The boy, however, went straight over to where she stood.

'We're sorry,' he said, collecting the ball under his arm. 'It was an accident.'

'Be off with you!' she said, trying to sound stern. The boy's manners had disarmed her. 'Or I'll call the police.'

The group needed no convincing. Hitting the window had punctured their fun. With a wave of his hand, the boy corralled those that remained over to the off-licence. One push on the door and they all bundled in.

I got out my phone and reviewed the pictures I'd taken. Most of them were too far away. They showed the boy as a blur; nothing more than a distant twist of royal blue. There were the odd one or two that had him in decent close-up, but they had captured nothing more than the back of his head as he lunged for the ball.

I heard the bell above the shop's door jamb ring out and looked up to see the boys re-emerge, clutching sweets and cans of Coke. They began to walk away, back in the direction from which they had come. I did a roll call. The boy was no longer with them. He must still be inside.

I approached the shop and pressed on the door. This was my chance to get a shot of his face. It didn't budge. Locked. I took a step back. The blind had been drawn and a 'Closed' sign now hung in the window. The guy must be on a toilet break or maybe he was out back, making the boy something to eat. Either way, I couldn't afford to hang around for too long. My work supper with Mr McDonald was at 6 p.m.

Resigned to coming back again some other time soon, I was about to leave when I had an idea. The shop might be closed, but what if the off-licence had a garden or a backyard where Keith let the kid out to play? What if the boy was there right now, messing around on his scooter or his bike? It would be cutting it fine, but I should have just enough time to take a quick peek and, hopefully, a better photo of his face. Then I'd be on my way.

15

The back alley stank of rotten food and urine. The cobbles had once been blue but were now grey, their edges curded with potato peelings and soft cardboard. I counted the gates as I walked, an assault course of wheelie bins, crates and empty drums of vegetable oil dotting my path.

Tramping past the flies and the dog mess, I tried to marry up the extra-wide loading doors, burglar bars and wooden gates with their high-street shopfronts. Reaching what I guessed to be the back of the off-licence I saw that, instead of a yard, a single-storey, flat-roof extension filled the space. Built out to the alley, the only openings in its red brick wall were a reinforced metal door and a long, thin window near the roof.

The window was six feet off the ground, but I wasn't going to let that stop me. I looked around. I needed to climb onto something high enough to allow me to see inside. I put my bag on the least grubby bit of floor, balanced my jacket on top and stashed my phone in the waistband of my skirt. Grabbing the nearest wheelie bin I could find, I rolled it under the window, its wheels giving out a deep, rumbling noise.

Unsurprisingly, I hadn't anticipated my day would involve me having to clamber on top of a bin and so this morning I'd decided to wear my black suede stilettos with the polished metal heels. My fallback footwear of choice whenever I had a particularly difficult meeting to attend or when, like today, I needed a bit of Dutch courage, I considered them and their spiky, weapon-like heels my armour, there to fortify me against whatever might come my way. Super-high (even for me), when I'd bought them the girl in the shop had referred to them as limo shoes (so precarious, beautiful and expensive they necessitated the wearer to be driven everywhere lest she damage them or herself). Now, looking at the dimensions of the bin, I realised I couldn't have worn a more impractical shoe.

Putting my hands behind me I tried to hoist myself backwards onto the lid. But the bin was empty and, almost immediately, it toppled onto its side, taking me with it. As I broke my fall with my hands, I heard the right underarm of my blouse rip wide open.

Dusting myself off, I reassessed. I needed something with a solid base to support me. Finding a bin packed to the brim with bags, I heaved it over to the window and placed a bottle crate next to it. Stepping up onto the crate, I put one knee onto the lid. The plastic buckled almost instantly. I waited for it to meet the top of the bin bags inside and, as soon as it had stabilised, I raised my other knee up. The bin's column swayed beneath me and, once it had settled into position, I grabbed onto the window ledge and peered inside.

What I saw was some kind of living room. Pine laminate covered the floor and the walls had been painted magnolia. A mismatched sofa and armchair were the main pieces of furniture; an airer with grey clothes drying on it, a dead-looking yucca plant, small chest of drawers and a TV being the only other things in the room. A framed photo sat atop the chest of drawers. Too far away to see in any real detail, it seemed to feature the boy and two other people, all wearing sunglasses and sunhats, aboard some kind of small boat. One of the men was on the large side. Probably the shopkeeper. But the other person was more difficult to identify.

I realised the TV was tuned to a cartoon channel and looked at the room again, more carefully this time. Lego was scattered next to the sofa, and now a small hand appeared, moving a toy ambulance back and forwards and around the bricks. The hand was part covered by a royal blue sleeve, hanging low on the wrist.

It was him. The boy.

Slipping my phone out of my waistband, I turned the camera on and held it up to the window. The boy's hand kept coming further and further out as he raced his toy faster and faster. I held my phone steady, willing him to break cover.

The hand disappeared from view for a few seconds and then re-emerged at the side of the sofa, this time pushing a miniature red racing car. He pushed it too hard, lost control and the car flew forward, out of his grasp. This was it. I held my finger poised on the photo button. He reached out to retrieve the car and as the back of his head came into view I began taking photo after photo. Just a bit more, just a bit more, I begged, snapping away. I could almost see the side profile of his face when I heard the back gate of a shop a few doors down being wedged open.

I climbed off the bin as fast as I could, my dismount levering open the lid, and as my heels clattered down onto the alley cobbles I caught a whiff of the rotten sweetness contained within.

'If it isn't my damsel in distress.'

It was the bloke from the café. The one who had helped me.

Wearing jeans and a pale green T-shirt that highlighted the dash of his shoulders, he smiled but then looked behind me, concerned, as though he'd realised it didn't make any sense for me to be out here.

I couldn't remember his name.

'Tommy,' he said, guessing the source of my confusion.

'Tommy. Of course,' I said, brushing off the old leaves that had attached themselves to my skirt.

'What are you doing out here?' he asked, his Glaswegian lilt more noticeable than the first time we'd met. 'On the hunt for another cold drink?'

I couldn't tell if he was being sarcastic.

'The shop was shut so I thought I'd try a short-cut back to the car.' I tried to sound ditzy. 'I got lost.' It was a weak lie and I couldn't tell if he'd bought it. 'Judging by that sign above the door it seems I'll have to find somewhere else to stop.'

He picked up the rubbish sacks, deposited them in a cylindrical industrial bin and came closer. When we'd first met I hadn't realised how tall he was, but now, standing next to him, I saw that he was at least six foot, if not more.

'I wouldn't worry,' he said quietly. 'Keith can't find any takers. He's likely to be there for a good few months yet.'

He looked me up and down, taking in my outfit, waist and breasts.

'How's the leg?'

'Fine,' I said, realising my bag and coat were still on the floor. I started to panic. What if he noticed them there and asked me why, if I was out here because I'd got lost, I'd gone and put all my stuff on the ground?

'Come on through to the caff and I'll make you a cuppa.'

There was no way I could take him up on his offer. If I was going to be on time for my meeting with Mr McDonald I needed to leave in the next few minutes. Still, for some reason I found myself hesitating.

'Can't. I'm on the clock.' I had to push the words out fast before I could change my mind. 'I've got one more appointment before I'm done for the day.'

'Shame,' he said absently. He was looking at me again.

'Which way is it back to the car park?' I asked, picking up my phone and bag as subtly as I could.

'That way.' Without taking his eyes off me, he gestured behind him with his head. 'Unless you want to come to the pub? Once you're finished, I mean? I'm due to close up soon, and me and Keith normally reward ourselves with a pint in the George and Dragon.' He looked at his watch. 'Knowing Keith, he'll already be there.'

I found myself staring at his mouth. Surrounded by the short, dark outline of his beard, his lips were wet and pink.

'I really should be going,' I said, filling my lungs with air. I needed to clear the fug in my head.

'Can't blame a man for trying,' he laughed.

I walked slowly, hoping he would go back inside and allow me to climb back up onto the bin. I wasn't sure if the photos I'd taken were any good and I wanted to get some more, just to be sure. But I hadn't gone far when I heard footsteps.

'Where are my manners?' he said, falling in next to me. 'I'll walk with you. Make sure you take the right turning.'

'That's very kind,' I said, trying not to sound irritated.

We walked in silence, me struggling to navigate the cobbles in my metal heels, Tommy whistling under his breath, until we reached the opening that led out onto the street.

'Goodbye then,' I said, keeping my voice light.

He nodded.

As I walked away, I got the feeling he was standing there, watching me go. I turned back to check. I was right. Backlit by the sun, he had his head cocked to the side, his arms crossed high against his chest. He acknowledged me with a tiny nod.

Hoping I might be able to sneak back for another photo, I turned to look round one last time as I reached the corner of the street. But he was still there, watching me, an unpassable black silhouette.

16

Back at the car, I got out my phone and opened the album of photos I'd taken. I planned to email the clearest ones through to Martin immediately.

I swept my thumb across the screen, moving through the twenty-five shots. They were no good. Either I'd held the phone too near and got a close-up of the window frame or else I'd held it so far away I'd caught my own reflection in the glass. I flicked ahead, hoping the others would be better. Finally, I came to a picture that depicted the room I'd looked down in on. I squinted at the image. I could just make out the child's hand at the side of the sofa. I scrolled through the remaining shots and there was his arm and shoulder, there the blond-haired top of his head.

There was only one photo remaining. My heart drumming, I prayed for it to show some or all of the boy's face. It was possible. I'd kept pressing the button right up until I'd had to jump down from the wheelie bin. But, as the picture loaded, I saw it revealed only the merest edges of the boy's hair and hand.

I slumped in my seat. It was frustrating but I had to go. My meeting with Mr McDonald was in fifteen minutes. I put my key in the ignition and started the engine.

As the motorway flew by in a blur of bleached grass verges and low, grey cloud, I let my thoughts go back to what I had seen through that window. In my head I rewound the boy's hand reaching out for the racing car and tried to freeze-frame the millisecond advance of his forehead, nose and chin as it emerged from behind the sofa. I found myself willing him to keep going, to keep pushing the toy further than he actually had. As if, by doing so, I could fast-forward to the point at which he fully showed himself and get the photo I needed.

The faint line of the Cleveland hills appeared on the horizon and I noticed that the other side of the motorway had emptied of cars, while my lane was congesting into long, lazy lines of traffic. I pressed gently on the brake pedal and soon I was bumper to bumper with the blue BMW in front. I could see the outline of the back of a bald man in a grey suit behind the wheel. My eyes travelled down the length of his car to the boot. On reflex, I began to wonder who or what might be inside.

And then, like toppling dominos, my thoughts went back to the day Lauren went missing.

That Saturday, Lauren had been playing outside the caravan on her bike while I stood at the caravan's tiny kitchen sink, washing tomatoes and boiling eggs for lunch. Mum and Dad were in the small living room, doing Sudoku. The meal all set, I went to call Lauren in. But she wasn't there. I found her bike abandoned, a few feet from the steps that led down from the caravan's front door. Tipped onto its side, the front wheel was still going, the spokes making a tick-tick-tick noise every time they brushed past the brake pad.

At first, I'd tried not to be too frantic. I'd wanted to believe it wouldn't be long before we found her underneath one of the caravans' crawl spaces, hiding behind the brick stacks the cabins rested on. But then, as the minutes had slipped by, a feeling had started to harden inside me, a feeling I knew to be true but that I wanted to ignore. A feeling that the moment to act had gone, that something tectonic had already shifted and changed and that there was nothing I could do to shift it back.

In the distance, on the other side of the motorway, I could see flashing lights and the backed-up traffic beyond. There had been a crash. One car was flipped onto its roof, the seam of the exhaust pipe running along its metal underbelly like the spine on an upside-down roast chicken. Behind it were four other cars, concertina-crushed into each other. The usual fire engines, ambulances and police cars littered the scene, but there were also other people in fluorescent yellow vests busy erecting a hoarding between my lane of the motorway and theirs. I wondered what they were doing, and then I realised. They were blocking the view. Martin had once told me how the emergency services had made this a policy after they discovered that a crash on one side of the motorway means an 80 per cent increase in the chance of a crash happening on the opposite side within half an hour. 'They can't help it,' he'd said, 'the drivers take their attention off the road to have a quick look and before you know it – bam!' He'd slapped his hands in the air. 'It's happened all over again.'

I cruised past the last of the smashed-up cars and soon my lane of traffic was back to its normal speed. Less than a mile later I pulled off the motorway and onto the road that would lead me to the restaurant where I was meeting Mr McDonald. I came to a halt at a set of lights and stared out at the row of houses to my left. One of the houses, a tidy pebble-dashed semi, had a large To Let board in the front garden, advertising its rental potential to passing traffic.

Worry knotted my stomach.

I planned to go back for a photo of the boy again soon, but what was to say he'd even still be there? Whatever Tommy had said to the contrary, the estate agent I'd seen showing that couple around seemed to mean business. What if, the next time I managed to make it over, I discovered the bloke running the off-licence and the boy had moved on? By passing up Tommy's invitation to come and have a drink I was missing out on what might be my only chance to find out more about Keith and the true identity of the child. The pub would be a chance to chat to him direct. He might say something to allay all my fears, something to reassure me that the child was not Barney. On the other hand, he might give away some detail, some scrap of information that would give me the confidence to override Jason's wishes and get the police involved.

My table with Mr McDonald was booked for five minutes' time. I'd already missed one meeting with him; to be late tonight would be bad form, but not the end of the world. He was an amenable fellow. Maybe I could stall?

A petrol station appeared on my left and I swerved into it at the last second, leaving the drivers behind me beeping their horns. I pulled up next to the cash machine, turned off the engine and sat there with my eyes closed. Listening to the radio, I tried to concentrate on the way the air felt as it went in through my nostrils and down into my lungs.

I got out my phone and dialled. He picked up on the first ring.

'Mr McDonald, Heidi Thursby. From Bullingdon's.'

'Heidi, my dear.' There was a murmur in the background. I heard the clink of glasses and the rattle of cutlery. He was already there.

'I took the liberty of choosing the wine. Do you like Montepulciano?'

'My favourite,' I said. This was good. If he started ploughing into the vino he might be more forgiving.

'I'm terribly sorry but I'm stuck in traffic. I'm going to be late.'

I screwed up my face, braced for his reaction.

'How late?'

'There's an accident on the A19 and the cars are backed up for miles.'

I hoped that, by telling him a half-lie, I'd sound more convincing.

'I suppose it can't be helped.'

'It can't,' I jumped in. 'Again, my apologies. You know how grateful I am that you've made time to see me. Especially after we missed each other last week. Stay where you are. I'll be with you as soon as I can.'

I checked my watch. I should have just enough time to get to the pub, have a quick drink and be back at the restaurant within the hour. I looped my way round the outskirts of the forecourt and set off back in the direction from which I had come.

17

Red paint flaked off the pub's doorframe and curtains hung brasserie-style from gold hoops over the windows. The curtains' lining faced out onto the street, revealing old condensation stains. Zig-zagging up and down the inside of the fabric they looked like a series of complicated brown graphs. Smoothing down my suit, I steeled myself ready and pushed on the door.

Inside, groups of men sat at small round tables and leant against the bar, their shoulders hunched and eyes glassy from an afternoon on the beer. Trying to ignore the fact I was being given a predatory once-over, I scanned the room. I couldn't see Keith and Tommy anywhere. My nerve began to wobble. Maybe coming here had been a mistake?

I was about to leave when I saw a little wooden arrow next to the toilets with the words BEER GARDEN burnt onto it in clumsy block capitals. I told myself I'd check out there and then, if there was no sign of them, I'd be on my way back to Mr McDonald and his Montepulciano.

The beer garden turned out to be a concrete patch of ground with a few benches and red velvet-covered stools that had been brought out from inside. I clocked Keith and Tommy straightaway. They were sitting at a table near the smoking shelter, Tommy with his back to me, Keith's head bent over a newspaper.

I thought of the boy playing on the floor of the back room of the off-licence. Had Keith left him locked in there alone while he went out to the pub?

As I got nearer, Keith looked up. When he saw me he did a double take, as if trying to place me, and said something to Tommy I couldn't quite hear. Tommy twisted round, smiled and beckoned me over.

'Thought I'd join you after all,' I said as flippantly as I could and sat myself on the bench next to Tommy. 'Mine's a glass of white wine.'

Winking the same way as the boys at school when they knew you'd snogged one of their mates at the disco, Keith signalled to Tommy, asking him if he was ready for another. Tommy nodded and, with that, Keith hoisted himself off the bench and went inside.

He'd left his newspaper on the table. Folded in two, it showed the top half of an advert for Center Parcs. It featured a family: a mother, father, boy and girl, splashing together in a bright blue swimming pool. Enlarged to fill the page, the oversized dimensions of the family's smiling eyes made them look unreal, other-worldly almost. I started to feel dizzy and, as I looked away, I caught Tommy's eye. He gave a tiny, almost imperceptible nod, as though he'd realised something I had yet to understand.

'So,' I said, acting as if we hadn't just seen each other in the back alley. 'How was your day?'

I caught myself. There was a flirtation to my voice I didn't realise until I heard it out loud. When had I decided to play it like this?

'Hot,' he replied and then paused, letting the word settle, 'and busy.' He smiled, his beard creasing up around his acne scars.

I felt myself smiling back.

Tommy reached towards my head and, for a moment, I thought he was going to cup my cheek so that he could kiss me, but instead he fished something out of my hair and held it up for me to see. It was a sweet wrapper. It must have got stuck when I fell off the wheelie bin. We stared at it like it was a rare butterfly, our faces close. But then I saw Keith returning with our drinks and directed my eyes to the left, indicating we had company. Quickly, we drew apart.

Keith retook his seat, the bench creaking and listing so far to his side that Tommy and I were raised a few inches in the air.

'You've got some size on you,' laughed Tommy, and I was surprised to see Keith's cheeks pink a little at the allusion to his weight.

'It's all right,' he joked, posturing that way men do when they want to hide their embarrassment. 'You can't help being jealous I'm such a magnificent hulk of a man.'

Sitting across from him like this, I took my chance to compare Keith's face with the three suspect photofits from Jason's file. I went through each of his features in turn, trying to find points of similarity, but there were none. He had almond eyes and long, saggy cheeks, but I decided any witness would almost certainly have remembered his nose. A protuberance so tiny it looked more like an afterthought than an intended, coherent part of his face, it was dead straight, his nostrils lizard-thin.

No matter. The fact remained. He was the one person in charge of or in close contact with a child I had recognised as Barney. And so I decided that, as I'd made the effort to come here, I might as well see if he could shed any light on my suspicions.

'So Keith,' I asked, 'how do you know Tommy?'

'The caff,' he said, patting his tummy. 'Someone has to keep me in bacon butties.'

Tommy laughed.

I figured my best tactic would be to try and catch him off guard. To ask a question about the boy out of the blue. If the question spooked him in any way, then it might be a sign something was up.

'How's the little lad?' I tried to sound as small-talky as I could.

I scrutinised his face, ready for any change of expression that might betray his guilt or fear. But, apart from seeming a little surprised that I'd mentioned the child, there was nothing.

'You must mean my nephew, Mikey?'

Taking a deep sup of lager, he began picking at the gold sovereigns that decorated his left hand; flicking his nail off the rings' latticework. I let my eyes drop down from them to the table. Keith had been resting his pint on his newspaper. The Center Parcs mother now had a series of dark, damp rings on her forehead.

'It's a nightmare keeping the little sod entertained,' said Keith. 'But unlike some of us,' – he nodded accusingly at Tommy – 'I try and help my sister whenever I can. I take him for her after school.'

I forced the best platitude I could – 'That's very nice of you' – and gulped at my wine, only to find my glass already empty.

'Underneath all that flab there's a heart of gold,' added Tommy.

I laughed. Too loudly by the looks on their faces. It was time for me to leave. What was I thinking, sitting here with two men I hardly knew? I needed to get back to the restaurant. I'd left Mr McDonald waiting too long already.

I looked around. The beer garden was now packed with people smoking and drinking, all men, and the temperature had dropped considerably. I searched for the door that led into the pub – the only way back out to the street – and saw that it was blocked from view by a large group of football fans having a few pre-match pints.

'So, champagne lady,' said Keith. He did remember me then. 'Live nearby? Got a nice big house over in Jesmond or something?' He said the place name in a posh accent.

'Heidi's not from round here,' said Tommy, jumping to my defence.

'She isn't?'

'She's from down south.'

I smiled gratefully. Next to him like this I was able to see how his beard stopped just short of his lips, leaving a neat line of skin around his mouth. Every now and again a flash of gold filling would peep out from the back of his teeth.

'Don't we know a lot about each other? You'll be telling me her star sign next,' laughed Keith. 'Now, if you'll excuse me,' he said, heaving himself off the bench, 'I might leave you two lovebirds to it.'

Lovebirds? I felt for the curve of my wedding band.

'Off to see your mam?' asked Tommy.

'Thought I'd pop in for a bit, see how she's doing,' replied Keith, readjusting his waistband.

'Give her my love.'

Keith nodded and I realised that, without that off-licence cage between us, my sense of him as a person was totally different. Up close, he had a vulnerability I hadn't noticed the first time, a vulnerability that meant he could never willingly hurt a child.

Not only that, after this afternoon, I now knew that the boy was in school. Happy and healthy, he had friends and was allowed to come and go from the shop as he pleased.

'His mam is in a hospice,' said Tommy, once Keith had gone. 'Hasn't got long left, by all accounts.'

'Oh?'

'They diagnosed her less than a year ago. Keith tries to visit every day.'

I stared at the tattoo of the naked, winged woman on Tommy's forearm. Her breasts were large, high and powerful, her figure hourglass.

My phone buzzed inside my bag. Mr McDonald. No doubt wondering where I'd got to. I felt my belly twist. I couldn't miss my meeting with him. Not again. I needed to leave, now.

'So,' said Tommy. 'Got any plans for tonight?' He lit a cigarette. 'Or do you have to get back to your husband?'

A chill wind gusted through the beer garden and I shivered. I'd left my suit jacket in the car and I could feel how my nipples were sticking out through my blouse.

A smile danced around Tommy's mouth and there it was again, that flash of gold.

'I have to get going,' I said, resisting the urge to cross my arms.

He licked his lips and for a brief moment I had the feeling he was playing me. That he had been all along. Suddenly, I felt like he knew exactly who I was, who I was married to and why I was so interested in Keith and the boy. That the two of them were in it together. My stomach curled in on itself. I had to get out of here immediately; I had to call the police. But then I stopped. If

Tommy did know that the boy in Keith's care was Barney and if he also knew who I was, it wouldn't make any sense for him to invite me into his world, would it? He'd be trying to push me away, not welcoming me in every chance he got. As soon as I started to think rationally, I felt better. No, I was just being paranoid, on edge from my Nancy-Drew-like attempt at detective work, that's all. Plus, I told myself, in the past I'd always been able to tell when people recognised me, even if they tried to hide it. You saw the click of satisfaction in their eyes. It was like they'd found a match, a key that fitted. I'd never seen that click with either Tommy or Keith. I was sure I was safe.

'I should get back,' I said again, as if, by repeating myself, I would make the words come true.

'If you must.' He blew a series of smoke rings up into the air.

But then, as I tried to get up off the bench I found he'd barred my way. I lost my footing and had to grab the table for support.

'Tommy, please,' I said, my mouth sticky from the wine.

After checking no one was looking, he reached his hand in behind the crook of my knee and gently ran his palm up my inside leg. Once my skirt started to bunch in the middle he brought his hand to a halt and left it there.

'Do you want me to stop?' he asked. His fingers were on my inner thigh, inches short of my knickers. 'If you want me to stop, say.' His hand was shielded by the top of the picnic table. He could go further and no one would see. 'What are you doing next Monday?' What was he asking me, what was happening? 'I want to see you again.' His hand was hot on my skin. 'Do you want to see me?' It took me a minute, but finally, I managed to say the word.

'Stop.'

And, although I said it very quietly, under my breath, he instantly removed his hand and swung his legs to the side, letting me go.

I staggered forwards and tried to push my way through the crowds of people towards the door that would lead me back into the pub. I was halfway across the beer garden when he shouted after me.

'Next Monday,' he said. 'I'll be in touch.'

Safe in the knowledge he had no way of ever contacting me, I turned back, ready to give him a generous smile, only to see him produce one of my business cards from his back pocket.

He must have taken it the day I got knocked over by the van.

Like a magician performing a trick, he wove the white rectangle between his finger and thumb, his eyes on me. Once he was certain I had properly registered its meaning, he returned the card to his pocket and went back to his drink.

18

The next morning I arrived at work to find Yvonne pacing the boardroom, her phone glued to the side of her head.

Boxed off from the rest of our floor by immaculate glass walls, the boardroom took up the entire left side of the office and was at once the most private and the most public place we had at our disposal. Dominated by a large oval table around which Yvonne was currently performing laps, its single non-glass wall was garish with framed colour photos of our clientele.

I went to my desk and turned on the computer. Within seconds, Nick appeared. He stood behind my monitor, smiling.

'Is there something I can help you with?' Nick had been assigned to my team a few months earlier. A junior sales rep, he was always first in the office and last to leave and liked to clog my inbox with unnecessarily long reports on every call and pitch.

'Have you had a chance to look at the Wetherspoon's spreadsheet?'

With coarse black hair cut close to his head and wiry sprouts on the backs of his hands, he had a tendency to wear shirts that were just that bit too small.

'Spreadsheet?'

'I sent it last night.'

'OK. I'll come back to you as soon as I have any feedback.'

I turned my attention back to the computer screen, letting him know we were done. He lingered for a few more seconds before wandering off, back to his side of the office.

Nick dealt with, I logged in and was all set to power through my emails when I heard Yvonne banging on the glass wall. I looked up and she pointed at me, then beckoned me inside.

Ignoring the craned necks and curious whispers of Nick and my other colleagues, I did as she asked. Taking a seat, I noticed a single white envelope on the table in front of her, face-side down. Yvonne had placed her index finger on its seal and was moving it around in small circles, the paper sliding easily across the varnished pine.

I gave her a hopeful smile. She didn't return the gesture. My mouth went dry. There was only one thing this could be about and that was last night.

After departing the pub, I'd finally made it to the restaurant only to discover that, having waited for over an hour, Mr McDonald had gone. I'd hoped to spend this morning doing damage control but, judging by the scowl on Yvonne's face, it seemed I was too late.

Nervous about the inevitable tirade to come, I began fiddling with the hem of my skirt and was hit by the sensation of Tommy's palm on my inside leg. My cheeks burned a hot, immediate red.

Opening her mouth slightly, Yvonne tapped her teeth together, apparently deciding how best to begin.

'Head Office said it was too soon for you to be promoted,' she declared with a wave of her hand, as though the board of investors were sitting right behind her. 'But I stuck up for you. No, I said. She's ready, I said. Trust me, I said.'

Wearing a green wrap dress that strained at the bust, Yvonne wore her short, henna-dyed hair in a side parting, smooth against her head.

'Then what happens?' she continued. 'One month into the new role and you think you can do what you like.'

Blotches began to appear on her neck. I'd seen this happen to her once before, after she'd disciplined a PA for stealing office stationery.

'That was Mr McDonald on the phone. He's decided to give the pubs and clubs contract to Calico Drinks. An outcome which is going to massively damage our' – she paused for effect – 'and *your* end-of-year targets.'

'Last night couldn't be helped,' I said. 'There was an accident on the A19. You must have seen it on the news.'

'But it's not just last night is it? The other week you had,' she lifted her fingers in the air to signal inverted commas, 'food poisoning. Which meant you missed the original meeting . . .'

'I did, I told you, I ate a dodgy sandwich,' I said, still hoping to persuade her none of this was my fault. I hated myself for having messed up so badly, but there was no way I could admit that to Yvonne.

'Sorry, Heidi.' She couldn't meet my eyes. 'I'm asking you to consider this your first formal warning.' She slid the white envelope across the table to where I sat.

'Yvonne. No.' I turned it right side up. There, in black capital letters, was my name. 'I'm sorry. Really. I love my job and I've always appreciated the way you've supported my career . . .'

'I don't want your appreciation,' she said. 'I want you to show up when you're supposed to. I want you to tell me it won't happen again.'

'It won't,' I said. 'I give you my word.'

Her anger spent, Yvonne seemed to collapse in on herself.

'Take a few minutes to compose yourself.' She placed a hand on my shoulder. 'Then go home. Take the rest of the day. Think of tomorrow as a fresh start.'

Looking out through the glass walls, I saw that a few people had gathered around Hayley, the receptionist's, computer. They seemed to be watching something together. Shooting the odd, sly glance in my direction, it was clear they were gossiping about what might have just transpired.

I smoothed down my skirt and pushed back my shoulders. I could not afford to lose this job. Jason's freelance teaching salary was unreliable – and negligible at that, which meant I was the breadwinner in a house where we were already overstretched on the mortgage. Plus, I was still planning to talk to Jason about trying for a baby. If and when I fell pregnant, I didn't want to be unemployed with no maternity pay to speak of.

I mustered the best smile I could, lifted my head high and opened the door. Acutely aware of my team's every shared look and halted conversation, I began the long walk back to my desk. I told myself they had no idea what had just happened. As far as they were concerned, my chat with Yvonne had been a targets catch-up. But they'd seen the expression on her face. They weren't stupid. Still, I made sure not to let my smile falter and, after grabbing my things, I wandered over to reception.

Hayley and a couple of others were watching a video embedded into a news site. Their reaction was such that they'd now attracted a small crowd, interested to see what all the fuss was about. Hayley explained that it was a jewellery advert that had gone viral and, at everyone's urging, she clicked play, starting the video over from the beginning.

I moved closer.

The video began with simple grey text on a white background that announced the ad's title: *The Unique Connection*. An acoustic guitar track started playing in the background and the shot cut to a large, airy warehouse, backdropped by high, wide windows. Six women entered the warehouse and lined themselves up in a row. Next, we were presented with a beautiful little girl. Aged four or five, she was wearing a simple white dress and had blonde corkscrew curls. We saw her eyes being gently covered with an ecru blindfold and then we were presented with more text, this time explaining that what we were about to see was an experiment. Was it possible for children to recognise their mother through touch and scent alone? As the girl began to move tentatively along the group, the row of women waited anxiously, her mother amongst them. One by one, the women bent down so that the little girl could touch and smell their hair and faces. The little girl felt for the hands and hair of the first woman and shook her head; she did the same with the second and again, shook her head. But then, no sooner had she got close to the third woman in the row, she smiled and removed her blindfold, confident this was her mother. The mother smiled, her eyes wet with tears, and then she drew her daughter in for a hug.

The ad came to an end and someone requested that Hayley play it again. I took my chance and slipped out the door unnoticed, as though my reason for leaving was nothing more ominous than a late lunch.

19

That night, I lay in bed waiting for Jason's snores to take on the long, low rattle that signified deep sleep. On the floor beside me was my handbag, a white envelope peeking over the edge. My formal warning.

There had been a time when Yvonne had given me a very different kind of letter: a job offer to come and work at Bullingdon's. That was over two years ago. Walking into the interview, I'd assumed that at some point she'd ask about Lauren or my relationship with Jason. That she'd want her own individual scrap of gossip to relay to her friends. As it turned out, she was nothing but professional. When we got up to shake hands and she still hadn't mentioned anything, I knew she wasn't ever likely to. I'd been right. And so, even though she had her faults I liked working for her. I wanted to keep on working for her.

I slipped my hand out of the duvet and pushed the envelope down to the bottom of the bag. From now on I needed to be more careful.

I slowed my breathing and tried to relax, but every time I closed my eyes I saw the framed photo in the room at the back of the shop. My mind began to race. It was the only picture in the room and Keith had gone to the trouble of framing it. That meant it was significant to him in some way. Why? And who was the other adult in the picture? I still had the four photo-composites of the suspects I'd taken from Jason's file: the people who'd been seen in or around the flats when Barney first went missing. Was there a chance that one of them could be a match?

I tossed and turned for another hour, restless with thoughts of the boy and my formal warning. Close to midnight I had an idea. I couldn't sleep, and so what if I put this time laid here awake to good use? Instead of fretting in the dark, I could go back to the shop now, in the middle of the night, and try to put my mind at rest. The time might even be to my advantage. Jason had an old pair of binoculars in the drawer downstairs and there was a torch in my car. I could look at the framed photo without interruption.

Sliding out of bed, I gathered up my clothes from the floor and stole across the carpet and out to the landing and the bathroom. I got changed in the dark.

I was almost ready when I fumbled with the lace on one of my trainers. The shoe dropped to the tiles with a thud. Across the hall, I heard Jason stir. Blood pounding in my ears, I waited to see if I'd woken him. There was nothing. Then I heard the telltale duvet rustles that meant he was turning onto his side. Only once I was sure he had properly settled did I finish getting dressed. All set, I tiptoed down the stairs and, after making a quick detour to the kitchen for the binoculars, I was out the door.

I worried that Jason might hear if I started the car while it was parked in front of the house and so I released the handbrake and let it roll backwards down the hill. As soon as I was a fair distance away, I put the key in the ignition. I hoped to get to the off-licence and back without Jason realising I was ever gone.

However, if he did wake, I was counting on the fact that there had been plenty of previous occasions when, unable to sleep, one or the other of us had gone out pacing. There should be no cause for concern.

The motorway was predictably quiet, and I made it to Gateshead in less than an hour. I parked on Coatesworth Road, a short distance from Wine City, got out and walked up to the shopfront. The LEASEHOLD AVAILABLE sign was still hanging above the shop's hoarding.

As would be expected at nearly two in the morning, the metal shutters were down, the door locked. However, despite the hour, there were some lights on in the flat above. Keith must still be awake. I'd need to be careful. I carried on to the end of the street, turned the corner and headed for the gap in the wall that led to the back alley.

As I moved forward into the darkness, I held the thin torch I'd brought in front of my body, but it was so small that it illuminated only tiny, ineffectual circles of light. Cursing myself for not thinking to bring something bigger, after a few minutes I gave up and turned it off. Gradually, my eyes began to adjust, and soon I could distinguish between the different gates and loading bays. Ten feet ahead was the brick extension that marked the back of the off-licence. I felt for the binoculars, on a strap around my neck, and continued on my way.

I was almost there when I heard rapid footsteps up ahead. A man was approaching from the opposite end of the alley. On instinct, I jumped behind a large industrial bin and crouched on the floor. Looking through the thin gap between the bin and the wall, I watched as the man slowed his pace. I worried it was because he'd seen me, but then I realised: he was counting doors. Tall and thickly built, he was completely bald and was dressed in jeans and smart shoes, his top half covered in a bulky Puffa jacket, the collar of which reached all the way to his ears.

He came to a stop outside the off-licence and took a step back, surveying the brick extension and first floor beyond.

Apparently satisfied with whatever he saw there, he moved in close to the door and raised his right hand, fist clenched. He banged hard three times, then stopped, listening. When a minute or so later there was still no response, he shook his head, disappointed, and then, as if he was sorry for what he was about to do, he began to bang on the door again. This time he didn't stop. The dull thud of his fist against the metal was relentless. Each slam resulted in a dull thump followed by a tinny crumpling; the impact's ripple effect on the door's loose, metal outer edges.

Finally, a light came on in the extension's single high, thin window. The metal door opened a crack, flooding the alley with a yellow glow.

The man in the alley held his fist in the air for a few seconds and then lowered it to his side. The skin on his head shone smooth and white.

The door was on the chain. A shirtless Keith peered through the gap.

'Robbie,' he said, scratching his belly. 'Long time no see. To what do I owe the pleasure?'

I noticed that, despite the pleasantry, he didn't remove the chain from its bolt.

'Where is she?' asked the man. He jammed his foot in the gap at the bottom of the door.

'Don't know.' Keith stopped scratching. 'Haven't heard from her in ages.'

'Don't lie, fat boy.' The man got in as close to Keith's face as the gap in the door would allow. 'I know you two. You're thick as bloody thieves, always were.' He thrust his hands in his jacket pockets. 'I'm going to ask again and this time I want you to tell me the truth. Where is my wife?'

'Like I said before, I don't know.' I heard the catch in Keith's voice. He was trying to sound brave, but this man frightened him. I remembered what he'd said to me about the shop the first time I went in there. The cage was good because it meant no one could get back there to beat him up.

The man laughed, a half-hearted attempt at nonchalance.

'I heard they let her have the kids back?'

Keith said nothing. The man tried again.

'They're my flesh and blood,' he said, his indifference forgotten. 'My son and daughter. I've got a right to see them.'

I wanted to keep listening, but I also didn't want to be stuck here when the man finished. If Keith was frightened of this person, then I definitely should be. I tried to get up and creep away, back the way I'd come, but I'd been crouching on my haunches for too long and my muscles had seized. I fell onto the metal bin I was hiding behind and it moved forward on its castors, letting out a low rumble.

Spooked by the noise, the man stopped ranting and looked over in my direction.

I tried to scrabble back into my hiding place, but it was too late.

'Who's there?' The man turned towards me and, as he did, he removed his foot from the gap. Keith took his chance and, with no interest in who or what might be lurking, slammed the door shut.

Realising what had happened, the man turned to the door and started to kick and punch the metal.

'Fuck, fuck!'

It took seconds to realise his efforts were futile and then he returned his attention to where I was trying to get to my feet.

His face was churned up, gunning for a fight, but then as I came into view his expression changed to one of confusion. He looked me up and down and then his face relaxed, as though he'd had some kind of revelation.

'Oi oi. What do we have here? Hello, sweetheart.'

Now upright, I started to back away.

'You interrupted something very important just now.'

There was still at least ten feet between us, but he was trying to close the gap.

'How about you make it up to me?' He tugged at the front of his belt. 'What's the going rate these days?'

I started to run.

Far ahead was the rectangle of orange light that marked my exit. If I could just get to the street, there might be people. I'd be safe.

I heard him laugh, hard and loud, and then I heard the friction-swish of his arms pumping against the insulated fabric of his Puffa jacket. He was in pursuit.

I tried to break into a sprint but I kept banging into things, my ankles twisting on the tin cans and wrappers underfoot.

'Don't cock-tease,' he shouted after me. 'Not tonight. I'm not in the mood.'

I turned around, trying to see how far away he was, but as soon as I stopped looking where I was going, I crashed straight into an empty drum of vegetable oil. The momentum sent me careening towards the ground. I only just managed to right myself in time and was nearly at the end of the alley when my foot slipped on a cobble. I went over on my ankle and something sheared in my foot. The pain was white-hot but I couldn't stop. He was gaining on me. Please let there be someone on the street, I prayed. Please let there be someone to help me.

I reached the pavement and, panting for breath, looked left and right. But the place was deserted. My car, I needed to get back to my car. I turned left and left again, back onto the high street, my footsteps brittle in the empty air. After a while I realised I could no longer hear him. I did a quick check, but there was no sign of him. He must have lost interest. My chest heaving, I slowed my pace to a walk.

I reached my car, got inside and locked the doors, but within seconds he'd reappeared from nowhere and began banging on my windscreen, swearing and jeering.

I fumbled with the key, trying to get it in the ignition, but I lost my grip and it fell into the footwell. The man's screaming and banging was getting louder.

Rummaging in the gloom, finally, my fingers came upon the key. I started the engine and was about to pull away when I realised there was a car parked directly in front of mine. I was blocked in. I turned around. There was nothing behind me.

Pushing the gear-stick into reverse, I sped away, my engine wailing. Undeterred, he started running after me.

I pressed harder on the accelerator and he slowed to a jog.

Checking the road behind, I saw that I was fast approaching the crossroads that marked the end of the high street. I would either have to stop or fly out blind, backwards into any oncoming traffic. I released my foot off the pedal while I tried to figure out what to do. But within seconds it was clear I'd made a mistake. The man had not, as I thought, tired of me and had decided to use my new, much slower speed to his advantage. He raced towards me, getting closer and closer. I saw that he had picked up a brick from somewhere. I looked around for help, but the street was empty. There was nothing for it. I closed my eyes, slammed my foot on the accelerator and flew across the different lanes, red lights, beeps, screeches and skids roiling in my wake.

Somehow, I reached the other side unscathed. I checked back on the man. Hampered by the now chaotic crossroads traffic, he'd stopped. He stood looking at me, weighing the brick in his hand, as though trying to work out how far he could throw it.

I turned the car around, put it into first gear and sped off down the street. I wasn't sure which way I was going. I didn't care.

20

As I put more and more distance between the man and me, I started to calm down. And, as I calmed down, I realised how stupid I had been. What would he have done if I hadn't managed to get away?

Too wired to go straight home, I decided to drive around for a bit while I tried to make sense of it all. I thought about the brick in the man's hand, held ready to throw through my windscreen, and shuddered. No wonder his wife didn't want to be found. Had she left him for another? Keith?

I braked at a set of traffic lights and my ankle screamed in protest. I drove on, paying no real attention to where I was going, and wondered what I'd seen tonight meant for the boy. The man had mentioned wanting to see his kids. Was one of those kids the boy in the shop?

Keith had seemed odd to me right from the off, secretive. I'd thought it was because he had Barney captive, because he had a child that wasn't his, but maybe his behaviour was off because he had something else to hide. Keith had told me Mikey was his nephew. Maybe he'd been telling the truth. Maybe he was harbouring his sister and her children from an abusive ex-husband. Maybe it was her and her children that he had to protect?

Taking the next turning on my left, I swung round the corner and found myself on a familiar street. Carla's new street. It seemed I'd driven here on autopilot.

As I approached the outside of her building, I slowed the car and tried to see if there were any lights on. It was almost 3 a.m. Unsurprisingly, all the windows in her flat were dark.

I pulled over and switched off the engine. Despite her numerous attempts to get in touch, we hadn't spoken since that night at the barbecue. Mark had stitched her up just as badly, if not worse, than me and Jason. Still scared of what I might say, I'd avoided her until now.

I rang her doorbell three times. The hall light switched on and Carla appeared in the gap between the chain and the door. Wearing a faded Levellers T-shirt that went all the way to her knees, she'd swaddled her shoulders in the red silk kaftan she used as a dressing-gown.

'Heidi?' she said, her voice croaky with sleep.

'I need to talk to someone.'

She blinked twice, not quite awake, and closed the door. For a moment I worried she was turning me away, that after all her ignored calls she'd finally lost patience and decided to wash her hands of me. But then I heard the metal jingle of her releasing the chain and the door reopened. She motioned for me to come in.

'I'll put the kettle on.'

I found I needed a few moments' peace ensconced round her kitchen table before I could relay the evening's events. Despite the hour and the fact I'd just knocked her out of bed, Carla didn't press for details. Instead, she sat there yawning, drinking her tea and reaching down to where Jasper slinked by her shins. It was one of the things I loved about her: she never felt compelled to fill our time together with noise; she never made me hurry out my words before they were ready. Sometimes I would lie on her osteopath's table while she manipulated my shoulder, and I would want to chatter and gossip and she would talk just as much as me. But then, there were other times I wanted to lie there quietly, or maybe even close my eyes, and then she would just do her thing, reaching her cool hands underneath my ribcage, trying to loosen the constriction there, and the silence between us never felt awkward or tense the way it often can.

'I went back to that shop,' I said, at last.

Giving me a look that said, oh, so that's what this is all about, she put down her mug and drew the kaftan around her chest.

'The one with the boy?'

I nodded, and then, suddenly desperate to tell her everything, I spoke quickly, expelling the sentences as fast as I could.

'I went there last week. I saw him coming home from school. I managed to get some photos, but they were no good. I went back but there was this man and I fell over –'

'Hang on,' Carla interrupted. 'You were there just now, in the middle of the night? By yourself?'

'There was a photograph of the boy and some other people,' I explained, impatient to continue. 'In the house. You could see it through the back window.'

'But why in the middle of the night?'

'I needed to get a better look. Without being disturbed. I needed to see if I could identify any of the other people in the picture.' I realised I was babbling and slowed down. 'But then there was this bloke. He thought I was on the game and when I told him I wasn't, he got angry and he chased me.'

'Chased you? Chased you how?'

'Down the street. He had a brick.' I mimed the way he'd held the weapon in the air.

Her eyes widened.

'I think we should call the police.' She went to get up, but I put my hand on her arm, stopping her.

'I don't want them involved. You know how the copper grapevine works. It would take five seconds for word to get to DS Gooder and he'd almost certainly mention it to Jason.'

'And where does Jason think you are right now?'

'I waited until he was asleep before I went out.'

Her face flashed with an anxiety I'd never seen before. Edging her chair in close to mine, she took hold of my hands. 'It sounds like everything has got a little out of control.' She gave them a squeeze. 'Maybe what happened tonight was just the fright you needed to make you stop.'

'To make me stop?' This I hadn't expected. 'What if I don't want to stop?'

Covering her eyes with her palms, she took a breath, lifted them up to her forehead and smoothed back her curls.

'How can I put this?' she said flatly. 'When you first told me about the kid in the shop, you said you showed Jason the boy and he stated definitively that the child was not Barney, right?'

'Right, but –'

'He was sure he wasn't Barney,' she reiterated. 'Listen to yourself. You spent the other afternoon spying on a child on his way home from school and tonight were almost attacked. Now you're in my kitchen ranting and raving about a kid you've seen up close what, all of once, twice?'

'Does it matter how many times I've seen him?' I threw my next sentence like a punch. 'How many times did it take for *you* to realise Mark was a journalist?'

I expected her to recoil, but instead she kept her gaze fixed on me.

'I'm sorry I was the one who brought Mark into your house, but the honest truth is him lying like that was not the end of the world. I know you probably don't want to hear this, but I was happy to be used. The sex was great. Looking back, there were a whole lot more pros than cons.'

Removing my hands from hers, I tried to get up but my ankle gave from under me. She was at my side in an instant.

'What's the matter?' She dropped to her knees. 'Are you hurt?'

'It's nothing.' I winced as she took my foot in her palm. 'I went over on it when I was running away.'

She rotated my ankle gently, right and left, and I cried out in pain.

'You're lucky,' she said once she had finished her examination. 'It's only a sprain.' She replaced it carefully on the floor. 'Ice it, keep it elevated and it should be back to normal in a few days.'

We sat there sipping our tea, the wind chimes tinkling outside the kitchen window.

'Sorry,' I said, for once unable to bear the silence. 'The thing I said about Mark.'

She chewed her lip.

'I think you need to consider the possibility that all this stuff with the boy has to do with something else,' she ventured. 'That maybe it's more about . . .'

'It's not,' I jumped in before she could go on. 'I know what you're going to say, and this is absolutely, definitely not about Lauren.'

I banged my hands on the table. 'Why will no one listen? Why will no one help? Barney could be there now, right in front of our bloody noses and we're not doing anything about it. Don't you see how ridiculous that is?'

I was about to go on, but something about the expression on Carla's face made me stop. Patient but wary, it was the same look I used to see on the doctor whenever he came to sedate me in the weeks after Lauren went missing. It was a look of compassion, a look that meant, I am here to help you but I also think you might be a little bit crazy.

I was suddenly and painfully aware of exactly what I must sound like. It was like stepping into a bath of cold water.

'OK,' I conceded, dropping my head into my hands. Carla was right. When you looked at the facts, this whole thing was preposterous.

'No more. Do you hear?' said Carla, reaching across for a hug. I nodded my assent and let my cheek rest against her shoulder. Her kaftan was warm and smooth to the touch.

I closed my eyes. In a little while I'd go home to my bed and my husband and then in a few hours I'd get up and go to work. And, I told myself, if I tried really hard, pretty soon everything would be just as it was before, as though I'd never laid eyes on that boy.

21

Saturday evening, and Jason and I were celebrating our wedding anniversary. Laid out between us were the remains of a curry: yellow poppadom shards and stray grains of pilau littering the white tablecloth.

Since the night I was chased, I'd left the boy in the off-licence alone. It hadn't been easy. Every time I thought I'd banished him from my thoughts the shop's LEASEHOLD AVAILABLE sign would flash into my head and, no matter what Tommy had said to the contrary, I'd be gripped with an awful fear that I was standing by and doing nothing while my husband's son was once more spirited away.

'To my lovely wife.' Jason raised his pint and I lifted my wine in response. 'Thank you for two wonderful years.'

The toast complete, I reached across the table for his hand and interlocked our fingers. Jason brought our crabbed double-fist up to his mouth and kissed both our wedding bands. Remembering him doing the very same thing in the registry office just after we were married, I smiled. Jason: my husband, my friend, my saviour.

I shifted around in my seat. I was wearing the new hold-ups, black lace bra and knickers I'd bought especially for tonight and, while I'd been sat down, the elastic stocking-tops had started to dig deeper and deeper into my thighs. I never usually wore stuff like this. It felt like too much of a prompt. Still, tonight's celebration was all well and good but it couldn't hide the fact recently something between us had fractured, just below the surface. And so, even though it felt like I was decorating the fissures and cracks splitting their way up our walls with patterned paper and fairy lights, I found myself doing it anyway. I found myself having to try.

It hadn't always been like this. We used to be the kind of couple that had sex anywhere, anyhow. On our first holiday together we went to Paxos, a tiny Greek island. Out for a walk one morning, we'd come across a deserted cove. To get to it we had to climb down a hill. We'd been kissing before we even reached the bottom. I remembered how the beach had these spine-bruising white pebbles that warmed our skin. As I'd climbed on top of Jason, I'd struggled to get traction on the scree and the movement had sent hundreds of the stones clattering down towards the sea. Sweat had pooled in Jason's clavicle, mixing with his sun cream. As we got close, he'd sat up, and the sweat and the cream had run down his chest in neat white lines. Afterwards, we'd waded into the water holding hands and the green seaweed had floated loose like grass around our calves.

'While I remember, I need a favour,' said Jason. He wet his forefinger with his tongue and used the moisture to pick up a stray piece of poppadom. 'You know I'm being assessed in December?'

I nodded. Jason was now booked in for the exam that, if he passed, would take him up to the next level of first-aid instructor.

'I want you to come and observe me teaching. I thought you could take notes, let me know if there's anything I can improve on.'

'I'll be there,' I said, giving him a mini-salute. 'What day is the class, Saturday or Sunday?'

'Actually, it's a Tuesday. I was hoping you might take the day off.'

'I don't know,' I said, already imagining Yvonne's face were I to ask for last-minute leave just over a week after my formal warning. 'I've got quite a lot on. Can't I come to your next weekend session?'

'You could, but the thing I really need to brush up on is my' – he stopped and sat up straight, ready to reel off the course's formal title – '"Communication With Mixed Age And Ability" module.' He relaxed again. 'Those classes only run during the week.'

I tapped my fingers on the table, not sure what to do. I hadn't told him about my warning and so he was oblivious to just how tricky things were at work. I looked across to where he sat with his eyes focused on the tablecloth. This exam was important to him. I'd find a way to make it work.

'In that case,' I grinned, 'I wouldn't miss it for the world.'

He looked up in surprise.

'Thank you,' he said, leaning across to give me a kiss. 'I knew I could count on you.'

I reached for the dessert menu and was about to offer it to Jason when I noticed the waiter seating a couple at the next table. The woman was heavily pregnant and, much to her dismay, the waiter was making a huge fuss, pulling out her chair and gasping at the size of her bump. We both watched in silence and, once the show was over, I made sure to catch Jason's eye.

'I'm not getting any younger and we're not always all that careful,' I said, alluding to our hit-and-miss approach to contraception. Most couples had 'the baby talk' at the start of a relationship, once things started to get serious, but when we'd first got together we'd been understandably distracted by other topics. Every now and again the subject would come up in conversation and we'd dance around it, an elaborate tiptoe that, despite my best efforts, never really went anywhere. I reached my foot under the table and pressed my leg against his. I was sick of tiptoeing. I needed to know where I stood on the matter. Where *we* stood. 'Do you think you'll ever want to become a father again?'

'Again? I still am a father.'

'I didn't mean that – you mustn't think that's what I meant.' I felt him move his leg away from mine. 'I meant, would you ever want another child. With me?'

'I don't know.' He spoke quietly. 'I wouldn't want Barney to come home and think I'd tried to replace him.' Registering the look that must now be on my face, he began to back-pedal. 'I'm not saying no,' he soothed, 'it's just – I wouldn't feel comfortable. Not yet, not until Barney is found. Otherwise, it would be like . . . like I was . . .' He faltered, unable to complete the thought.

Like you were admitting he was dead, I thought, finishing it for him.

As the waiter began to clear our plates, Jason took the opportunity to stand up and was about to disappear off to the loo when he stopped in his tracks. He retook his seat, an odd expression on his face. He seemed frightened, pissed off and embarrassed all at the same time.

'Of all the nights,' he muttered, taking a sup of lager.

He was looking at something or someone behind me. I shifted round in my seat to try and see.

'Don't. You're being too obvious,' he said, slinking low in his chair.

I pretended to get something out of my handbag on the floor and while I was there inclined my head slightly.

'Heidi, don't,' he said again.

I scanned each section of the packed restaurant. Shiny red paper covered the walls, and the spaces between the tables and high-backed chrome chairs were marked by a series of mirrored pillars. As my eyes roved past the corner near the aquarium, I realised what the problem was. Jason's ex-wife, Vicky, and her best friend, Mandy. They were taking off their coats and accepting menus from a waiter.

Vicky was dressed in skinny blue jeans and gladiator sandals and a black T-shirt hung off her left shoulder, its sleeves shredded into a fringe, a tiger design made up of spattered purple paint and sequins on the front. With long black hair, a tiny frame and perfect, doll-like features, Vicky was always adorned with clothing embellished with some kind of sparkle, glitter or studding. Mandy, meanwhile, was sporting a purple Lycra mini-dress and huge false eyelashes.

As well as being Vicky's best friend, Mandy was also Barney's godmother. She had been the matron of honour at their wedding, and when Vicky and Jason had divorced it had only been natural she take Vicky's side.

It seemed likely they hadn't clocked our presence yet.

I came back up to where Jason was glowering in his seat.

'We can get the bill and have our dessert at home,' I said, trying to pacify him. I tugged at my hold-ups. It felt like they were cutting into the tops of my thighs. 'We shouldn't let them spoil our night.'

But it was too late. I'd lost him.

Without waiting for the bill, Jason put down three £20 notes and stood up, ready to go. He didn't stop to let me get my bag and coat and, with my ankle still sore from the fall the other night, I struggled to catch up.

He got to the bar (the halfway point between Vicky and Mandy and us) and paused. In order to leave the restaurant we would have to walk right past where they were sitting. Jason grabbed my hand in his and went for it, striding forwards, his head held high. My ankle was killing me, but I didn't dare complain and so I hobbled along next to him as fast as I could. We were free and almost clear when we heard them go quiet. Jason hesitated for a split second but managed to keep going. He was reaching for the door handle when Mandy muttered something that sounded like 'freaks' under her breath. It was all Jason needed. He retraced his steps until he was standing over Mandy.

'What did you say?'

At first I thought she was going to deny it. She looked scared and caught off guard and for a moment I gave her the benefit of the doubt. Maybe we'd heard her wrong. But then there was a ripple of hardness around her mouth that travelled all the way up to her eyes and it was clear she had decided to go through with it after all.

'You heard me.'

'Not quite, Mandy, love,' said Jason, his voice sickly sweet. 'That's why I'd like to hear you say it again. To my face.'

'Mandy, please,' said Vicky, trying to defuse the situation. But Mandy dismissed her with a wave of her hand.

'Go on Mandy, say it,' challenged Jason.

I realised he had yet to let his gaze stray in Vicky's direction.

But now Mandy's cheek had started to wobble. Most of the restaurant were watching and the manager was hovering by the bar, all of them sensing something big was about to kick off.

'I thought so.' Jason turned and went to leave, as though he'd won.

'You know she's had to start seeing the doctor again,' Mandy shouted after him.

'Mandy, shut up!' shouted Vicky.

Jason stopped and, although he kept his face forward, I could tell he was listening to every word. Jason had told me that, in the past, Vicky had been prescribed antidepressants.

Mandy made eye contact with me and held it while she delivered her next line.

'He said she could do with being able to talk to someone who truly understands what she's going through. You know, someone like you, Jason.'

I felt my gut contract.

Vicky hid her face in her hands.

Jason shook his head and I could tell he was trying to make out he didn't care, that Vicky meant nothing to him, that her plight was no longer his concern.

It was a struggle but, eventually, he managed to turn away and walked out of the restaurant into the night. He didn't wait or hold the door.

Mandy shot me a sly look of triumph and went back to her menu.

22

Sunday morning, and I woke to the sight of Jason on the floor. Already in his shorts and T-shirt, he was busy putting on his trainers.

'You're up early.'

'I need to clear my head,' he said, pulling his laces so tight the skin on his hands blanched a temporary grey.

'Will you be gone long?'

'Not sure,' he said, velcroing his iPod holder to his bicep.

'What about later?' I asked. 'Maybe we could drive out to the country, have a pub lunch?'

Making an 'mmm' sound, he stood up, placed his right leg on the bedside table and inched his head towards his knee. While he waited for the hamstring to capitulate, he reached down and zipped up the lightweight jacket he favoured for particularly long runs. Repeating the exercise on his left leg, he plugged in his white earbuds and, after giving me a kiss goodbye, somewhere between my cheek and mouth, he disappeared down the stairs.

The whole time he'd been getting ready I'd kept my face normal, my voice cheery, but as soon as I heard the front door close I nested the duvet up and over my head.

Jason didn't want a baby. Not until Barney was found.

I knew that, with the help of IVF, some women managed to

conceive well into their forties. But I also knew there were no guarantees. The longer we waited, the older I got, the harder it would be. Maybe it had been naive to think he'd want us to have a child together, but still, until last night I'd thought, I'd hoped. I burrowed further into the quilt, trying to lose myself in sleep, and had just begun to drift when I was startled awake by the phone.

Reluctant to leave my cocoon, I reached out my arm, patting the floor until I came upon my handbag. Plunging my hand inside, I yanked it out and hoisted myself up to sitting.

'Hello,' I said, breathless from the effort.

'Have I caught you in the middle of something?'

'What? No, no,' I said, disoriented. 'I was in bed and...' I stopped mid-sentence, realising I had no idea to whom I was explaining myself. 'Who is this?'

'Tommy.'

'Tommy?'

'Told you I'd be in touch.'

My business card. He took it that day.

'You're being all shy,' he said when I didn't respond. 'But I bet on the other end of that phone you're smiling that lovely smile. Like sunshine, it is.'

I remembered the pressure of his hand on the inside of my thigh.

'I'm calling to see what you're up to tomorrow night? I know this lovely little pub. Out in the country: Lamesley Pastures. The Ravensworth Arms. You can see the Angel of the North through the windows of the snug.' He waited a beat. 'It has some lovely rooms upstairs.'

I thought about the other men I'd come across like him in the past. Men who, even as teenagers, are full of secrets and experience. Men who you sensed, just from the weight of their palm on your hip, had always known what to do.

'I'm washing my hair,' I said, trying to make it clear I wasn't taking him or the prospect of infidelity seriously.

'I'm going to be there anyway, so you don't have to give me an answer now. Just come along on the night if you feel like it.'

'Got to go,' I said, hanging up.

Stretching back under the duvet, I flipped onto my front, intending to sleep. My eyes closed, I became aware of how the edge of my nightie had ridden up, leaving the silk hem to rest against the curve of my bottom. I shifted slightly and the material moved higher. My thighs were warm against the sheet. Turning my head to the side, I flexed my feet and, digging my toes into the mattress, I pushed my hips forward. Slipping my hand down underneath the weight of my body, I began to move, slowly at first and then faster, greedy for the end. My breath grew shallow. As soon as I came I burst out laughing: a strange, high giggle that seemed to suggest both delight and horror in equal measure.

Now wide awake, I got out of bed and stood in front of the mirror. One of my nightie's spaghetti straps had fallen away and was dangling low on my arm. I gave my other shoulder a shrug, releasing the strap that hung there, and my nightie fell to the floor with a swoosh. Stepping out from the silky pile at my feet, I moved in close to the mirror and turned on the light.

After studying the faint purpling on the front of my hip (the last of the van bruising) I turned side-on, trying to imagine my body through Tommy's eyes. My arms were scrawny and pale blue thread veins speckled the backs of my thighs. I poked at my breasts. They weren't too bad: high and round, even after I'd lost all the weight. I wondered how they'd fare were I ever to have another baby.

I pinned my hair into a bun, put on my dressing-gown and went in search of breakfast. Dousing the cornflakes in milk, I cupped the bowl in one hand, grasped a spoon in the other and began to wander around the house, slurping cereal as I went. It wasn't long before I found myself outside the door to the spare room.

I spooned in another mouth of cornflakes. Less than ten feet away from where I stood, sitting in the dark, were five lever-arch files' worth of Jason's case notes. Case notes that might contain something to connect the off-licence or the man that ran it to Barney's disappearance.

I felt my hand press down on the door handle.

The filing cabinet stood in the corner, next to the desk, its polished steel dulled by the grey morning light.

Managing to resist its pull, for the moment at least, I veered to the opposite side of the room and the world map stuck to the wall. Positioned next to the line-up of Barney age-progression photos, the map's continents and countries were pierced with hundreds of multi-coloured drawing pins. Stepping over Jason's old bag of welding tools, I moved closer and ran my finger over the pins he'd clustered everywhere from Thailand to Tobago. It was odd. While the police had conceded it was entirely possible Barney had been trafficked abroad, they had no definite theories either way and, as such, had continued to plough just as much manpower into domestic leads. Still, the longer Barney was missing, the more international sightings there were. Every now and then there would be a flurry of people claiming to have seen Barney in a Madrid petrol station, Moscow supermarket or at the front of the queue for Disneyland's Thunder Mountain. And, when the fancy took them, the twenty-four-hour news channels were just as bad. Reporting on 'a blond-haired boy seen with a group of older men at a Gibraltar ferry port', they would go on to pick over the details with sound bites, outside broadcasts and graphic reconstructions for days on end. Sightings of Barney in the UK meanwhile, continued to dwindle.

My eyes roamed over the map of far-flung and familiar places before eventually coming to a stop on the United Kingdom. Ours was a strange-shaped island. Like a foetus turned on its side, its too-short hands seemed to be poking out into the amniotic Irish Sea, its toe dipped down into the English Channel. Was Barney out there, somewhere in the big wide world, or was he still here, in the UK, less than fifty miles from where he was last seen?

I stepped back into the middle of the room, my eyes once more drawn to the filing cabinet and the prospect of what lay within.

Placing my cereal bowl on the desk, I curled my fingers round the top drawer's curved metal handle and pulled. Planning to pick up where I'd left off, I grabbed the file at the back marked 2010 and tried to lift it out. But I'd forgotten how heavy it was and, as I fumbled to get a grip, the folder tipped back into the cabinet and onto the contents of the locked drawer below. Reaching in with my right arm, I picked it up and tried to move it back out through the hole. But it wouldn't budge. Its corner had caught on something. Stretching my other arm in to help, I grabbed the folder with both hands and gave it a tug. Finally, it came free. Breathing a small sigh of relief, I put the file on the desk and pushed the cabinet closed. But the drawer was barely halfway shut before it stopped, unable to go any further. Opening it back out, I squinted into the gloom, trying to spot the source of the problem. There was an object blocking its way. I must have dislodged something in the locked drawer below. I stretched in again and tried to free the obstruction. But, whatever it was, was just out of reach.

I looked around for something to help. A collection of pens, a ruler and a pair of scissors filled the desk tidy. All useless. Scanning the rest of the room, my eyes soon fell on Jason's old bag of welding tools. Made out of thick burgundy canvas, its sides had been covered in oil and grime when Jason had first dumped it in here. Now though, having collected a few years' worth of dust, the bag had a grey, furred coating. Crouching down on my knees, I tried to pick it up, but it was too heavy and so I tipped it forward instead. A blowtorch, drill, metal clamp, oversized screwdriver and a few other tools I couldn't identify tumbled out onto the carpet. I considered the C-shaped clamp. That might work.

Holding on to the clamp's screw, I pushed the hook deep inside and swatted around in the dark. The cabinet's metal frame had just begun to cut into my shoulder when I felt the end of the clamp brush against something. After a few more goes, I managed to get a purchase on it and pulled the obstruction up and forward to the point where I could grab hold of it with my other hand.

Rubbing at my shoulder, I inspected my haul. I had expected to see something you wouldn't want a potential burglar to have easy access to. Instead, I was faced with a thin, black, A4-size folder, the front cover of which was plain except for a single white sticker. Written on the sticker, in red block capitals that I recognised as Jason's handwriting, was one word. I stared at it, trying to understand what it was I was seeing. VICKY. The one word written on the folder said VICKY.

23

I backed away from the desk, as though what was inside the folder might do me harm. I scrambled for an explanation – Jason kept it under lock and key, but maybe it contained important paperwork relating to his and Vicky's divorce and subsequent financial arrangements? I thought back to last night, in the curry house. The way he hadn't been able to meet her eye. On the other hand, maybe the folder was more personal. Full of old love letters and ticket stubs he'd been unable to part with. Evidence of their relationship, of his old feelings for her, that he didn't want me to see.

Placing my finger under the folder's bottom corner, I shuffled the contents out onto the desk and took a seat.

Starting with the piece of paper on the top of the pile, I saw that it was a mobile phone bill addressed to a Mrs Vicky Thursby and was dated June 2010 – the month before Barney went missing. Studying it in more detail, I saw the bill listed every number she had phoned over a twenty-eight-day period as well as the duration and cost of each call, and that two numbers in particular had been highlighted wherever they appeared on the sheet in fluorescent yellow marker.

I put the phone bill to one side and did a quick inventory of the remaining documents. As well as a map showing the location of Jason and Vicky's old house, I found Vicky's bank statements for the period January–June 2010, a photocopy of a crumpled petrol receipt for a garage situated twenty miles away in Thirsk and a list of names and times in unfamiliar handwriting.

Why had Jason collected these things together? Surely he didn't think Vicky had anything to do with Barney going missing? He'd always told me that, like the police, he believed everything she'd said happened that day and was angry at the way she'd been vilified in the press.

And how the press had gone for her.

Although Vicky had never strayed from her story, certain sections of the media had made sure that there was always a question mark over her involvement in Barney's disappearance. Ultimately, as far as they were concerned, it all came down to Mrs McCallum's witness statement and the fact she couldn't recall Barney ever having been in her flat that day.

They had ignored the old lady's deteriorating memory and instead developed a series of increasingly fantastical theories about what might or might not have happened. Through underhand sources they had discovered that, although Barney's fingerprints and hair had been found in Mrs McCallum's flat, as per Vicky's story, the police had not been able to establish whether the traces were from that day or previous weeks' visits. On top of all that, they had revealed how Vicky had suffered with postnatal depression in the months after Barney was born. Putting the two together, they'd concocted a scenario in which, somewhere between Vicky's last appointment and her journey to Mrs McCallum's flat, she had accidentally or intentionally hurt Barney and, after disposing of his body, had made up the whole disappearing-into-thin-air story in order to protect herself.

Looking back, I thought that the press and internet forums latched on to Vicky in the way they did because they were otherwise at a loss as to what might have happened. To have had a child vanish defied all rational logic and spoke to our greatest, darkest fears: specifically, the fear that, no matter how hard you tried to protect your babies, someone or something could take them and there was nothing you could do about it. By casting Vicky as a potential suspect, flimsy evidence aside, they had been able to explain away something that otherwise terrified them and their readers.

I looked again at the collection of documents Jason had decided were so important he'd kept them locked away. Had he realised something about Vicky's story that the police had missed? If so, how long had he thought this? He would almost certainly have told Martin about any possible new leads, whether they involved her or not. But then, maybe he had gone to the police with his theories and maybe they had been dismissed?

I didn't hear the door open.

'What are you doing?'

It was Jason, back from his run.

I jumped. Trying to stand up and turn to face him all at the same time, in my haste I knocked the cereal bowl flying. Milk and soggy bits of cornflake splatted onto the documents spread out on the desk and began dripping onto the carpet below.

I looked around for something to mop up the mess, but Jason was already pushing me out of the way. He slipped off his T-shirt in one easy movement and began dabbing at the pages.

'Why are you going through my stuff?'

I went to answer but my head was so crammed with the implications of what I'd just found that I couldn't speak.

'Heidi, I asked you a question,' he said, trying to salvage the damp sheets of paper.

'I wanted to refresh my memory,' I said. 'To look through your files and see if there's anything that might have been overlooked.'

'Why the sudden interest?'

He'd cleaned up as much of the milk as he could and, for the first time, he took in exactly what it was I'd been looking at. He froze. I held my tongue, waiting for him to explain. But he said nothing. Coming back up to standing, he screwed his soiled T-shirt into a ball and went to leave.

'Why have you got a file on Vicky?' I asked in the strongest voice I could muster. 'And why are you keeping it in a locked drawer?'

He paused for a second and then, trying to make out like he hadn't heard me, kept going, headed for the stairs. I followed behind.

'What does it all mean?' I shouted after him.

But still, he ignored me. A cocktail of worry and anger began to form in my stomach. Trailing him into the kitchen, I tried again.

'What's going on, Jason?'

I watched as he filled a pint glass with water from the tap and then drank it down without stopping. Once the glass was empty he wiped his mouth on the back of his arm.

'Do you think Vicky had something to do with Barney's disappearance?' I asked, trying to goad him into conversation. Still he acted as though I wasn't there.

Retreating to the opposite side of the kitchen, he placed his forehead against a cupboard and after taking some deep breaths in and out through his nose, he thumped the worktop with both hands and set off towards the hall.

'I feel like I'm going to say or do something that I'll regret.' He lifted his Adidas hoodie off the coat rack. 'I need to go out for a bit.' He fed the top over his head and reached his arms up through the sleeves.

'What? Jason, no,' I said, following behind. 'Look, I'm sorry, OK? I was just trying to help.' I tried to grab hold of him but he took a step back and my hands fluttered around his sweatshirt. I moved towards him and tried again, pinching and pulling at the fabric until finally, he gave one of my hands a hard slap.

The sound shocked us both.

'I don't want your help,' he said. 'Don't you get it? I don't fucking want it.'

He didn't bother to slam the front door. As he jogged away down the hill it swung back and forth on its hinges in the wind before a big gust caught it, making it fly shut with such force it made the whole house shudder.

24

It took me a few minutes to realise why I'd woken up. I'd been having a dream in which I was in the off-licence with the boy. I was thirsty. Somehow, I'd managed to get round to the other side of the cage where the boy was being kept, and there I'd discovered an enormous bottle of water. It was the boy's water, but I was so thirsty that I took it from him. I'd only planned on having a sip and then giving it back. But, when I drank, I discovered it was the coolest, sweetest water I'd ever tasted and so then I took another sip and another. It seemed that, no matter how much of the water I consumed, I couldn't quench my thirst. At first, I thought the dream was my body's way of telling me I was dehydrated, the way it sometimes does if you've eaten too much salty food. But then I felt the spit rushing in my mouth and I knew I had woken because I was going to be sick.

I got out of bed, went to the bathroom and knelt in front of the toilet. As I waited for the first hot sting of acid in my throat, I realised how quiet the house was, and yesterday's events floored me all over again.

Afterwards, I'd waited in all day and then all night, hoping for Jason's return. By midnight, there was still no sign of him and so I'd tried to go to bed. But rest had proved impossible. Lying there, I'd found myself paralysed by the same feeling I used to have in the years before we met. It was as though the marrow had been scraped from my bones, as though I was a hollow woman, desiccated and lighter than air.

I still found it impossible to believe Jason might think Vicky had anything to do with Barney's disappearance. That he would ever consider her capable of hurting her own son. But then, sometimes mothers did kill their children. On purpose or accidentally. In their right mind or not. I thought about the locked drawer and the folder it held. Maybe Jason knew things about Vicky and her history that meant he couldn't totally disregard the possibility she had been involved. Maybe he suspected she had been to blame all along.

The boiling in my abdomen was getting worse. What had I eaten to make me ill? No doubt the wine I'd drunk to help me sleep had something to do with it, but then, I'd only had a couple of glasses. Maybe I'd had more than I'd realised or maybe the bottle was off. That happened sometimes. As my stomach began to pulse I braced myself, ready. Before long, whatever it was inside of me that was wrong was out and it was all over.

My knees shaky, I grabbed hold of the towel rail and used it to pull myself up to standing. And then it happened.

I don't know if it was the acrid smell in the air, or the fact that for the first time in ages I'd spent last night alone, but I found myself remembering one particular day when Lauren had been sick. She must have been three or four years old. The sounds of her retching had woken me and I'd gone to her room to check on her. Bleary-eyed, I'd tried to clear the vomit from the carpet: all smushed up pitta bread and pasta shells from her dinner the night before. I remembered how some of its wet warm had grazed my knuckles as I scooped it up with the cloth.

But then I'm not sure that 'remembering' is the right word for the way that that particular image had come into my head. I mean, how *do* you describe it when you suddenly recall something you haven't thought of since? Something so banal and everyday that it dissolved from your brain almost as soon as it happened? I had many precious memories of Lauren stored away, memories that I liked to turn over like jewels in my hand, enjoying them again and again. But, until now, I'd always thought they were finite, that I'd gleaned my mind for every last drop of her. So, to have something like this come back to me was such a peculiar and unexpected treasure. It felt like I had found a bit of unwatched home-movie footage at the bottom of a cupboard.

I went back into the bedroom, to where my phone sat on the dressing table, and checked for missed calls. But the screen was a blank. Where had Jason spent last night and when was he going to get in touch? I resisted the urge to call around his friends and ask if any of them had heard from him. Something told me I'd be better off keeping this to myself.

Then I had a thought that, even as it formed in my brain, I tried to dismiss.

What if he'd spent the night at Vicky's?

He could have asked for refuge: a blanket and the sofa and time to sort out his head. She would never refuse him.

It was 4 a.m. I could drive over there now and see if his car was outside.

25

Swathes of fog rolled low on the ground and old leaves rucked brown against walls and fences. The sun had yet to come up but sparrows were already chittering in the trees. Blanketed by the warm air thrumming from the vents and the dashboard glowing blue and red in the gloom, I drove on towards my destination.

I reached the entrance to Vicky's cul-de-sac and slowed to a crawl. Parking on the opposite side of the street, some distance from her house, I turned off the engine and sat there in the dark. Populated by identical semi-detached houses, the close seemed to radiate with yellow-coloured bricks, the white gabling around each front door like a fluorescent marker, there to semaphore each resident's home. Every house, including Vicky's, was dark, the day to come still sandbagged by closed curtains and drawn blinds. I listened to the clicks and creaks of the car engine cooling and got Lauren's compass out of my bag. Holding the silver disc in my palm, I completed an inventory of every parked car. There was no sign of Jason's Golf.

I breathed out, long and slow, and gripped the steering wheel. Once I'd recovered myself, I looked at Vicky's house, trying to imagine Barney playing football on the crunchy gravel in the drive. Vicky and Jason had bought the place when they got engaged. When they divorced, he'd let her have it as part of the settlement.

My mouth was still coated with an acid, sour residue, the after-effects of my earlier bout of sickness. I searched out the roll of mints I kept in the well beneath the handbrake and my hand brushed against a sheaf of papers. I popped a mint into my mouth and unfolded the four sheets of A4. They were the photo composites of the unidentified people seen in or near Ashbrook House around the time Barney went missing. I must have left them in here the day I brought them to the off-licence. I made a mental note to replace them in Jason's files before he could notice they were gone. One by one, I held the male faces up to the weak, grey moonlight. Reassured they didn't pass any resemblance to Keith, I folded them back together. Why none of the people pictured in these photofits had ever come forward remained a mystery. Some speculated that it was because they were involved in Barney's disappearance, others thought it was because they didn't exist, because they were a figment, imagined out of thin air by eager witnesses desperate to offer something, anything that might help.

I'd just placed them in my coat pocket when Vicky's front door opened. I scrunched down in the seat, my ears full of the whump-whump of blood being moved fast around my body. Had she seen me? Was she coming out to ask why I was spying on her?

My hand on the ignition, I was about to leave when someone appeared in the doorway. Too tall to be Vicky, the person was shrugging a coat up onto their shoulders and looking right and left, sizing up the neighbouring houses. They stepped out onto the drive and I realised it was a man.

Jason?

I watched as he stopped and turned back, apparently in response to someone still inside the house. Vicky appeared on the step. Her black hair loose around her shoulders, she was wrapped in a long white dressing-gown, the collar drawn up against the cold. The man retraced his steps and Vicky brought up her hands, drawing him in for a final kiss. To reach her mouth, the man had to bend down low. As he came back up to standing, he angled his face ever so slightly to the left and the street light caught on his profile. I gripped the compass hard.

The man kissing Vicky was Martin. DS Martin Gooder.

My first feeling was relief. It wasn't my husband on the doorstep. This soon gave way to shock. Vicky and the detective were together. Or they had been last night. I wondered if Jason had any inkling there was something going on between them? If he had, then he'd never once mentioned it to me. As far as he was concerned, since their divorce, Vicky had remained single. Would he be jealous?

They finished their goodbyes and the detective lolloped off into the dark, the dangle and swing of his arms and legs making it look like they were only loosely attached to his torso.

He was on the other side of the street to where I was parked. Still I hunched as far down in my seat as I could; I came back up to sitting only once I was sure he'd gone.

The watery dawn light was just starting to show over the rooftops. I checked back on Vicky's house. Every window was dark, her front door closed tight.

26

Back home, I went through every room, checking for signs of Jason. If he'd been here while I was out, he'd left no trace. My search complete, I slumped on the small chair in front of our dressing table. I needed to get ready for work, but first I decided to give Jason one more try.

Dialling his number, I used my other hand to feel in my bag for Lauren's compass. As his phone began to ring, I rubbed my thumb against the disc's serrated edge and was just warming the metal in my palm when his voicemail kicked in. I let myself listen to the recording for a few seconds and then I hung up and tried again. Maybe he hadn't been able to make it to the phone in time. But once more he didn't answer. I decided to leave a message.

'Where are you? I'm worried.' I softened my tone. 'I'm sorry, Jay. I shouldn't have gone through your things. At least let me know you're OK.'

As I hung up, I caught sight of my reflection in the dressing-table mirror. My eyes were swollen and the smattering of grey at the edge of my hairline seemed to have seeped from my scalp overnight. I looked all of my thirty-nine years and more. I grabbed a face-wipe and began to clean the tears from my cheeks. At least Jason hadn't taken a bag. His things were still scattered amongst my perfume bottles and tubs of moisturiser. I looked at his tin of deodorant, tube of ChapStick and hairbrush, dense with old strands of blond hair. He'd have to come home soon, if only to get a change of clothes.

On compulsion, I scrolled through my phone again, hoping there might be some call or text message I'd missed the first time around. But of course, there was nothing. The last person to contact me had done so yesterday morning from a withheld number. Tommy's number.

I considered Jason's hairbrush. Some of the blond strands snagged in its teeth still had the white root-plugs attached. I'd watched enough TV to know that the root was the part of the hair they used for DNA testing.

I looked at the withheld number on the screen.

It had been weeks and still, I was unable to forget the child from the off-licence.

I imagined Jason's face were I to be able to come to him with the wonderful news I'd found his son.

Maybe Tommy's phone call was an opportunity? Maybe he was the one person who could help me get definitive proof as to the boy's identity? If I could make Tommy believe that his interest in me was reciprocated, then I'd be able to visit and spend time with him – and hopefully, through his association with Keith, get access to the child, all without sounding any warning bells.

I got to my feet. I was a fool to let this chance pass me by. I needed to get closer to the boy. Without the metal security cage between us. Without spying on him in the street. Tommy. Tommy was the key.

27

I spent the rest of the day at work checking and rechecking my phone as though, if only I looked at it enough times, I could make it ring. But it had remained infuriatingly silent and now, as I returned home to find there was still no sign of Jason, a new and horrible collection of fears began to take shape.

In two years of marriage we'd never gone this long without talking. Did it mean I'd overstepped a mark there was no coming back from? And what of the folder I'd found? What else might he be keeping from me?

I got changed in a daze and as I got back in the car, I kept reminding myself I had a plan. A good, solid plan. All I needed was some of the boy's DNA. Proof. Proof would put everything that was wrong, right. For the next few hours at least, I decided to keep my mind focused on that.

I was less than a mile away when I saw the Angel of the North. Scarecrowing up out of the dusk, it stood next to the motorway, beaconing me in. I took the next turn-off and soon I was on a narrow B road, framed on both sides by high black hedgerows. I navigated the weaves and dips of what quickly became little more than a bumpy countryside lane. The car's headlamps cut through the darkness. Before long, I saw a sign advertising the pub Tommy had described. I slowed down and hunched forward over the steering wheel, searching the gloom for the entrance. Around the next corner my headlamps picked out a tall wooden pole, a square board announcing the pub's name amidst an elaborate coat of arms insignia. The Ravensworth Arms: Public House and Inn.

I pulled into the car park and got out. In front of me was the pub. A long, narrow building built out of sand-coloured stone, its ground floor was ablaze with light. Meanwhile upstairs, thick curtains swagged the windows of what were presumably the hotel rooms for hire. Undeterred by the chill October wind, a collection of smokers stood by a bench near the far end of the building.

I headed for the small door set forward into an eaved vestibule and tried not to lose my balance as my metal-heeled stilettos sliced into the car park's softer sections of grass and mud. Inside, orange lights burned in bowl-like glass shades fixed to the ceiling and the air was warm and hop-scented. A few people at the bar looked over at me and whispered. There was no one dressed in anything more formal than a jumper and jeans. I must look odd standing here in my high heels with my hair curled and pinned.

I scanned the pub from left to right. Tommy had said he would be here tonight with or without me, but it was almost 9.30 p.m. I was two hours later than the specified time. I started to worry that I'd come all the way here for no reason when I saw him. Sitting apart in a snug situated towards the back of the room, he was nursing a pint in front of a fire. I approached where he sat. Wearing jeans and a thick green fleece, he seemed so at ease in his own skin and to so completely own the space he occupied, that it felt like a shame to disturb him.

It took him a few seconds to notice my presence.

'Heidi,' he said, sitting up straight. He seemed relieved to see me. Maybe he wasn't quite as blasé about my coming tonight as he'd tried to make out.

'Hi,' I replied, with a small wave.

He shuffled over to the far side of the sofa and patted the newly empty spot, encouraging me to sit down.

But I'd no sooner perched next to him than he got to his feet. He finished the remainder of his pint in one.

'White wine, right?'

I caught a waft of his aftershave. Nothing like the clean, metallic scent Jason liked to wear, it had a cinnamon kick that reminded me of the way the house smelt at Christmas.

He went to the bar and was soon back with our drinks. As he handed me my glass, I saw a plaster on his thumb.

'What did you do there?' I asked, brushing it lightly with my forefinger.

He waited before answering, as though he wanted to see how long I was willing to let my hand remain touching his.

'Cut myself chopping some onions at work,' he said. 'Had my mind on other things.'

I met his eyes with a smile and he retook his seat next to me. The fire was banked high with slack and the coals glowed amber in the grate. I tried to stop the side of my body from pressing into Tommy but the sofa was small and after a while sitting tense and upright, I became uncomfortable and so I let myself relax in next to him.

The pub crowd that surrounded us was a mixture of lone men supping pints at the bar and groups of friends and couples at the many tables arranged about the place. The air murmured with laughter and easy conversation. I watched as the people at the table nearest to us got up, ready to leave. Two couples – a middle-aged husband and wife and a much older pair, sporting grey hair and glasses; it was clear from the way the younger couple were helping the others on with their coats that they were either their parents or grandparents.

I turned to Tommy.

'Do you have family round here?'

'They're mostly in Glasgow.' He shrugged. 'But then, I think family is what you make it.' He laughed to himself. 'Or who you make it.'

'You don't ever wish you were like Keith?' I said, trying to find a way to turn the conversation to my advantage. I could tell by the look on his face that this was too much of a volte-face but to stop now would make it worse. 'You know, with his Mary Poppins routine.'

'You mean him looking after Mikey?' he asked carefully.

I nodded, relieved. He wasn't fazed by my random change of direction.

'Sure. Helping your family is an important thing. The most important thing. Keith's sister works shifts. Stacking shelves. Not easy when you're a single mum.'

I thought back to the exchange I'd witnessed between Keith and the man that night in the alley. Robbie, that's what Keith had called him. He must be the ex-husband.

'Does she have just the one kid then, his sister?'

'She's got two others. You've met Kimberley already, I think. She works for me. In the caff.'

The chubby girl behind the counter. She'd been there the day I got knocked over by the car.

'Then there's Jake. He's still at school. Mikey is the youngest.'

'Three?' I said, failing to hide my surprise. 'She has three kids?'

'That's right.' Tommy stopped and considered me with a strange half-smile.

That night in the alley Robbie had mentioned two children: a son and a daughter. Where had this third child come from? Of course, it was entirely possible that Keith's sister had had a baby either before or since her marriage to Robbie.

'Being a single parent is tough.' I thought back to how it had been raising Lauren on my own. Even with Mum and Dad to help, it was hard and often lonely. 'Divorce?'

'More complicated than that. She was married but he used to knock her around, whether the kids were there or not. Social services got involved. She stuck by him and in the end they took the kids off her, into care.'

'That's awful.'

'It was a long time ago, now. Being without them messed her up. You can imagine.' He paused and, even though I was certain he had no clue who I was, I felt myself bristle, suddenly paranoid that this was some reference to how I'd coped without Lauren. 'But then she managed to sort herself out. She left him and moved away, somewhere he'd never find her. Then she fought to get her kids back.'

'What about the husband?' I asked. 'Where is he now?' I wondered if Keith had told Tommy about Robbie banging on the door that night.

'He's inside. Not for what he did to her,' he said, anticipating my next question. 'Though he would have more than deserved it. No, he's just one of those bad lads, into all sorts.'

I thought of the fear I'd heard in Keith's voice in the alley, how he'd tried to cover for his sister. He was clearly a good person and the story he'd given me was looking more and more plausible. His sister was real, as was one of her other children, Kimberley. Had I got this whole thing horribly and completely wrong?

My eyes began to close. The last twenty-four hours were finally starting to catch up with me. I let my gaze rise up, beyond the fire, to a framed picture of the Angel of the North on the wall. With its rusty-red steel and wings spread wide, the sculpture looked majestic, magical even. It reminded me of something, but I couldn't think what. Then I remembered. I looked down at Tommy's forearm and the winged siren woman he had tattooed there. The anchor draped across her body had a tangle of roses running along the width of its crown.

'One for the road?' He gestured at my empty glass.

'I'm driving.'

'We could always stay here.' He motioned to the floor above.

'Nice try.' I smiled. 'But I don't think so.'

He reached for my hand. Slowly, he curled each one of his fingers through mine. His palm was papery dry. I looked down to where our hands now lay, intertwined on his leg, and was struck by the memory of Jason's face just before he'd walked out. His lips had been half-pursed, his eyes soft. At the time his expression had made no sense. But now I knew what it meant. Pity. That was it. He'd felt pity for me.

I looked back at our hands, still together. I could feel the heat of Tommy's skin through the fabric of his jeans. I waited a beat. I didn't move my hand away.

The bell rang for last orders and then time. People began gathering their things, ready to leave, and we joined the exodus into the car park.

Outside, the cool night air was a shock to the system. I was wearing a jacket made out of thin cotton and, almost immediately, my teeth began to chatter.

'I don't want to go home just yet.' He motioned to a jeep in the far corner. 'Shall we talk in my car?'

I hesitated, but then I reminded myself that the whole purpose of my coming here tonight had been to make him trust me. The things I'd learnt about Keith and his sister were useful, but I'd need more to be truly satisfied.

'I should be getting back.'

'Go on.'

I gave him a shy smile. It would serve Jason right if he got home and discovered I wasn't there. Let him worry.

'Just for a bit.'

I followed him over to the jeep and, after opening the passenger door for me, he went round and got in the driver's seat.

Inside, the jeep was immaculate and had that chemical, pine smell cars get when they have just been cleaned. My teeth were still chattering and so he turned the heating on high. It blared loudly from the vents and soon the car was sickly warm.

'That's better.'

We sat there in silence, watching the other cars leave. The earlier cloud cover had given way to thin, wispy contrails, and the crescent moon shone through them, high and white in the sky. I knew I should try and find some way to bring up the topic of Keith and the boy again, to use my time here to my best advantage, but every question or opener I framed in my mind sounded too weird or obvious.

'I'm glad you decided to come tonight,' said Tommy, sliding his hands up and down the outside of the steering wheel.

I watched them turn out the lights in the pub one by one and was trying to work out how to respond when I felt him reach over and stroke my left cheek.

I went to protest, only to discover I'd already moved my face in close to meet his hand. I pulled my head away.

'What are you doing?'

'Depends. What do you want me to do?' he asked, lowering his hand to my chin. He turned and tilted my face so that I was looking at his lap.

He had an erection. Part of me registered that, alone with him in his car like this, I'd left myself vulnerable. For a brief moment I let myself imagine how Jason would feel if something bad were to happen to me.

Using one hand to keep my face turned towards him, with his other hand, he began stroking himself through his jeans, making me watch, daring me to take over.

When I didn't, he stopped what he was doing and reached his hand in between my thighs. Spreading his fingers out against my flesh, he paused and looked at me.

'What do you want?' he asked again.

Apart from the odd few stragglers, the car park had now emptied.

He moved his hand up towards my knickers and, as he made contact with the cotton, I gasped at the realisation of my own wetness. He'd just started to edge my underwear to the side when a car swung past in the lane to our right, their headlights flashing directly through the windscreen. I startled and squeezed my legs together. Patting my hand against the car door until I found the lever, I grabbed it and pulled hard. When it didn't open, I tried again and again. He must have put the auto-lock on.

'Open the door,' I said, wriggling away from him. 'Please!'

'Fine,' he said, withdrawing his hand and bouncing back into his seat. He pressed a button and, as soon as I heard the doors click, I stumbled out into the dark.

Sobbing, I collapsed onto the grass and mud, my dress tangled up around my waist. I got to my feet and began walking towards my car, trying to make it back before the clouds covered the moon and cast everything into darkness.

28

I drove home slowly, my head clotted with filmy images of Tommy's fingers on my thigh. Pulling up outside the house, I saw the hall light was on. I felt a rush of happiness. Jason was back. But then, thinking about what had happened tonight, what I'd let happen, the rush was replaced with a sharp, cringing shame.

Inside the hall I felt a draught. The back door was open. Heading through to the kitchen, I saw that the garden's security light had been triggered. Fixed above the window, its sensors were designed to respond to any kind of movement – burglars, foxes, squirrels – and would switch on for a brief, timed period before switching off again. Moving to the open door, I saw Jason. Sitting on the bench underneath the apple tree, he had his head bowed low.

I stepped out onto the gravel path that cut down the middle of the lawn and as my heels crunched against the tiny stones, he looked up. Wearing an oversized T-shirt, and tracksuit bottoms that looked borrowed from someone else's wardrobe, he blinked a few times as if to make sure it was really me.

'Where have you been?'

'I went out with Carla.' With my make-up and mascara smeared all over my face I knew I must look a fright. Hopefully he'd put it down to the tears I'd cried in his absence. 'Are you OK?' I asked. 'I was worried.'

He didn't respond and so I took a seat next to him. Together we stared at the back of our house: the arrangement of the bedroom windows and kitchen door like eyes and a nose that had been cut into the flat, red brick. Drawing down my gaze, I saw that the security light had attracted a group of floury-winged moths. I watched as they battered their furred bodies against the bulb's hot glass.

'I'm not proud of that file,' said Jason eventually. 'When the papers used to say those things about Vicky . . .' He stopped, unable to voice the actual allegations. The garden had been free of movement for a few minutes and so the security light clicked off. We found ourselves in darkness. 'I was so desperate to know what happened. I wanted an answer. Any answer.' He shook his head in rebuke.

'And what did you find?'

'Nothing, I found nothing.'

He dipped his head to his chest.

'Maybe you did find something? Maybe you just didn't realise it? Have you told Martin about any of it? He and the team might pick up on something you thought was unimportant. We could talk to him and –'

'But I did. I did mention it,' he said, cutting me off at the pass. 'He took one look and said there was nothing in the file they weren't already aware of.'

I remembered the way the detective had left Vicky's house that morning, checking over his shoulder before he ventured out into the dark.

'What was it exactly you were suspicious of?'

'Certain things. They didn't make sense.' He took my hand. 'Look, I'm embarrassed enough. Can we just leave it at that?'

I thought about the length of the kiss I'd seen Vicky and the detective share on the doorstep. Martin had known and supported her through the worst five years of her life. No doubt he cared for her very deeply. He'd already risked his job by starting a relationship with someone involved in an ongoing high-profile case. If anyone found out, he was liable to be suspended, or worse. So how far would he go to protect her? How far would he compromise himself to stop her from being hurt?

I leant in and pressed Jason's cheek against mine. My nose filled with his sweet, glandular tang. It was wonderfully familiar but then, almost instantly, I reached for the memory of Tommy and his cinnamon musk. I felt like I was about to disintegrate, but then Jason squeezed me into an embrace so hard and so tight that all the air was pushed from my lungs. He started to rock me, backwards and forwards. The movement activated the security light and still he kept rocking, our eyes shut against its hard, yellow glare.

29

The following week, despite the fact that it hadn't gone down well with work, I'd taken a day's leave to come and observe Jason teach.

While I took a seat at the back, apart from the rest of the students, Jason shut the door, sealing us all in for the morning. A mixed bunch, the room spanned everyone from Kappa-clad adolescents to eager pensioners.

'So,' he began with a clap. 'You're here because you want to learn how to be a good first-aider. You want to know how to help, and possibly even save, those in need.' He was wearing an old denim shirt, rolled up at the sleeves, and my eyes kept being drawn to his forearms. Wide and solid, they were seamed with fat veins: his wrists thick and strong. 'I'm going to start by talking to you about *the* most important piece of information I want you to take away today. I want to talk to you about how important it is to not help someone.'

He raised his hands in front of his chest.

'I know. Not helping someone. It sounds strange doesn't it? It goes against all your natural instincts, but what I want to drill into you is how vital it is to make sure you yourself are not in any danger before you even think – even think,' he repeated, emphasising his words by slicing the side of his hand through the air, 'of going anywhere near someone in need.'

His voice took on a mysterious tone.

'Enough of me yapping. I always think the best way to learn anything is to put it into practice in the real world.'

At this, he got up and walked out of the class. Everyone watched him go, puzzled. The students looked at each other nervously and then Jason began shouting from the corridor.

'Help! There's someone hurt out here!'

They waited a few beats more before two of them got up and ran out. The rest soon followed in their wake. After watching them leave, I got to my feet and made my way into the corridor, where the class were gathered around a stairwell.

As I got near, I could see what they were all looking at. On the floor was a man. Covered in blood, his limbs were splayed out at different angles, his skin pallid, eyes closed. A rickety-looking stepladder had been staged next to his right leg and a set of frayed electrical wires dangled from the ceiling.

Standing apart from the scene, hands on his hips, Jason watched as his class took in the drama. One of the students, a woman in her sixties wearing a jumper with a picture of a pink poodle on the front, went to ask him a question, but Jason beat her to it.

'What have we got here?' he asked the class. 'What should we do to help this person?'

The first time I'd ever come to watch him teach and I'd seen someone apparently hurt like this, I'd been shocked. That had soon changed into an appreciation of the special effects. I now knew Jason hired members of the local amateur dramatic society to play his various 'victims' and that he taped small bags of fake blood inside their clothing. These bags had little tubes that fed out to various parts of the body to make it seem like blood was leaking from their veins or dribbling from their mouth.

Jason suggested the class role-play the situation and as they did what he asked, I marvelled at how, not that long ago, he'd been the kind of person who would struggle to apply a simple plaster, let alone teach someone else how to perform CPR. In actual fact, his interest in first aid hadn't come about till he was well into his twenties, after Barney had first gone missing. On a contract to repair a bridge on the Tees, they'd needed an extra first-aider on-site and Jason had been one of the men sent on a course. He'd loved every second of it and by the end of the first day he was smitten. Six months on and he'd started evening classes; one year after that he'd qualified. Despite the huge drop in salary, it wasn't long before he'd jacked in the steel and turned to teaching full time.

The role-play exercise reached its conclusion and I watched as the actor got to his feet and went around the group introducing himself. It was funny. Even though everyone knew he'd been playing, there was still a real sense of relief he was OK.

As the class milled around, laughing and talking about what had just happened, I took the opportunity to get some fresh air and check in with the office.

Outside, I headed for the row of metal benches that lined the edge of the college, sat down and got out my phone. As well as a host of emails from clients, there were also a few messages from Yvonne. Written in the same curt tone, she took every opportunity to make it clear she was unhappy about my having today off. I knew she couldn't discipline me for taking a day's holiday, but I also knew that, as far as she was concerned, I should be working twenty-four-seven to try and get back on track.

I answered as many emails as I could and was thinking about returning inside when I became aware of someone watching me. Looking up, my eyes locked with a tall, jacketed man loitering by the smokers' shelter. Hands thrust deep in his pockets, he had dark wavy hair and a way of standing, with his shoulders erect and his head held to the side, that I found familiar. It was Mark, the journalist who'd inveigled his way into our barbecue.

'You've got some nerve,' I said, stomping over to where he stood. 'I assume it's no coincidence you're hanging around on the same day my husband teaches a class.'

He looked down at his feet and, for a moment, he seemed embarrassed to have been caught out.

'I was hoping I'd bump into him.' He scuffed his left shoe against the base of the smoking shelter. 'But not for the reason you think. I wanted to apologise. I know what I did might've seemed wrong, but I stand by what I said. I really think an interview would help the search . . .'

'Wrong! You know it seemed wrong?'

He held up his hands in defeat.

'I get it, OK? You're angry. And you've every right. But, like I said, I wanted to say sorry.'

'So, what? You were hoping for something juicy? Some exclusive from behind the scenes?'

He looked off into the distance as though he hadn't heard what I'd just said.

'I've been looking into Barney's disappearance. The days that followed. There are certain things, things Vicky did, that make no sense.'

'You're full of it. If this is your weird, roundabout way of baiting me into an interview, then I suggest you go back to journalism school.'

'Ask him. Jason. Ask him if their marriage was as solid as they made it out to be back then.'

I started to walk away.

'I mean it when I say that some fresh press could help Barney's case.'

I stopped, marched back to where he stood and pushed myself so far into his face that he had to take a small step back, away from me.

'Don't for one second try to pretend this is about finding Barney,' I said. 'You come here and make nasty allusions that make no sense. You don't care about him or Jason. All you care about is yourself.'

He crooked his lips into a half-smirk.

'Why are you so worried about one silly interview?'

'What do I have to be worried about? I think we all know the worst thing that can happen to a person has already happened to me.'

He looked off into the distance.

'What age are you now, Heidi? I'd have thought you'd need to get a move on if you and Jason are to start your own family together.' He said the words as though he was making an observation about nothing more than the weather. 'Is it because you can't?' He paused. 'Or is it because he won't?'

It was like he'd kicked me.

'I feel sorry for you,' I said, walking away before he could see my tears. 'Make sure you're off the premises before Jason's class is over or I'll call security.'

'You have my number,' he shouted after me. 'If you ever change your mind.'

I waited until I was as far away from him as possible, out of sight, and crouched down against the nearest available wall. I reached in my bag for Lauren's compass and squeezed my eyes shut. It took some time for my body to stop shaking.

Back in the classroom, Jason was in full-throttle teaching mode. As I retook my seat, he caught my eye. Waving my phone in the air, I shook my head and mouthed the word 'work'.

While I was gone, he'd moved on to the theory part of the course, the part for which he expected to come under particular scrutiny come his assessment in December.

'So,' he began, cueing up a DVD. 'We all have different chances of survival in different situations. Our relative age, fitness and health can massively affect whether we live or die.'

He gestured at the TV screen. Paused on an American news bulletin, it showed a female newsreader about to speak. To the right of her head was a small picture of the next story: a snowy riverbank and the flashing red lights of an ambulance.

'Children are massively resilient. With children, accident or disaster situations can be a whole different playing field.'

Jason waved the remote at the screen.

'Take the case of Jake Schneider. He was only four years old when, while playing with friends, he slid down a bank and fell into a freezing lake in Canada. He couldn't swim.' Jason paused, letting the frightening reality of the situation sink in. Once he was satisfied that everyone was suitably anxious, he carried on. 'It took twenty minutes for the fire services to get there and pull him out.

Twenty minutes. So what do you think? Did he survive, or not?'

The woman in the pink poodle jumper raised her hand.

'The human brain cannot survive any longer than four minutes without oxygen, so there would be no way he lived,' she said.

Jason nodded.

'You'd think so, wouldn't you? To argue otherwise would be daft, right? To argue that a four-year-old child who couldn't swim would go on to live after twenty minutes under water in a freezing lake would be mad.'

He got to his feet.

'Let me tell you what actually happened. As soon as Jake enters the water,' – he mimed something going from a great height onto the ground – 'he starts gulping in mouthfuls of liquid. But then, as his body submerges, the mammalian dive reflex kicks in, shutting off his windpipe and preventing any further water from entering his lungs or stomach.'

Jason let his hand sink to a spot just below his hips, symbolising Jake lying at the bottom of the lake.

'Now Jake is under water and he is freezing. And, as would be the same for any of us here, his heart rate and brain function all shut down as a way of preserving his core body temperature.' He motioned to his own chest, mouth and head to illustrate his words. 'In its rapidly cooled state the brain doesn't need very much oxygen and can remain undamaged much longer than the usual four minutes. In effect, the body goes into suspended animation. However, despite all of this, if any of us adults had been at the bottom of that lake, we would have died. But what happened to Jake?'

He looked around the room.

'Anyone?'

The class was mute. He grinned in anticipation of the crescendo he was about to deliver.

'Children have larger heads relative to the rest of their body than adults, much larger, meaning they lose heat more quickly. Add to this the fact that children's temperature regulation systems aren't as well developed as they are in adults and you have the reason that Jake lived to tell the tale.'

A few of the students looked at each other, confused.

'Let me put it simply,' continued Jason. 'If an adult had gone into that lake for that length of time, they would be dead. However, four-year-old Jake's body went into suspended animation almost immediately, which meant that his organs and brain were protected and preserved almost immediately, which meant he could stay down there for much longer than four minutes without being brain-damaged, which meant he could be brought back to life.'

There were still a few puzzled expressions.

Jason spoke his next words very slowly.

'The combination of Jake's age, the coldness of the water and the fact that when a child is going to drown they usually submerge very quickly means that a cold child drowning has a fifty per cent better chance of survival than any adult in the same situation.'

The woman in the poodle jumper raised her hand in the air again. It seemed that, despite her earlier knock, she wasn't going to go down without a fight.

'Mr Thursby?'

'Yes?'

'Isn't it true to say that Jake wasn't drowning? I mean, if he lived, which you say he did, then he wasn't drowning was he, he was merely underwater?'

Jason frowned.

'What do you mean?'

I started to feel nervous. This woman was challenging a fable Jason had clung on to and nurtured for God knows how long. She was saying his story was flawed.

The woman shimmied her shoulders.

'To say that someone is drowning would mean that the end result is death and so, well, wouldn't it be more accurate to say a cold child under water has a good chance of survival?' She sat up a little straighter. 'To say he was drowning, if you were to look at the meaning of the word, it tells us how things turned out, it tells us that the boy died.'

'Maybe,' said Jason, ejecting the DVD. 'But the official medical definition of the word drowning does not equal certain death.'

He put the DVD back in its case and began pacing up and down the room, a curl of a smile on his face.

'A cold child drowning.' He said the words carefully, absorbing the feel of them in his mouth, and then, quoting the definition he'd learnt off by heart, 'Drowning is the process of experiencing respiratory impairment from submersion in liquid. It does not imply fatality, or even the necessity for medical treatment.'

He moved in close to the poodle-jumper woman.

'So, you see, the end result is not death. His fate is not already decided.' His face was glowing, beatific in the late morning sunshine. 'It's all still to play for, all of it.'

31

While Jason packed up his classroom, I went to wait in the car. I got into the passenger seat and pulled out my purse. I'd forgotten all about Mark's business card until he'd mentioned it this afternoon. I found it tucked between my driving licence and Tesco Clubcard.

Jason had just appeared through the double doors of the college when my phone began to ring. Thinking it might be something to do with work, I answered quickly.

'Heidi Thursby speaking.'

'It's me.'

Tommy.

'I hadn't heard from you. I wanted to check you were OK?'

'I've been busy.'

'Heidi the busy bee.' He laughed to himself.

Jason would be getting into the car at any moment. But then, when I looked, I saw that he was still standing outside the college. He'd been accosted by the poodle-jumper woman from his class.

'I'd like to see you,' continued Tommy. 'Pick up where we left off.'

My breath caught in my throat. I had thought that, after the way I'd behaved the other night, he'd want nothing more to do with me.

I checked back on Jason's progress. He had his head cocked to one side and seemed to be genuinely interested in whatever it was the woman wanted to talk about.

'What do you say?' pushed Tommy, a wobble to his tone I hadn't picked up on first time around. 'Shall we arrange another get-together?' And there it was again, that giveaway lilt. 'Heidi?'

Jason had extricated himself from the poodle woman and was back on the move. It would be only a matter of seconds before he was at the car. I kept the phone pressed to my ear, Tommy's breath crackling down the line.

I left it as long as I dared. Holding out until the very second Jason appeared at the driver's door. And then with that, I pressed the red button, cutting Tommy off, and turned to Jason with a smile.

32

'Thanks again for coming today,' said Jason as he stowed his teaching materials on the back seat. He got in beside me and, after hooking his arm around the back of my headrest, reversed out of the parking space. 'I need to make a quick stop.' He pulled onto the main road. 'I've got to drop Barney's fire engine at Vicky's.'

I shook my head, not sure I'd heard him right.

'You've got the fire engine with you?' They usually exchanged the toy every other Monday, like clockwork. Today was Tuesday.

'I'm late getting it back,' he went on, 'and she's not best pleased.'

We pulled up outside Vicky's house and Jason went to retrieve the toy from the boot. I'd just relaxed back into my seat when I noticed Jason beckoning for me to join him. I raised my hands in the air to signal my confusion. I'd never been into Vicky's house before and she had never been into mine. It was an unspoken rule and, I felt, quite normal, in fact, for the divorcée and the new wife never to enter each other's territory. Right now though, Jason seemed to feel differently. He marched back round to my side of the car and opened the door.

'I want you to come with me,' he said, unable to meet my eyes.

'What? Why?'

'Please. I'll explain later.' Reaching in, he undid my seat belt, helped me out and began pulling me down the garden path.

'Jason, what is this about?' I asked as he rang the doorbell.

Before he could answer, Vicky appeared.

'You're a day late,' she said. 'A whole day.'

She had yet to notice me standing behind him.

'It's not fair,' she said. 'We agreed.' She had lost weight in the weeks since we'd last seen her that time in the curry house, and there were pale grey smudges underneath her eyes.

'I left a message. I got held up yesterday,' said Jason, quietly. 'Then I had to work.'

He handed her the bag with the toy inside and she pressed it to her body. After a few moments she looked up and it was then that she registered my presence.

'Don't suppose there's any chance of a cup of tea?' asked Jason, as though me being there was the most normal thing in the world. 'I'm parched.'

Open-mouthed, Vicky looked at him and then me, like this was some kind of trick. I held my breath, waiting for the insults to fly, but it seemed Vicky had decided to go with whatever was happening, however strange. Still clutching the bag to her chest, she headed to the kitchen.

As Jason crossed the threshold, I turned around, intending to bail and go back to the car, but he held my hand firm.

'Heidi, no.'

'But . . .'

'Heidi, please.'

I let him lead me into the living room. He sat down on the sofa but I remained standing.

'What's going on? This is weird.' I was about to continue but was silenced by Vicky coming into the room.

'The kettle's on.' Seeing me, she stopped for a moment, as though she'd forgotten I was here, but within seconds she'd righted herself and slumped in the armchair. Realising I had no choice but to sit this one out, I took my place next to Jason.

'Were you teaching today?' Vicky asked. Her hair was loose around her shoulders and now she took a section of it between her fingers and began twisting it tight like a rope.

'Yes, I've been putting in the hours.' He looked at the room as he spoke. 'I need to practise for my assessment and the extra cash is good. Especially as we've got the holiday round the corner.'

'Holiday?' asked Vicky. She twisted the hair even tighter; it started to pull at the white of her scalp.

'We're going to Gran Canaria for two weeks.' He grabbed my knee. 'Winter sun. All-inclusive.'

'Gran Canaria.' For the first time since she'd entered the room, Vicky looked me in the eye.

'We go away on 20th November. The 20th for two weeks, isn't it, Heidi?'

He turned to look at me for affirmation and it was then I realised why he'd wanted me to come and watch him teach today. He must have planned it all along. If I came with him to his class then I'd be with him when he dropped off the fire engine.

He cleared his throat.

'So, Vicky, the two weeks we're away would normally be my two weeks with the truck,' he explained. 'What do you want to do? Do you want to keep it for a month and then I have it for a month?' I could tell he was working hard to keep his tone casual.

Jason had realised the date clash a few weeks after we'd booked the holiday. He'd been looking at the calendar and when he worked it out he had seriously considered taking the truck with us to the Canary Islands. But then he'd worried about it getting damaged in the suitcase or being stolen from the room and soon he'd decided that the best solution would be for them to adjust their custody arrangement. This, however, required Vicky to play ball. He was terrified Vicky would insist the two weeks we were away were his, whether he was around or not. I'd assumed he'd cleared it with her ages ago, but now I realised he must have been putting it off for as long as he could. Today, he must have hoped that, if he brought me here, she'd be less likely to make it an issue.

'What do you think?' asked Jason.

Vicky smiled sadly to herself in a way that I didn't understand. She was about to reply when there was a loud rapping at the front door. We all started.

'Vicky! Vicky, are you in there?' shouted a woman through the letterbox.

Vicky stood up and sighed. She tugged at her skinny jeans and I noticed how much they gaped at the waist.

'What does she want?' She went to leave the room, but then, remembering we were there, took a few steps back to explain. 'It's that Margaret from the end of the road. I won't be long.'

As she went into the hall to see to Margaret, Jason and I remained where we were.

'Are you all right, Maggie? What's the matter?' She sounded only mildly concerned.

'It's my hair dye. I thought I'd try the Magenta Sunrise this time, but I think I left it on too long and it's burning my scalp. Can you help?'

'You silly mare,' laughed Vicky. I could hear her putting on her jacket. 'Won't be long,' she shouted back to us and then we heard the front door slam.

Out of the window we saw Vicky running down the path behind a woman with a towel round her shoulders, purple dye dripping from her hairline down the sides of her face.

I waited for Jason to do something. When he didn't, I decided to take the bull by the horns.

'Shall we go?' I stood up. I was glad this woman Margaret had come knocking. It gave us the perfect excuse to leave immediately.

'I don't know,' said Jason relaxing into the sofa. 'I'm not sure if Vicky took a key.' He tucked a few stray strands of hair behind his ears.

I looked at the toy, still in its bag, centre stage on the coffee-table.

'Why were you late with the truck?' I asked. 'Surely you want to get in Vicky's good books so that she'll be nice about the holiday arrangements? She's not likely to accommodate you now, is she?'

Jason hung his head.

'I know,' he said quietly. 'I just needed one more night with it.'

'You should explain that to Vicky. She'd understand.'

'Maybe,' he shrugged. 'Maybe not.'

He got to his feet.

'Are we leaving?' I moved towards the hallway, happy to be on our way.

'What? No. Sit down.' He directed me back to the sofa. 'You stay there. I need to check something. I won't be a minute.' And with that, he went into the hall with the ease that only comes from having once inhabited a place.

'Check what?' But it was too late. He'd already disappeared up the stairs.

Alone in Vicky's house for the first time, I looked around, trying to imagine her and Jason in it together, living here as man and wife.

A three-piece brown leather suite, and a beech sideboard and coffee-table dominated the room. The walls, meanwhile, were skimmed plaster, painted magnolia. The cream colour scheme continued around the bay window, where Vicky had hung thick cotton curtains from a chrome pole that had twisty spiral flourishes at each end. I sniffed the air; there seemed to be a Glade plug-in freshener in every available socket and they gave the room a rich, sickly smell. Apart from a grey vase on the sideboard containing three decorative sprigs of wood, the only other ornamentation were the framed pictures of Barney.

Curious for a better look, I got up and traced my thumb along the mantelpiece, lined with photos three deep. A few of the pictures had Jason in them. I picked one and took it over to the window so that I could study it in more detail. It was the kind you get taken at a professional studio and it featured Vicky and Jason against a white background with a baby Barney in a nappy on the floor, two milk teeth peeking out of his bottom gum. Jason's hair was shorter than he wore it now and he was as skinny as a colt.

I stroked Jason's face through the glass with my finger. He and Vicky both looked so young. Probably because they were. Having got together at school, everything else followed on from there. They were engaged by eighteen, married by twenty and Vicky was pregnant with Barney at twenty-two.

They'd celebrated their fourth wedding anniversary a few

weeks before Barney went missing. One year later, one year of him being gone, and the marriage was over. Jason told me they'd done everything they could to carry on, but that being together meant they were never able to think or talk of anything else except Barney. It had paralysed them. While on the one hand, Vicky was the only other person in the world who could truly understand what he was going through, on the other, the fact she was Barney's mum meant he never had any respite.

We met a year after their divorce. I was under no illusion as to why we worked as a couple. Jason needed someone who could understand his loss and pain, and I did, truly. But, at the same time, my loss was different from his and so, with me, he would always have the space to breathe.

I put the picture back where I had found it and moved over to the largest photo on display. Positioned next to the armchair where Vicky had sat, it showed Barney modelling a junior Middlesbrough Football Club kit. The shorts were way too big for him and he could barely hold the adult-sized football under his arm, but he looked so proud.

Was this the boy from the off-licence?

For a moment I considered asking Vicky for help. I could tell her what I'd seen. Ask her if she recognised the child as Barney. But no. It would be too weird. And besides, to go to her behind Jason's back with something like this would be such a betrayal. He'd never forgive it.

I was about to go and sit back down and wait for Jason when I saw a thin line of silver poking out from the armchair's seat cushion. Vicky's mobile phone.

I couldn't help myself. Wedging it out of the sofa, I flipped it open, found the envelope symbol and clicked.

Most of the messages were from her mum and friends. I opened a few but they were all fairly boring and meaningless. I went to scroll down, but I must have pressed too hard because the texts went zooming up the screen and before I knew it I was looking at messages from a few weeks back. I was about to start the laborious process of scrolling forward when I noticed a text message from someone called 'Jason'. I tried not to let it worry me. I knew that Jason had to stay in touch with Vicky because of Barney. The text was dated Sunday 3rd October. The day after our wedding anniversary.

'Are you OK? What Mandy said about you going back to see the doctor – is it true? Anything I need to be worried about?'

Vicky's reply was there, right beneath it.

'Am fine. Mandy shouldn't have said anything. Just had a rough few days, that's all. xxx'

It meant nothing. Of course he'd checked to see if she was OK. It was in his nature.

I closed the message and returned to her inbox. She seemed to have saved lots of messages into a separate folder. I opened it. They were all from someone she'd entered into her phone as 'MG'. DS Martin Gooder.

I opened the most recent exchange. They were the usual texts you'd expect to see between a romantic couple. They were either busy arranging their next tryst or reminiscing about their previous time together, but then I came across an odd sequence of messages. The first was dated a few weeks earlier and was from Vicky to Martin.

'It's getting worse. I need to do something.'

Below was the detective's response.

'No. You can get through this.'

Vicky's reply followed.

'I keep thinking about how old my baby would be now.'

'It wasn't your fault. None of it.'

There followed more messages of reassurance from the detective. It seemed she was having a particularly hard time of it at the moment. It sounded like the disappointment of the Turkish sighting a few weeks ago had more than left its mark.

As I wedged the phone back into the armchair cushion, I noticed the time. It was almost three. I'd been so engrossed in my snooping that I hadn't realised how long Jason had been gone.

'Jason?' I called out as I climbed the stairs. Silence. 'Jason?' I said again. The whole house was fitted out in a thick cream carpet that muffled the reach of my voice. 'Where are you?'

I made my way across the landing to the only open door. Inside was a small bed with a blue spaceship duvet cover and a plastic bumblebee night-light on the table next to it. Barney's room. Sitting cross-legged on a rug by the window was Jason, reading a well-worn copy of *Where the Wild Things Are*. It was as if I'd stumbled upon a grown-up version of Barney, come home at last.

'You OK?'

He looked up from the book with a dreamy expression, but then went back to his reading.

Coming to sit down next to him, I began stroking his back, softly at first and then with more pressure. The room smelt of polish and the rug beneath us bore the telltale stripes of having being recently hoovered. I looked around. On a low-level brass hook on the back of the door was a small blue-and-red fleece dressing-gown.

I wanted to lean into Jason for a cuddle, but I couldn't because of the way he had his legs crossed. Instead, I began tracing my thumb over the burn and scorch-mark scars that pocked his wrists: a hangover from his welding days. He'd explained how these burns couldn't be helped. That, no matter how hard he'd tried, there was always a bit of neck or that thin, delicate skin on the underside of his wrists that would end up exposed to the sparks that flew back from the welding torch. He'd said that, when they hit you, they felt like tiny stings.

'I love you. Do you love me?' I asked, trying to get my face in his line of vision.

I kissed him on the cheek and then the neck, but still he kept on reading. Waiting until he'd turned the page, I kissed him on the mouth and began unbuttoning his jeans. He tried to stop me, but I kept going. I reached down to his boxers, slipped the flat of my hand underneath the elastic waistband and began rubbing at his penis. I could tell he was trying to fight it, that he wanted his body to ignore me, but he was becoming harder.

'Heidi, no,' he said, his eyes coming into focus. Once more, he tried to brush my hand away, but this time I held his wrist tight. With my other hand I took the book off him.

'No. Not here,' he said, his eyes closing.

I pushed him down so that he was lying flat on the floor and straddled him. Pulling down his boxers, I pushed my knickers to the side and then we were together. I looked at the bumblebee night-light. After all this time, had the bulb inside stopped working or did Vicky make sure to replace it? I started rocking faster and then slower, taking him to the edge and then bringing him back again, over and over.

I came a few seconds before he did. I took a moment to get my breath and then, my limbs loose and lazy, I rolled off and onto the floor next to him. As Jason tidied himself back into his jeans, I looked up at the ceiling, my dress still around my waist. Decorated with those stars and moons that glow in the dark, it seemed to be the only part of Barney's room that Vicky had forgotten to keep clean. Cobwebs furred with dust hung down in clumps from the lampshade, and grey streaks marked every corner.

Jason got to his feet and, without waiting for me, thundered out of the room. The cobwebs swayed in the temporary breeze. A few seconds later and they'd resettled, back into the position they'd held for years and years.

33

I placed the lasagne in the oven, poured myself a glass of Sauvignon Blanc and took a seat at the table. Soon, the air was heady with the smell of baked garlic and tomato.

Jason was upstairs, revising. He wanted to study right up until dinner and so, to kill time, I reached for the local free paper. But the words and pictures did not interest me and soon my thoughts began to drift, back to the text messages I'd seen on Vicky's phone. On the face of it, the exchange between her and Martin was straightforward. Barney went missing when he was in Vicky's care. She, quite understandably, still felt guilty. That was hard to live with. But there was something about their exchange that didn't sit quite right, something I couldn't put my finger on.

Abandoning the paper, I decided to make a start on the salad. I chopped the lettuce, cucumber and tomato and arranged the mixture on two plates. I dressed Jason's portion with olive oil and salt and pepper and, as usual, left my portion untouched.

I'd struggled with my weight ever since I was a teenager. Until Lauren went missing and the subsequent loss of appetite, I'd been what was politely referred to as a 'big girl' and I'd been OK with that. I liked to eat and as my dress size used to testify, I never denied myself. Lauren had revelled in my pillowy stomach and thighs. Whenever she saw me in my underwear, she'd grab hold of my midriff and with the same screwed-up face people adopt when they marvel at a chubby baby, she'd declare, 'Mummy, you are so lovely and squishy!' But Jason had only ever known me like this: slim and fit. Of course, he knew what I used to look like, but our relationship had been predicated on me as I was now. We'd never spoken of it, but I sensed that it would never do to break those terms.

The salad sorted, I started to lay the table. I'd wait right up to the last minute before calling him down to eat, give him as much time as possible. He was so committed to passing this exam and to his subject. It was hard to imagine what he was like in the years before we met, when he still worked as a welder. The steel was in his blood – a family trade – and had, by all accounts, been a huge part of his social life. Yet after Barney went missing, he'd left it all behind without, it seemed, a second glance.

I looked at the two fire-blankets and portable defibrillator fixed to the wall next to the cooker. On occasion, his passion for his new profession had bordered on obsession. The defibrillator had not come cheap but, within weeks of moving in together, Jason had insisted we invest. A square red case, it had curved edges and a black carry handle. Not unlike the carry-on luggage favoured by 1950s air hostesses, it was emblazoned with a white heart symbol, a slice of lightning through its middle. As soon as it had arrived, Jason had given me a tutorial. Inside was a surprisingly simple-looking kit: a pair of scissors to cut off clothing or underwired bras, two pads with adhesive stickers and the machine itself. A small grey box, it had two buttons: one green, one orange. Jason had reassured me that if I attached the pads to a person who was not, in fact, in cardiac arrest then the machine would not fire. He'd said that the pads were designed to check for arrhythmia before administering a shock.

He liked to keep the box hanging dead square next to the fire-blankets, but now I noticed it was balanced at a funny angle. It often got knocked as people brushed past. I readjusted it into position, but no sooner had I centred it back onto its hook than it slid down to the right again. Something inside was making it list. I lifted the case off its hook, set it on the table and opened the catch.

There, wedged in next to the grey box, was a folder I'd seen once before. Jason's Vicky folder. I stepped back from the table, confused. And then, wanting to check it was in fact the very same as the one I'd found in the filing cabinet, I opened it up. There was the mobile phone bill, with the same two numbers highlighted; there the receipt for petrol from a garage just outside Thirsk.

Jason had moved the folder. Not only that, he'd hidden it. Somewhere he thought I'd never find it. Why?

I spread the contents on the table and did a quick inventory. There were two pieces of paper that I couldn't remember seeing before. Had I missed them the first time round? Or were they new additions to the file? The first document was a calendar for the year 2010. The year Barney went missing. Various dates were circled in red in the months prior to his disappearance. The second document was an invoice. Dated one month after Barney disappeared, it was for a procedure listed only as 'Event (general anaesthetic)' from the Nuffield Hospital for £643.

I heard movement on the floorboards upstairs. Jason was getting ready to come down for dinner. I looked at the papers splayed out in front of me. I had more than enough time to put the folder back together, replace it inside the defibrillator and return it to its usual position on the wall. He'd never know I'd found his new hiding place. But no. I felt a prickle of defiance. I wanted to know what was going on.

I placed the folder neatly on the table and left the open defibrillator case next to it. Then I sat and I waited.

A few minutes later and Jason bounded down the stairs. He came into the kitchen and went straight over to the fridge for a beer. I sat perfectly still. Oblivious to the folder, he came up behind me and kissed my neck. Then, as his eyes travelled over my shoulder and down onto the table, I felt him stiffen.

'I get why you hid this before,' I said, as he started to scoop the documents back into a pile. 'But why hide it again?'

The papers safely back inside the folder, he gathered it up to his chest.

'It's hard to explain.'

'Try.'

An acrid smell began to fill the air. The lasagne had been due to come out of the oven twenty minutes ago.

'What are the calendar dates about?'

'Can't I have some things that are just for me?' He was indignant. 'Why do you insist on us sharing everything?'

'What are you keeping from me?'

'Keeping from you?' His face was red. 'You're paranoid, do you know that?' He tapped his finger at the side of his temple.

The burning smell was getting worse. Thin wisps of black smoke started to snake their way through the thin gap at the top of the oven door.

'Jason, you can tell me anything.' I softened my voice. 'I'm your wife. Please, what is going on?'

'Nothing.' He retreated back out of the kitchen and up the stairs, the folder clasped to his chest.

I looked at the defibrillator case, abandoned on the table, its cavity exposed.

At that moment the smoke alarm registered the burning lasagne. Its regular high-pitched shrill began to ring out through the house. I turned off the gas and left the ruined lasagne to cool. The smoke alarm continued to pierce the silence. I didn't cover my ears.

34

We spent the rest of the evening avoiding each other, and by the time I left for work the following day we still had not spoken.

Early afternoon and I was holding a meeting in the tiny breakout area by reception. Designated for internal, impromptu get-togethers, the space consisted of a square of different coloured carpet, four chairs and a flipchart. And because it was flanked by the receptionist, Hayley, discussions were punctuated by the constantly ringing phone and subsequent 'Hello-Hayley-speaking-how-can-I-help-you?'s.

'Let's go through it one more time,' I said, pushing the flipchart sheets back over the top of the easel. 'I'll open, thank them for coming and then, Stacey, Colin and Nick,' – I pointed to each of them in turn – 'you three will take over.'

Stacey and Colin nodded their assent, but Nick kept his head low, focused on doodling in his notebook.

'Nick, is that clear?'

He continued to scribble for a few more seconds – long swirly lines that spread across the page like leaves – before looking up.

'Crystal,' he smirked, raising his pen to his temple.

'Remember,' I said, taking care to speak loud enough for them all to hear but not so loud that I disturbed the rest of the office, 'when it comes to our pricing structure, we don't want to put them off, but we don't want to mislead them, either. If we get it right, this has the potential to be a huge contract.'

Stacey and Colin leant forward in their seats, eyes wide at the prospect of such a big win. Junior sales reps, they were both at least ten years younger than me and dead keen. However, although they worked hard, they seemed to lack the shark-like ambition and confidence of someone like Nick. I tried to encourage them as much and as often as I could.

'Colin, you're next up.' I motioned for him to come and take my place by the flipchart. 'Would you like to take us through the differentials and then –' Before I could go any further, I was interrupted by my mobile. I'd balanced it on top of a pile of folders on the floor and as I let it ring out to voicemail, it vibrated its way off the side and toppled onto the carpet.

'The figures involved are critical –' I said, trying to regain my train of thought. But once more, my phone's electronic trill cut me off mid-flow.

'Do you need to get that?' asked Nick. 'Seems important.'

Picking it up off the floor, I checked the screen. I didn't recognise the number. Keen to avoid any more distractions, I turned it off completely.

'Sorry,' I said, my hands fluttering around my neck. 'Where was I?'

'The figures,' said Nick.

'The figures, yes,' I said, forcing my hands down to my hips. 'We need to show we can deliver for under ten per cent and Colin has worked out a way we can do that.' Colin had just got to his feet when the reception landline blared.

Hayley answered and, after a brief exchange, she held the phone towards me.

'It's for you.'

'Take a message?'

Hayley returned the phone to her ear but after a murmured exchange she was soon back to trying to hand me the receiver.

'What is it?'

Hayley scanned the breakout area, hesitant to verbalise whatever it was in front of the others.

'They say it's urgent. Something to do with Jason.' She chewed on her thumbnail. 'They won't take no for an answer.'

Ignoring the shared glances rippling through my team, I took the phone.

'Heidi, it's Tesh,' said the person on the other end of the line.

'Tesh?'

I hadn't seen him since that night at the barbecue. For a moment my head was filled with the image of him doing the flamenco around our garden, a pair of meat tongs held above his head like castanets.

'I'm in the middle of something,' I whispered, shielding the receiver with my hand.

A dash of red bobbed at the edge of my vision. Yvonne. She was standing in the doorway to her office, watching me.

'It's Jason,' said Tesh. 'I need you to get over here right away.'

'I'm at work,' I whispered.

'I don't want to get the police involved,' said Tesh, 'but if we leave it much longer I'll have no choice.'

'The police?'

'He got on-site somehow. He's on the roof.'

For a moment, everything seemed to pitch.

'He's refusing to come down.'

He gave me the address and I handed the phone back to Hayley. Turning to face Colin, Stacey and Nick, I ignored their looks of brazen curiosity and collected my things.

'I've got something I need to take care of,' I said brightly. 'We'll pick this up later.'

Grabbing my bag and coat from my desk, I went over to where Yvonne stood, her mouth twisted into a dense bud.

'I need to dip out for an hour or so.' I kept my voice light. 'Won't be long.'

'Everything OK?'

'Personal emergency.'

She tutted.

'What about Monday? You weren't in yesterday and you said you were going to spend all of today and tomorrow preparing.'

'Don't worry, we're all set.' I shuffled my arms into my coat. 'And like I said, I won't be long.'

I went to leave but I hadn't gone more than a few steps when I heard another tut.

'You know, if you're finding it all a bit much,' she said, 'Nick has offered to step in and share the load.' She stopped, giving herself the time to stand back and properly observe the impact of her next sentence. 'He's very keen.'

'I don't need anyone to share the load,' I said, giving her a firm smile. 'I can handle it just fine.'

35

It had started to rain. Holding my coat over my head, I ran to the car and got in. Tesh had told me to come to a building site based out by Seal Sands. On the other side of the river, it should have been no more than a twenty-minute journey, but the roads were slick with spray. I drove only as fast as I dared.

Reaching the track that ran alongside the site, I scanned the wooden hoardings that fenced its perimeter and headed for the tall white cement cylinder Tesh had said marked the entrance.

Pulling inside, I found Tesh standing by the cylinder, waiting to greet me. I got out of the car and he led me to the shelter of a nearby overhang.

'Thanks for coming so quickly,' he said, water dripping off the tip of his hard hat.

'Where is he?'

'Up there.' He pointed to the half-built power station on the other side of the site. 'He's been on his own for the last half-hour.' Tesh's cheeks reddened. 'I had to bring the other lads in because of the weather.' He nodded at the Portakabin to his left. Muddy puddles were already forming in front of its doorway. Not everyone though, it seemed, had retreated indoors. A single figure paced up and down next to a gap at the side of the cabin. A man wearing heavy blue overalls. The back of his neck, head and underside of his chin were decorated with a tattoo of leaved branches and fruit that originated somewhere beneath his overalls. Every now and again he would glance up towards the top of the power station, as if he were checking Jason was still there.

Tesh tugged at his fluorescent yellow jacket. 'Our insurance, it doesn't really . . . I shouldn't really . . .' He coughed and tried again. 'Jason is an old mate. I didn't think it would do him any favours to go and make it all official.'

'What happened?' I asked, looking up to where the structure's end met the sky. Already its metal skeleton of rivets and bolts reached a hundred feet. The thought of him alone up there made me dizzy.

'He must have sneaked his way in when we were on lunch. When we went back on shift one of the lads saw him.' He handed me a hard hat. 'I realise he knows his way around a site, but still – do you think you could persuade him to come down?'

'You want me to go up there?' I'd been expecting to talk to him on a radio or to wave at him from the ground.

'I'll clip you to the guard-rail. You'll be safe.'

'I'm not great with heights.'

'It's you or the Old Bill.' He crossed his arms. 'You decide.'

I took another look at the power station roof. Rain bounced from its clean horizontal lines.

'I'll do it.'

Immediately, Tesh took charge. He led me over to a small lift fixed to the side of the structure, opened the door and gestured for me to go inside. Following behind, he bolted us in and pressed a button. As the lift stirred into action, there was a low rumble of thunder in the distance. I shivered. My coat was already drenched through and I could feel how the hard hat's clumsy plastic shell had flattened my hair into a damp mess.

'Has something happened?' broached Tesh as we made our ascent. 'I know things are always difficult, but has something upset him recently?'

'That kid out in Turkey,' I said, as the ground grew further and further away. 'He got his hopes up. We all did.'

We reached the top and Tesh pressed a red button. The lift came to a halt. We were now on the roof of the power station's main burner. Aside from the box we stood in, we were totally exposed. Oblong in shape, every side of the roof boasted a sheer drop down to the ground below. My legs felt like they were about to buckle. Resisting the urge to turn and go back the way we had come, I looked out to where the river's mouth met the North Sea. The water's surface was fat with the incoming tide, its expanse a slurry brown.

Putting a harness over my coat, Tesh pulled the straps tight and hooked me onto a safety wire that connected to metal runners bolted to the length of the roof floor.

'I'll leave you to it,' he said as he swung the gate open. He handed me a radio. 'Shout when you want to come back down.'

Squinting against the rain, I saw a figure sitting on the corner edge of a girder, legs dangling. The figure was not wearing a safety wire. Jason.

I didn't want to shout and scare him, so I followed the path prescribed by my wire's metal runner. My knees were liquid, but still I forced myself to put one foot in front of the other. Once I was close enough for him to hear me over the weather, I said his name.

'Jason?'

Nothing.

The thunder was overhead now and as it boomed there was a whip-crack of lightning that divided the sky in two. My insides rolled. His boots seemed way too heavy to be hanging over the side like that.

I needed to get nearer to him and so I got down on my bottom and shuffled forward until we were side by side.

'Jay?' The wind pushed his name back into my mouth and I coughed. 'Look, I'm sorry about yesterday, about the folder. But I hadn't gone looking for it on purpose, I promise.'

Still nothing.

I followed his gaze down, to the ground below. Its pull surprised me. There was an inevitability to the drop. It made me feel strangely calm. It would be so easy for us both to surrender to it. So easy for me to unclip my wire, take Jason's hand and let ourselves fall off the edge. I wondered how the concrete would feel against our skin as we landed. I thought it would probably be like jumping into a cold pool; the way the pain was hardly noticeable if you just dived in without thinking and swam a lap to get warm.

'I hit him. Did I ever tell you that?'

It took me a while to tune into the fact that he was telling me what was wrong. I rewound his words in my head, tried to process their meaning.

'If you're upset we can talk about it. Just not here. It's not safe.'

'It only happened the once. I smacked him on the bum.' He used his thumb to rub at the girder between where we sat. The join in the weld was slightly raised and bumpy, like the keloid flesh of a scar that had healed. 'We were crossing the road together and he let go of my hand. He almost ran into the traffic.' He continued to rub at the girder, oblivious to everything but his need to recount what had happened. 'I grabbed him just in time, but I was so scared. I don't know why I did it. I was angry, I guess. You should have seen the look on his face. Pure betrayal. He never forgot.'

'Oh, love,' I said, wrapping my arm around his shoulders. He rested his head in the crook of my neck.

'I miss being on-site. The lads. The weather.'

'You do?'

I'd always been under the impression that the first aid had been a welcome escape. That he was a reluctant participant in the family trade. But then, maybe I'd never asked.

We sat there like that for a while, huddled together for warmth.

'I don't want to go on holiday. To Gran Canaria,' he said eventually. 'We'll probably lose our deposit but I can't face it. Not right now.'

'Is that what all this is about?' I said, relieved. 'Why didn't you say something sooner? Of course we can cancel. We can go some other time.'

He buried his head deeper into my shoulder and I put my arm around him, trying to shield him from the wind and rain.

'What if we never find him, Heidi?' His hair was sodden and as he pressed himself close, some of the droplets dripped onto my neck and down my back. 'I don't know how much longer I can do this.'

'I know,' I said, holding him close.

We were both soaked through, but we stayed together like that for a while yet, the river ribboning out to the sea below and nothing else around us but the roar of the wind and the constant pellets of rain, clanging hard against the steel.

36

At home the next morning, I woke to find myself lying on my side, my hands gripping the top of Jason's arm.

I eased out of bed, tiptoed over to where my suit hung on the back of the door and tested the fabric between my thumb and forefinger. Still damp from the storm we'd sat through. The rain had mingled with my perfume and it smelt bad, like flowers that have been too long in their vase. I'd need something else to wear today. I opened the wardrobe and ran my hand along the line of suits sheathed in dry-cleaning bags, the thin plastic clicking against my nails before shushing back into place. Selecting a navy skirt suit, I set about freeing it from its cover.

All dressed, I went to shut the wardrobe, but the door was caught on something. A quick rummage revealed a bag bulging with bikinis, sandals and sarongs. I'd been accruing them ever since we booked the holiday back in June. One of the sarongs had exploded over the side, its floral turquoise print loud against the murk. I shoved it back into the bag, my fingers lingering on the soft cotton. When I'd found it in the shop I'd imagined wearing it over a bikini to lunch, my skin sea-salt tight after a morning at the beach.

We'd been on the roof of that power station for nigh on two hours before Jason had let me help him over to the lift. I'd driven us home, guided him upstairs and, after peeling off his soaked jeans and shirt, pushed him back onto the pillows. The duvet had been where we'd left it that morning, scrunched at the foot of the bed. As I'd brought it up to his waist, his eyes were already closed.

I looked over to where Jason lay. His arms were on top of the quilt, tucked close to his body, his palms surrendered upwards. It reminded me of a yoga class I'd tried once. At the end of the session the teacher had made us get into exactly this arrangement and had told us it was called the dead man's pose. I pushed the bag as far back into the wardrobe as it would go.

I slipped on my heels and scooped up my handbag. I wanted to stay home and keep an eye on him, but after failing to come good on my promise to return to the office yesterday, there was no way I could ask Yvonne for any more unplanned time off.

Giving Jason a kiss, I headed downstairs and out the door. My stomach rumbled. I was hungry, but breakfast would have to wait. I wanted to get into work early and there was an important stop I needed to make on the way.

My breath clouding white on the morning air, I got in the car and started the engine. As far as I was concerned, Jason going up on the roof like that had changed everything. I was no stranger to the dark days that both of us dipped in and out of from time to time. They were an inevitable part of life without our children. But being with Jason on top of that power station was the first moment I'd ever felt like I might lose him to them. And so, last night, as I'd lain there listening to him breathe, I'd decided that I needed to do something, anything to help. Even if that something meant going back on my word.

I approached the small bridge that would take me over the river from Thornaby to Stockton and found myself caught in a line of rush-hour traffic. Before long I came to a complete standstill. From where I sat, I could see the river's edge. A single swan was floating near the bank, hard white on the black water. Suddenly, it took off and flew away downriver. I wondered what had disturbed it and then, in answer to my question, the nose of a pleasure cruiser emerged from underneath the bridge. Gulls were racing alongside its starboard side, so close to the water that the tips of their claws skimmed the surface.

Somewhere ahead the lights changed and I was on the move again. Reaching the roundabout, I drove past my usual turn-off, taking the one that would lead to the end of the high street nearest the police station instead.

No matter how many weeks had passed and whatever I might have seen to the contrary, I'd never dropped my suspicions about the boy from the off-licence. I'd been just about able to live with it, but then yesterday had happened. I could no longer in good conscience continue to ignore those suspicions. If there was even a sliver of possibility that I could put Jason out of his misery, then I had to try.

Taking everything into consideration, I'd decided my best bet was to once more ask Martin for help. He and his team were the only people who could find out, quickly and cleanly, if there was anything more to my hunch than mistaken identity. I'd give a statement to the investigating officer on the case and make it official. I knew they'd ask to interview Jason and that he would be angry with me for going behind his back but so be it. I was resolute. They had to look into the background of the boy and his supposed uncle, and they had to do it soon.

I parked up, got out and buttoned my coat. The road was lined with chestnut trees drooping with conkers and apart from a tabarded street cleaner sweeping drifts of rotten leaves, the pavement was deserted. I could just see the corner of the station in the distance. A squat two-storey Victorian building that had long since had its sash windows replaced with thick white uPVC, the station's entrance was marked by grey stone steps ballasted on either side by low walls that curved down and out to the pavement below. Hoping to catch the detective at the start of his day, I set off towards it at a trot.

I'd almost reached the beginning of the low wall when I noticed a small figure approaching in the opposite direction. Veering from side to side, he or she seemed to be looking for something. As I got nearer and the features of the person came into focus, I stopped dead. Wearing a beige mackintosh over what seemed to be pyjamas and mumbling to herself in urgent little whispers was someone I knew. Vicky.

Instinctively, I hid behind the nearest tree and peeped out from its trunk. Stripped of her usual mascara, lipstick and blusher, her tiny features had been swallowed up by the white expanse of her face and her hair hung in greasy panels down her back. She shuffled towards the stairs that led to the station entrance and it was then I saw she was clutching something red and blue to her chest. A child's fleece dressing-gown. I'd seen it once before, a few days ago, hanging on the back of Barney's bedroom door. Cuddling it into her face and saying words I couldn't make out, she trudged up the stairs and went inside.

Intrigued, I waited a minute and then I, too, climbed the steps. Looking through the glass doors, I saw Vicky standing by the reception desk. Hopping from one foot to the other, she kept showing the officer on duty Barney's dressing-gown. The officer seemed to have realised who she was and was gesturing for Vicky to take a seat in the waiting area. Giving the bench in question a cursory glance, she went and stood by the locked door that led into the station instead. There she continued to shift her weight from one foot to the other, the dressing-gown held close to her chest.

The door next to where Vicky stood buzzed open and Martin appeared. Not wanting to interrupt whatever was going on, I stepped to the cover of the wall and, once I was out of sight, inched my head as far back as I dared.

Vicky had placed herself directly in front of the detective and was busy pushing Barney's dressing-gown towards him. Martin looked from Vicky to the garment, confused. But then he seemed to recognise it and his face softened. Gently, he directed the dressing-gown back to Vicky, only for Vicky to once more shove it back at him. Her eyes wide, her lips began moving fast, shaping a torrent of words.

At this, the duty officer and two other reception staff stopped what they were doing and began watching the exchange with undisguised curiosity. Martin must have also found whatever Vicky was saying quite odd, because now he turned to his colleagues with a smile followed by an eye-roll that suggested he was trying to make light of the situation.

But then, when he turned back to face Vicky I was surprised to see his eyes narrow. Shaking his head so slightly that I found myself questioning whether or not I'd imagined it, he seemed to be trying to signal something to her he thought she would understand. He seemed to be giving her a warning.

What was she saying? Something about their relationship? Something that might expose their affair to his colleagues?

But Vicky didn't register his warning or, if she did, the consequences of ignoring it did not worry her, because she continued to babble and to press the dressing-gown hard into the detective's body. Trying to maintain a semblance of control, Martin put a placatory arm around her shoulders and began urging her towards the exit. He'd only gone a few steps when the duty officer shouted a question in his wake. Batting away his colleague's enquiry, the detective adjusted Vicky's mac so that it covered her shoulders and continued on his way.

It took me a few seconds to register that Vicky and the detective were now heading in my direction. I looked from the steps to the concrete path that hugged the front of the police station, trying to work out whether I should hide or escape. Deciding there wasn't enough time for me to make it back down to the pavement without being seen, I realised my only option was to retreat to the right of the doorway and flatten myself against the wall.

I'd only just got into position when the door opened, Vicky's chatter escalating in speed and volume as they crossed the threshold.

'I can't do this any longer,' she kept saying.

'Keep your voice down,' said Martin, steering her towards the steps.

One backward glance and they'd see me for sure. I looked around, searching for something to hide behind. But there was nothing. I was totally exposed.

They reached the pavement and, despite Martin's motions to move away from the police station, Vicky refused to budge and continued to jerk the dressing-gown towards him. They were too far away for me to hear exactly what they were saying, but every now and again the odd word or phrase would carry on the air.

'. . . want to tell them,' said Vicky. '. . . not right . . .'

She reached the dressing-gown up to her face and pressed it into her eyes. She'd started to cry.

'. . . what good . . . achieve nothing . . .' said Martin, patting her awkwardly.

Finally, Vicky seemed to give in to the detective's coaxing. I watched as she let him lead her away from the station. Once they'd turned into a side street, I, too, made my way down the steps to the pavement.

I thought again of the text messages I'd seen on Vicky's phone. The poor woman was obviously plagued by guilt. I recognised the feeling. Left unchecked it could destroy a person.

Yesterday, being on the roof of that power station, I'd felt like I'd been given a glimpse into a horrible potential future. A future in which I lost Jason to the hopelessness of the situation and now, this morning, I'd seen Vicky who, it seemed, was already gone.

Martin would need time to recover from this encounter. I could come in and make a statement at the end of the day. I decided to call him from work and headed back to the car.

37

I got to the office half an hour earlier than usual. I was glad. Hopefully, my being there before everyone else would go some way to compensate for the fact I'd had to leave so suddenly yesterday.

I swiped my fob against the square plastic reader and, hearing the click, pushed my way through the swing-doors. Stopping to turn on the lights, I was about to make my way over to my desk when I saw that Yvonne and Nick were already in. Standing in the small alcove that housed the office kettle, fridge and microwave, they both blinked and looked to the ceiling in surprise as the lights creaked and flickered into fluorescence.

'Morning,' I said, the word coming out as more of a question than a greeting.

'Heidi,' said Yvonne, fiddling with the tie on her wrap dress, 'did you manage to sort out your . . .' – she paused, searching for the right level of disdain – 'family emergency?'

'Kind of.' I made my way over to where they stood. 'Apologies again for disappearing on you like that.'

The last part of my sentence was drowned out by Nick slurping loudly from a giant coffee mug. White with a black copperplate 'N' printed on the front; he'd brought it in from home.

'You said you were going to come back,' said Yvonne.

'It took longer than I thought. It was complicated . . .' I faltered.

Again, Nick took another slurp of coffee.

'You couldn't have let me know?' said Yvonne. 'After you left I had an email from an old colleague who works at Caulfield and Co. They tried and failed to win the Griffiths account last year. She gave me some great pointers. I wanted the team to work them into our pitch. I got everyone together. We waited for you.' She let the implication of her words hang in the air. 'But then I decided to stop waiting.'

'I'm so sorry, really.'

I thought of my formal warning letter. My name printed on the envelope in thick black capitals. I knew I was being too vague, that I needed to find a way to get across the seriousness of the situation, but I couldn't tell them what had happened. I wouldn't. I didn't want the events of yesterday to be traded around the office like a piece of juicy gossip, or worse, with some journalist. But more than that, I didn't want to tell them because to do so would feel like a betrayal, of Jason and our bond.

'It was tricky – there was nothing I could do . . .' I said, trying and failing to come up with an alternative explanation.

'As it turned out, we were fine,' she snipped. 'More than fine, actually.' She gave Nick a wink. 'Nick stepped up. He'd been working on some new ideas in his own time and they turned out to be exactly what we needed.'

'Sounds great,' I said, trying to sound enthusiastic. I gave Nick a smile that didn't match the rest of my face.

Thinking we were done, I went to leave them to it. It had been an hour and a half since I'd left Jason asleep in bed and I wanted to make sure he was OK. I might not have been able to stay home and keep an eye on him, but that didn't mean I couldn't keep checking in by phone. However, as soon as I went to make a move, Nick put down his giant mug and cleared his throat.

'You're too kind, Yvonne,' he said. 'I ran through a few random thoughts I'd had,' he said, turning to me. 'That was all.'

Flexing his shoulders so that the fabric of his shirt strained and pulled against his chest, he waited until there was a click from his spine before continuing.

'You keep telling us we need to pull out all the stops and so I thought, if we're going to hit our end-of-year targets then we all have to go the extra mile.'

'You are so right,' I said, stepping away from the kitchenette. I let my bag fall to my desk with a thump. 'A good point, well made.' I reached down and turned on my computer. 'Better get to it.'

Determined not to let Nick's blatant attempts at one-upmanship rattle me, I spent the rest of the morning – apart from a couple of brief calls to Jason – with my head down. The inside steer Yvonne had gleaned from her friend was brilliant, but it meant our entire pitch now needed tweaking. It was fiddly work but it had to be done. I knew I'd probably spend most of the coming weekend getting it perfect for Monday, but that was OK. Nick wasn't wrong when he said that winning the Griffiths account was critical to our sales targets. What he didn't realise was how much I personally also had riding on the whole thing. If it were to go well then it would almost certainly help keep any further warning letters at bay.

I finished adding text to one of the new presentation slides Yvonne had requested and hit *save*. I'd decided to hold off calling Martin until lunchtime. Hopefully he'd persuaded Vicky to see a doctor. Jason had said that, in the past, Vicky had taken tablets: first for postnatal depression and then, later, to help her cope with Barney's disappearance. Judging by what I'd seen this morning, it seemed she'd stopped taking them or that her medication needed to be reviewed.

It was coming up to two o'clock when Yvonne announced that she was popping out to grab a sandwich. As soon as she was gone, I grabbed my phone and got up from my desk. Pushing my way through the swing-doors, I took a left down the corridor and headed for the stairwell at the side of the building. Secluded and rarely used (the other people in the building tended to take the lift), it would give me all the privacy I needed.

After tucking myself into the corner, I dialled the detective's mobile.

'Martin,' I said, when he picked up. 'It's Heidi. Jason's wife.'

He didn't respond. In the background I could hear muffled chatter and ringing phones. I let a few more seconds pass and then, when he still hadn't said anything, I tried again.

'Is now a good time to talk?'

'Of course. How can I help?'

'I'm not sure when you last spoke to Jason but he's been having a hard time of it these past few days.' I had planned on telling the detective how Jason had sneaked his way up to the top of the power station. I'd thought that it would help him understand why, despite what I'd said in the past, I was once more asking for his help. But now, when it came down to it, I found myself unable to say the words out loud. 'I keep thinking about that boy,' I said, getting straight to the point. 'The one I told you about. From the off-licence.'

'I remember.' His voice was low and steady. It gave me the confidence to continue.

'I've changed my mind. I want you to investigate.'

'And Jason?' he asked gently. 'Does he know about this change of heart?'

'Not yet.'

He paused and for a moment I had a terrible fear he was going to tell me that he couldn't help.

'I'll need you to come in.'

'I know.' I thought of the leasehold sign above the shop. 'How long do you think it will take before the team can start looking into it?'

'Once you've made a statement? Not long.' I heard a rustling noise, like paper being moved across a desk. 'We can start the background and sex-offender checks immediately and we should be able to get someone out to the off-licence in the next few days.' He stopped and I heard the sound of footsteps and a door opening and shutting. When he spoke again his voice had dropped to a whisper. 'We can hold off on getting Jason to make a statement for a day or so, but we will need to talk to him eventually. Do you understand?'

'Don't worry, I'll make sure I'm the first he hears from.'

We arranged that I'd come down to the station later that day and then we were done. Giddy with relief, I headed out of the stairwell and back through the corridor, towards the office. The wheels had been set in motion. Whether my suspicions turned out to be right or wrong, at least I'd done everything I could.

38

It didn't take long to give my statement. Sitting across from the senior investigating officer, I recounted the first time I'd seen the boy, when he appeared behind the shop's metal cage, and then detailed the subsequent two occasions on which I'd managed to get a look at him. I also told him about the search I'd done on my work database and the name of the school I thought the boy attended. The whole process was surprisingly simple. The officer took notes and then, once I'd checked and signed the document, I was done.

I returned home smiling. The burden was gone. As soon as the police started asking questions it wouldn't matter what Keith said to try and put them off the scent. If anything was amiss, if the child was Barney, they'd soon smell a rat.

I spent the rest of the weekend trying to find a good moment to tell Jason, but it never seemed like the right time. While I sat at the dining table, tapping at my laptop and frowning at dense, numbered printouts, Jason lay mute on the sofa, drifting in and out of sleep. I knew I was delaying the inevitable, but seeing him like this continued to unnerve me, and every time I tried to broach the topic he feigned tiredness or found a way to leave the room. Then, late on Saturday, he took himself off to Vicky's. It was almost her turn with Barney's fire engine and, even though I remembered the truck as being his for another few days at least,

I didn't say anything. Instead, I let his need to be near her flicker and flap at the edge of my vision, like a bird I knew was there but couldn't quite see.

Monday morning rolled around all too soon and, even though the Griffiths pitch wasn't until three, I made sure to be at my desk by seven. Armoured for the day in my metal-heeled stilettos, a red jersey dress and fitted black jacket, I was thinking about making the first of many coffees when an email popped up in the corner of the screen. Planning to read it and the rest of my inbox once I'd loaded up on caffeine, I gave it a quick glance and was heading for the kitchen when something about the sender made me look again. Sharon Hannah. The name was familiar, but why?

Intrigued, I clicked on the envelope icon. The message was written in a turquoise copperplate font I realised I'd seen once before. I dropped my gaze to the bottom of the page. And there it was, her email signature: Mrs Sharon Walsh (née Hannah). Sharon Hannah. The Tyneside rep I'd contacted the night after I'd first seen the boy. She was back from honeymoon.

'Hi Heidi. I was so thrilled to get your message,' she wrote. 'I don't think we reach out enough to our sister-company colleagues over here in retail! Regarding your Wine City query, I'm afraid I don't remember much of the visit itself and certainly nothing about counterfeit alcohol. My schedule is mega hectic; sometimes I can visit eight shops in a single day!'

Any excitement I'd felt dissolved. I wasn't too disappointed. I'd always known my contacting her had been a long shot.

'Anyways, if they are selling bootleg products they won't be for much longer,' she continued. 'Word on the grapevine is that the Wine City has been taken over by Costcutter. As I hear it, the shopfitters are due to go in there any day now. Best wishes, Sharon Walsh (Mrs).'

Trying not to panic, I called Martin.

'You must have read my mind,' he said, answering on the first ring. 'I was about to phone you.'

'You were?'

'A couple of officers went out to that shop yesterday.'

My centre of gravity seemed to tilt.

'What happened?'

'Nothing. The place was closed up.' His voice was flat, matter of fact. 'They asked around. Seemed the bloke –' He stopped, and I heard the notebook rasp of a page being turned. 'This Keith Veitch. He moved on just over a week ago.'

I felt sick.

'Did you look into him? Keith?'

'We did.' The detective answered brightly, as if he'd just secured the correct answer on a quiz. 'He's not on the sex-offenders' register and he doesn't have a record. Not so much as a parking ticket.'

This failed to reassure me.

'Don't you think it's suspicious he just upped and left? Can't you try and find where he went?'

'Actually, it's neither suspicious nor sudden. We talked to the estate agent and it seemed the guy had the leasehold on the market for a while. It was all planned and above-board. Normal, in other words.'

'What about the school the boy went to?' I was starting to feel desperate. 'Did you check with them?'

'Yes, but we didn't have much joy. The officers went to see the head teacher this morning.' Again he stopped, apparently consulting his notes. 'Mikey, the boy you saw, gave notice to the school last week. It seems like he and his mum have left town too. Most likely with Keith.'

'Did the school have any paperwork on them?'

'You've seen the area. Kids in that school come and go all the time. The local authority has one goal: to get people to put and then keep their kids in education. They never push families to produce birth certificates or that kind of thing.'

'What did they know about the family?'

'Mikey's mum did pick-ups on occasion and there was an older sister, too. But it was usually his uncle. His mum stacks shelves at the Aldi, does a lot of shift work. There was also another brother, Jake, but he was in the senior school.' He lowered his voice and I realised I was being handled. 'The mum worked and the uncle helped with childcare.'

Slipping my hand inside my bag, I felt around until my fingers came across the smooth, heavy weight of Lauren's compass. I worried the disc around my palm and tried to steady my thoughts.

'What about neighbouring businesses? Keith was friends with a guy who runs the greasy spoon a few doors down.' I hadn't included the various meetings with Tommy in my original statement. 'He might know where they've gone.'

'We canvassed the nearby area. Everyone said the same thing. Keith had been trying to offload the shop for some time. Mikey was his nephew. Keith babysat him after school. They would see his mum come and go. End of story.' He cleared his throat. 'Sorry,

Heidi. I know you think you saw some kind of resemblance, but everything checks out.'

I released Lauren's compass back into the depths of my bag.

'It must unsettle you, the fact he's gone, but hopefully we've managed to put your mind at rest.'

We said goodbye and I sat staring at my desk, struggling to absorb everything Martin had said. Behind me, the swing-doors creak-swooshed. It was Nick.

'Oh,' he said, when he clocked me. 'You're already here.'

Wearing a sky-blue shirt tucked into his trousers, he'd cinched his waist with a black leather belt. After pouring coffee into his person-alised mug, he came over to where I sat, his fingers obscuring the 'N'.

'I worked up a couple of extra pie charts over the weekend,' he said, taking a sip. 'Yvonne said they might come in useful.'

'Thank you.' I pretended to study my computer screen. I needed to organise my thoughts and to do that I needed to be alone, but when I looked up a minute later I saw he was still there.

'Is there something else?'

He didn't respond. I followed his gaze to the framed picture of Lauren on my desk. Taken by my dad, it showed her in a yellow mac and red wellington boots. Standing slap bang in the middle of a muddy puddle, she was sticking out her tongue and waggling her hands by her ears. Every time I looked at it I remembered how, when we'd got home, she'd peeled off her sodden socks and jeans and snuggled under a blanket on the sofa. Mum had the gas fire on full and the living room was warm, dusk just starting to settle. Lauren had accepted a mug of hot chocolate, burrowed a little further under the blanket and taken a long, loud slurp of the warm drink. Then she'd turned to me and, with all the world-weariness of a little old lady, had said, 'That's better.'

'Nick,' I said again, louder this time, 'I asked if there was anything else?'

'What? Yes, actually.' I realised he was blushing. 'I wanted to say how much I admire your husband. For never giving up hope.'

It felt like something had caught in my throat. Like Yvonne, my colleagues never mentioned Lauren or Barney. In fact, most of them seemed to find it confusing I was even at work. This wasn't unusual. Many people find it odd that Jason and I have to earn money; that we still have to do things like pay the mortgage and council tax. This simple fact embarrasses them. They actually go red in the face when they realise. It's as though, when they imagine some awful tragedy befalling them, they also assume someone somewhere will make sure they don't ever have to go back to the real world, to grubbing around for overtime to cover that month's electricity bill. They seem to think they'll be able to retire from life and all its obligations to grieve in peace.

'We have to keep looking,' I said, repeating Jason's mantra. 'No stone unturned. Barney is out there somewhere.'

Nick nodded, his brow furrowed in empathy.

I realised I was nodding along with him. I got to my feet and Nick took a step back, confused.

'I've left my USB stick at home,' I said, putting on my jacket. This was a lie. The USB was in my bag, under my desk. 'I need it for the presentation this afternoon.'

I had to talk to Tommy. I was sure I could get more out of him than the police. Maybe I could get him to let slip where Keith and his sister had taken Mikey and the kids. It was still early. I could go and make it back in time for the pitch with hours to spare.

'If Yvonne asks, will you make sure to tell her I won't be long?' I said, heading for the door.

'Don't worry,' smiled Nick. 'You can count on me.'

39

I turned onto the high street and studied the horizon. Even from this distance I could see the shop's metal shutters were down. I parked, went over to the door and peered through the letterbox. At the back of the shop, behind the cage, I could see empty shelves: dirty marks on the wall where the confectionery display used to be. I drew my gaze forward and saw that a pile of unopened post had started to collect, take-away menus and free newspapers splaying out across the floor.

I bit down on the inside of my cheek. Soon I could taste blood. I should have acted sooner. I should have trusted my instincts.

I turned towards the café, its fried-food reek clashing with the clean morning air. Keith and Tommy. They might enjoy a pint together from time to time, but how close were they really?

I set off down the street, the rat-tat-tat of my metal stilettos loud on the empty concrete. As I got closer I started to imagine what it would be like to see Tommy again and my pace slowed. Eventually, I came to a complete halt.

The last time we'd spoken I'd hung up, and as for when I last saw him in person: just thinking about it made me blush. I looked back at the abandoned off-licence, old leaves already starting to fur the gap where the shutters met the pavement. I had no alternative. Pulling my jacket straight, I smoothed my dress and forced myself on.

Inside, the red plastic two-seaters were full of people eating cooked breakfasts and drinking tea, the sizzle of egg and bacon providing a backtrack to their quiet conversation.

I approached the counter and was greeted by a hip-level mass of frizzy bleached hair, bobbing around by the till. I leant over and saw a girl on all fours, busy picking up a scattered pile of serviettes. Sensing my presence, she heaved herself back up to standing and brushed her hair out of her eyes. My breath caught in my throat. It was Kimberley. Keith's niece. She was still here.

'Is Tommy around?' I asked, trying to contain my surprise.

'Depends,' she said, eyeing my jacket and dress. 'Who's asking?'

I took in her thick dark eyebrows and small, black eyes. There was something about her face, her features, that reminded me of someone. I wondered why the police hadn't questioned her when they came out here to do their canvassing. Maybe she hadn't been on shift that day or maybe she had lied to them about her connection to Keith. Whatever the reason, her being here was a good sign. It meant it was likely Keith and the boy hadn't gone far. Maybe all wasn't lost after all.

In the kitchen beyond I noticed someone reaching inside one of the metal fridges. Obscured by the door, all I could see were the bottom of their black-and-white-checked chef's trousers and black trainers. Tommy. My heart stuttered in my chest.

'A friend; a friend is asking,' I said loudly, waiting for Tommy to recognise my voice. At that, the fridge door closed shut. My heart beat a little faster. But the person who emerged wasn't Tommy. Instead, I found myself staring at a young black guy wearing a back-to-front baseball cap.

Kimberley watched my reaction with amusement.

'He's upstairs,' she volunteered, apparently deciding to take pity on me. 'In his flat.' She nodded at the entrance. 'Back out the way you came, first on your right.'

I did as she said and, after finding the door in question, I knocked hard and waited.

Nothing.

I was about to knock again when I heard someone pounding their way down the stairs. Fighting the urge to run and hide, I pulled my face into a smile.

The door opened and then there he was, blinking against the bright morning sun. His chest and feet were bare; it seemed I'd woken him.

'You.'

'I was in the neighbourhood.'

He crossed his arms and I noticed how his forearms were a tanned, golden brown, his chest white. The contrast was so sharp it made it look like he was wearing a T-shirt.

'I did not expect to see you again.'

'I stopped for a drink at the shop,' I said, my voice shaky. 'But it seems to have closed down?'

He smiled.

'You better come in.'

Relieved he hadn't, after all, shut the door in my face, I followed him up the narrow stairs. When I reached the top I found myself in an open-plan kitchen and living space, empty except for an L-shaped black leather sofa and an enormous plasma TV on the far wall. There was only one photo on display; a small, square snap framed in silver, it sat on a shelf next to the TV. I moved in close to the photo. It featured three children: two boys and a girl standing outside a terraced house. The washed-out oranges and yellows of the print and the boxy, thick-fringed haircuts suggested the photo had been taken some time in the late sixties or early seventies. In the picture the children had their arms wrapped around each other, their eyes screwed up against the sun.

I picked it up, wanting to study it more closely.

'Who is this?'

'Me and my brother and sister.' Gently, he took the picture from me and replaced it on the shelf.

I sniffed the air. An old fried-food and washing-powder smell seemed to have sunk deep into the walls, floor and ceiling.

Tommy headed for the small kitchen that took up one corner of the room and began to fill the kettle.

I walked over to near where he stood and leant against the fridge.

'Has Keith moved?'

Getting two mugs out of a cupboard, he set them to one side and used a spoon to tap out a rhythm on the kitchen counter while the kettle boiled.

I'd gone in too fast. I tried a change of tack.

'Sorry I haven't been in touch.' I moved closer, forcing myself into his eyeline. 'How come you're not at work?'

He smirked and shrugged his shoulders. It was as though my presence both bored and entertained him.

'Isn't this your busiest time of day?'

Again he said nothing. Instead, he searched my face, as though looking for an answer or for a truth of some kind, and then, when that proved fruitless, he reached both of his hands up to my head. I thought he was going to pull me in for a kiss, but instead, he smoothed my hair back away from my face. Then he did it again and again, so hard I could feel my roots pulling on my skull. After a while, the repetition became enjoyable and I was just starting to relax when he darted his head forward, as if trying to scare me. I couldn't help but flinch. He laughed and lunged again. This time he put his mouth to mine.

He tasted of cigarettes. As we kissed, the friction of his beard against my skin created a burning sensation. He seemed to be enjoying it but then he withdrew and pushed me away, back against the kitchen counter. Removing my jacket, he pulled down the sides of my dress, the soft jersey material coming away easily from my shoulders. He looked at me for less than a second and then moved on to my bra straps, slipping them off and down onto my arms. With two tugs, he freed each of my breasts and then, as if his time was up, he stopped and took a step back.

I stood there half-naked from the waist up, the flat's central-heated air blowsy on my body. I wanted to cover myself, or to at least cross my arms over my chest, but I sensed that to do so would be to fail somehow.

Tommy stared at my breasts and I felt my nipples harden. He registered their change with a smile and then, without saying anything, he went back over to the kettle and began pouring the tea.

Smarting with a humiliation I didn't quite understand, I pulled my bra straps and then my dress back up into place.

Tommy handed me a mug and came and stood alongside me.

'OK then,' he said, taking a sip.

'OK,' I repeated, not sure what had just happened.

'You asked about Keith.' A muscle twitched underneath his right eye. 'I told you about his sister, Jenny. Seems her husband's out of prison.'

'Oh?'

Tommy eyed me carefully. It felt like he was trying to decide whether or not I could be trusted with the next piece of information.

'We had the police round here the other day, asking questions.' I studied the flickering muscle under his right eye. It was a tiny movement, barely noticeable. 'We reckon her ex told them some lies about his and Jenny's custody arrangement. Naturally we all kept our mouths shut.'

'But Kimberley is still working in the caff?'

'Why are you so interested in Keith and his family?' He smirked. 'A lesser man might get jealous.'

I considered telling him my suspicions about Mikey. Confessing that it was actually I who had called the police. But no. Keith's reason for upping sticks was entirely plausible. It all made sense. The realisation left me both reassured and deflated.

He clicked his teeth.

'Got any plans for tomorrow night?' he asked, as though the last few minutes had never happened. Going over to the sash window next to the sink, he lifted his arms up high and rested his hands and forehead against the glass. 'There's a fireworks display in Ropner Park.' He looked down at the street below. Keeping his hands on the window, he turned to look at me, his eyes slitted against the bright sun. 'We could go together?'

Keith and the boy's disappearance made sense but still, there was something about that kid, something I couldn't let go. I had to be sure. Kimberley continued to work for Tommy. That meant he still had contact. He was the key.

I moved across the kitchen until I was stood directly in front of him. I reached my hands up to his shoulders and dipped my fingers into the scoop of his clavicle.

'Sure,' I said as soon as I saw the beginnings of a smile on his face. 'I'll be there.'

40

I floored it all the way back to the office, the cigarette flavour still on my tongue. I opened the window a crack and the space around me filled with motorway roar. Remembering the feel of the air on my skin when Tommy pulled down my dress, I shivered. I opened the window a little wider. There would come a point soon when I'd have to think about the things that had gone on between us, when I'd have to acknowledge the things I'd let him do. But for now I found that it was like looking directly into a very bright, blinding light; a light so strong that even just to glance at it would be to bruise your eyes. And so until then, until I was ready, I decided it best to keep looking off to the side, into the corners, where that same light did nothing more than flare and shadow on the walls.

I arrived back at the office just before eleven. Planning to use the time between now and the pitch to check in with my team and give the presentation one last going over, I pushed through the swing-doors, ready to get everyone keyed up for the day ahead. But, apart from Hayley in reception, the place was a ghost town. For a moment, I considered the possibility a practice fire alarm was in progress and that everyone was outside, on the grassy square next to the building. Then I saw them.

Sitting around the boardroom's large oval table, the sales team were turned to face Yvonne and Nick, who were standing either side of the plasma screen, pointing at what looked like the third page of my presentation. Wearing a purple and white zebra-print wrap dress that pulled at her bust, Yvonne had moussed her short, hennaed hair close to her head.

I thought that maybe they were doing a rehearsal of some kind, but then I saw the three people at the opposite end of the table. Two men and a woman. Surrounded by the lion's share of coffee, pastries and flowers. The buyers. The Griffiths account. The pitch was already in progress?

Panic rising in my throat, I tried to rationalise the reasons behind what I was seeing. The meeting had been in my diary for nearly a month. Had I somehow got the time wrong?

Hoping I hadn't missed too much, I was on my way to the boardroom when Hayley bolted from her desk and ran ahead of me.

'Um, you're not to go in,' she said, blocking my way.

'Why on earth not?' I said, unable to take my eyes off the scene in the boardroom. I tried to move past, but Hayley sidestepped to the right, once more placing herself in front of me.

'Yvonne said you're to wait out here until they're done.'

'The meeting wasn't till this afternoon.'

'They called first thing,' she said. 'They've had some crisis at Head Office. They were going to cancel completely, but then Yvonne persuaded them to bring the pitch forward.'

I watched as Yvonne reached down to the laptop and pressed a button, bringing the next slide onto the screen. As she came back up to standing I caught her eye. She shook her head, a tiny warning shake, and then, without drawing breath, she continued to address the room.

I watched the remainder of the pitch play out from my desk. I knew every beat of the presentation, and through a combination of lip-reading and mime I found I could anticipate almost exactly which point they'd reach next. Yvonne and Nick seemed to have decided to do the whole thing as a two-hander. Laughing in all the right places, they made sure to offer each other perfectly timed supportive nods and eye contact. They made a good team.

The PowerPoint complete, they took questions and, after a brief discussion, the three-strong Griffiths contingent looked at their watches, smiled their thanks and got to their feet. It was all over.

I stayed where I was until Yvonne and Nick had seen them out and then I went over to where they and the rest of the team stood by reception. Shouty laughter and jittery backslapping filled the air.

Ignoring the hush that fell as soon as I got near, I prodded Nick on the shoulder.

'I knew you were ambitious,' I said, loud enough for everyone to hear. 'But I never thought you'd stoop this low.'

Nick looked to the floor.

I turned to Yvonne.

'Did he tell you I was in here first thing? Did he tell you I'd nipped home to get something for this, for *my* presentation?'

I prodded Nick again.

'At least have the balls to look at me.'

He lifted his head, a pained expression on his face. He opened his mouth, about to say something, but Yvonne raised a manicured index finger, silencing him.

'If you must know,' she said. 'Nick begged me to call you. He said you'd worked hard on this pitch and that you should be the one to deliver it.' She smoothed a palm over her stiff hair. 'But I wouldn't let him.'

I looked at Nick, trying to understand.

'I'm not going to ask why you weren't here,' continued Yvonne. 'I'm not interested in any more of your excuses.'

'But I was here,' I said. 'I was the first one in.'

'Clear your desk.'

My throat tightened.

'What?'

'You heard me. You're finished.'

My throat grew even tighter. I tried to speak, to argue my case, but no words would come. Tears blurred my vision. I took a step back towards the exit and knocked into the water-cooler. Nick put out his hand to steady me and then I was on my way, the swing-doors swooshing shut, the sun at the end of the corridor guiding me out to the car park beyond.

41

The alarm went off at its usual time. I got out of bed and headed for the shower. Huddled under the hot jet I closed my eyes and tried to ignore the lumpen knot in my stomach.

I hadn't told Jason I'd been fired. I couldn't figure out how to explain the chain of events without also confessing to how much effort I'd put into my investigation of the boy from the off-licence. In the end I'd decided to hold off until I could find a new job. Hopefully it wouldn't take too long. In the meantime, I'd decided to pretend to go to work as usual. This morning I planned to drive to a shopping centre somewhere out of the way. I'd spend the day wandering department stores before arriving back home at my normal time. Tomorrow would hold more of the same.

I was towelling myself dry when the door opened.

'The police just called,' said Jason, blinking against the light. He was wearing boxers and an old Goonies T-shirt, his right cheek still pleated with creases from his pillow. 'They want me to give a statement about that kid in the shop, the one from ages ago.' He sounded more confused than angry. 'They said you asked them to look into it?'

I wrapped the towel around my head and reached for my dressing-gown. The knot in my stomach twisted a little tighter.

'I was going to talk to you.' Towards the end of the sentence my voice began to give way. 'I know you said we should leave it alone.'

'But,' he said, 'you didn't?'

'That's right.' I tried to sound more defiant than I felt.

He moved over to where I stood, circled his hands around my waist and kissed my cheek.

'Heidi,' he said, softly. 'That child is not my son.'

I knew I should let it go. He was handling it well. Better than I could have hoped. I realised that, were I to say nothing more, there was a chance we'd be able to sweep all this under the carpet.

'It's been five years.' My face was pressed against his chest and so I spoke the words into his T-shirt's thin cotton. 'Have you considered the possibility that Barney has changed so much you may no longer be able to recognise him?'

I felt his arms fall away from my hips. He took a step back and shook his head; his eyes narrowed.

'What did you say?'

I knew I should stop, that I should pay heed to this new flint in his tone. My body heard it. Quickening my veins with blood to run and hide, it knew there was something wrong. But there was another part of me that remained deaf; a part that wanted to keep going.

'Maybe if you could talk to the child or interact with him somehow?' My words spilled out so fast they had to clamber on top of one another. 'Maybe that would help you recognise him and maybe that would help him remember you?' I was jittery with enthusiasm. 'The guy who runs the place claims he's his nephew, but I don't believe him. I –'

'His nephew? How do you know that?' His eyes flashed. 'Don't tell me you went back?'

Reading my silence for the admission it was, he shook his head. 'You have got to be kidding.'

'No stone unturned Jason. I had to be sure.'

Hearing his own words quoted back at him, he grimaced.

'Since you made your little report, how many man hours do you think the police have spent on this line of inquiry?'

'What?'

'How many hours?' He folded his arms. 'Come on, hazard a guess.'

'I'm not sure, I never thought –'

'That's right, you didn't think.' He shook his head. 'The more time that passes, the fewer resources the police have to devote to Barney's case. I want them to spend every second of that precious time on real leads. Not investigating a child I have already seen and discounted.'

'But –'

'On real leads,' he said. 'No more, Heidi. That's it. They said this man has moved on and that you're asking them to try and track down where he might have gone. You have to promise me you won't bother them with this again.'

'But Jason –'

'If you can't promise me, then I'm done.' He looked to the floor. 'We're done.'

'No.' I pressed myself against him and tried to arrange his arms back around my waist. 'Don't say things like that.' But he kept his arms limp and no sooner had I placed them on my hips than they fell away, landing heavy at his side.

'Yes.' He seemed surprised, as though it was the act of saying the words out loud that had made him realise his true intentions. 'I can't see any other way to make you understand.'

Again, I pushed myself into him and tried to place his arms around me. It was like trying to scale a smooth, flat wall.

'OK,' I said. 'No more police.' I felt him relax a touch, a tiny almost imperceptible give. I pushed harder, scrabbling to fit his embrace.

42

I stood outside the park, trying to decide whether or not to go in. The fireworks display had yet to start, but the bonfire's flames were already established, their orange tongues licking at the feet of the guy.

I'd spent the day wandering around a shopping centre, raking over this morning's row in my head. I knew I had to stand by my promise not to waste any more police time. Still, I couldn't walk away from the boy just yet. Not when there was a chance I could pursue things alone, with Tommy.

I strode through the gates and headed for the bandstand at the top of the hill. The temperature was close to freezing. Shivering, I buttoned my coat all the way to the top and bunched my scarf high around my neck. I thought back to our last encounter. How easily he'd pulled my dress away from my shoulders. My teeth began to chatter. The shivering was getting worse. I pulled the scarf a little higher.

I reached the top of the hill and looked down at the scene below. The park was packed with people, the grass underfoot flattened and muddy. As well as the bonfire burning bright in the large field, there was a multicoloured Ferris wheel, waltzers and a smattering of food trucks offering milky tea and baked potatoes. I turned back towards the bandstand and scanned the milling crowds. It didn't take long to clock Tommy. Wearing a black donkey jacket over a thick-ribbed polo neck jumper, he was smoking a cigarette, his shoulders hunched against the chill.

I made my way over to where he stood.

'All on your tod?'

I'd caught him off guard. His face broke into a huge smile.

'I was.' He took a last drag of his cigarette. 'But not anymore.' He peered over my shoulder, towards someone or something.

Confused, I turned to look. Lumbering over to where we stood, his slip-on trainers no match for the muddy grass, was an out-of-breath Keith. Sporting a large black-and-white-striped bobble hat, matching scarf and grey duffel coat, he looked like an overweight schoolboy.

'Sorry I'm late,' he huffed. He had yet to notice my presence. 'I was at the hospice.'

'How's she doing?' asked Tommy.

'They said it's a matter of days.'

'Anything I can do?'

Keith shrugged.

'You remember Heidi,' said Tommy, guiding me forward.

'Hope you don't mind me tagging along?'

'Not at all, darling,' said Keith. He gave Tommy an approving wink. 'The more the merrier.' He looked back, towards the hill he'd just climbed. 'Speaking of which.'

I followed his gaze just in time to see a small blond head appear over the edge of the summit. Waving a sparkler, he was busy drawing yellow shapes in the air and hopping from foot to foot in a kind of excited jig.

The boy.

Tossing aside his now extinguished sparkler, he came and stood next to Keith, who drew him in to his hip and ruffled his hair.

Hit by the same gut-rush of recognition as before, I had to fight every instinct I had not to hoist him over my shoulder and make a run for it. Up close, his face was longer and slimmer than in any of the pictures I'd seen of Barney (but that was to be expected with the age he was now) and his hair (a fine, white blond when he was taken) had darkened and thickened into the exact sandy yellow that covered Jason's scalp. A small crescent-shaped scar decorated his right cheek. I felt a pinch of doubt. Barney didn't have any scars. But then he could easily have got the mark at some point in the last five years. It meant nothing.

I was trying to order my thoughts when another two people appeared in the boy's wake. One of them I recognised as the chubby girl from the café and the other was a tall, acne-ridden lad of eleven or twelve.

'And this is our Kimberley and our Jake,' said Keith, giving them a wave.

Once again, I was struck by the feeling I'd had when I last saw Kimberley in the café. She reminded me of someone. But who?

I nodded hello and then took myself to one side of the group. It was all as Tommy had said. Keith hadn't, as I'd feared, fled the country. Instead, he and his sister had gone on the run, not for any of the reasons I'd thought, but because of her abusive ex-husband and the threat he posed. I looked at the silly hat Keith wore. The oversized bobble wobbled every time he moved his head.

'I was just saying to Keith,' said Tommy, trying to involve me in the conversation. 'The caff's not the same without him just down the road.'

'Don't listen to him,' said Keith, putting a conspiratorial arm around my shoulder. 'He doesn't miss me.' He patted his belly. 'He misses my need for a bacon and egg sarnie every morning.' He turned back to Tommy. 'Profits taken a bit of a dent?'

Tommy was about to reply when there was a loud crack above our heads. The fireworks display had begun. We all jumped and turned to face the opposite hill. Purple, blue and silver fizzled down through the night sky.

I watched as Kimberley retrieved her phone from her coat pocket and held it up in the air, ready to selfie against the background of sparkling fireworks. Adjusting her ponytail, she pouted and pressed the button. A small blue square appeared in the middle of the screen and the camera zeroed in on her small, porcine eyes and neat, snub nose. She looked to be sixteen, maybe seventeen. Her features were almost fully established; her chin, cheeks and forehead markers on the tipping point of what would be her final, adult face.

And then it hit me. The reason I felt like I'd seen her somewhere before.

The realisation was so intense I had to stop myself from shouting out.

I stole another look at Kimberley, my brain struggling to recalibrate. She was busy uploading her selfie, her face illuminated by the screen's blue glow.

All this time I'd been focused on Keith, convinced there must be some connection between him and Barney's disappearance.

And there was a connection. I'd just been looking for it in the wrong place.

A series of spectacular golden rockets started to rat-a-tat-tat their way into the heavens. The boy tugged on Keith's hand.

'Keith,' he said, trying to get his attention, 'I'm hungry.'

Keith placed his hand to his ear.

'I can hear roaring. Was that a lion?' He looked to his left and right, pretending not to see the boy. 'Has a lion escaped from the zoo?'

The boy giggled and wrapped his arms around Keith's waist.

'There it is again,' said Keith, hoisting the boy up into a piggyback. He swung round, pretending to search the nearby area. The boy clung to his shoulders, laughing. 'There must be a lion. Is he hungry?' He scratched his head, thinking. 'Does he want steak and chips? All lions love steak and chips.' The boy squealed in delight.

Finally, the boy let out a loud, 'Roar!' directly into Keith's ear. Feigning shock, Keith jumped and in one quick movement returned the boy to the floor and drew him into his side.

I remembered the second time I'd tried to go back to the off-licence. The day I met Tommy. In my possession I'd had the four photofits I'd taken from Jason's file. Composites of the people who had been seen in or around Ashbrook House on the day Barney went missing, they contained drawings of three men and one woman.

It turned out I'd had blinkers on. Self-inflicted blinkers.

The boy was still hassling Keith and Tommy for food. I stepped into their eyeline.

'I'm hungry, too.' I knelt down to address the boy directly. 'Do you want to come with me and get a hot dog?'

Tommy gave me an odd look. I couldn't get a read on it. It was as though he was trying to communicate something he thought I'd understand. Maybe he'd been hoping the two of us would go out for dinner together once the display was over and didn't want me to ruin my appetite?

I grabbed the boy's gloved hand.

'You lot want anything?' I asked, already moving away.

Keith looked to Tommy for the answer.

'No thanks,' said Tommy, sending us off with a wave. 'We'll wait here. Don't be long.'

We set off down the hill at pace. Unable to distinguish between the bangs and cracks searing the air above our heads and the hammering in my chest, I tried to process the fact I was alone with the boy. Keith seemed unconcerned that we'd gone off together. Was that because he thought I didn't know his secret or because he genuinely had nothing to hide?

'It was nice of your uncle to bring you tonight,' I said as we reached the row of food vans. 'Could your mum not come?'

The boy looked at me blankly, that way kids do when they're a bit shy, and turned his attention back to the explosions in the sky.

I tried another tack.

'Does he look after you often?'

'Look after me?' he asked, like I was stupid.

He spoke with a mild Geordie twang, but apart from that, his accent was fairly neutral. Unplaceable almost.

'What would you like?' I asked once we were in the queue.

'Are you Tommy's girlfriend?'

'Am I what? No, no. We're friends.'

He cocked his head.

'You talk funny.'

'That's because I'm not from round here. What about you? Where are you from?'

But his attention was elsewhere. We'd reached the front of the queue. I bought two hot dogs and handed one to the boy. He lifted it to his mouth and before he took a bite, we shared a smile. I was the first to look away.

I'd been so close to giving up, so close to accepting defeat. What if I had? What would have happened to the child then?

I looked back up the hill to where Keith, Tommy, Kimberley and Jake stood laughing and taking pictures of each other on their phones. They looked like any other happy family, here to celebrate Guy Fawkes. It was no wonder Kimberley seemed familiar. I had, after all, spent hours studying her features. Or, rather, those of her mother.

The fourth photofit. The woman with frizzy hair, snub nose and small, round eyes. Despite multiple witnesses remembering seeing her around and about the flats that day, this woman had never come forward to rule herself out of police enquiries. The likeness to Kimberley was unmistakable. Mother and daughter.

Now I had all the pieces, it was easy to put them together.

Tommy had told me that Keith's sister, Jenny, had been in an abusive relationship. He'd said that, when she refused to leave her husband, Kimberley and Jake had been taken into care for a period of time. That it had, understandably, left Jenny messed up. Then that night in the alley, her ex-husband had mentioned only two children to Keith: a son and a daughter. Jake and Kimberley.

I could only guess at the detail of what happened that day at the flats, but it seemed most likely that Jenny had been there. Taking Barney had been opportunistic. Presumably, to replace the children she missed so terribly.

It was circumstantial. I'd need to see Jenny to be certain. But my theory made sense, I was sure of it. All I needed was proof.

The boy finished the last of his hot dog and wiped at the smears of ketchup around his mouth. I looked at the top of his head, his thick blond hair. The same sandy yellow I woke up next to every morning.

I waited until the next squeal of fireworks and then, just as the rocket exploded into the heavens, I reached forward and tugged out a few strands.

He yelped and spun round.

'Ow!' He rubbed the spot I'd just scalped. 'What did you do?' he asked, and then, less certain and searching behind me for another culprit to blame, 'What did you do?'

43

Later that night I lay in bed, unable to sleep. Plagued by the stomach cramps that tend to precede my period, I cuddled a hot-water bottle to my abdomen and tried to process the evening's events. The exhilaration I'd felt at figuring it all out had gradually given way to calm determination. I had a theory; now all I needed to do was prove it.

At the end of the fireworks display I'd given Tommy a chaste kiss on the cheek and, at his behest, promised to meet him for dinner a few days later (a promise, now I had a sample of the boy's DNA, I had no intention of keeping).

Soon I would know for certain whether I was right or wrong. Soon I might be able to give Jason back his son.

I pretended to leave for work at the usual time. In my bag was the boy's hair. After yanking it from his head last night I'd stored it in the only vaguely sterile place I had to hand: Lauren's compass. This morning I planned to drive to the local shopping mall and buy one of those over-the-counter paternity kits.

Inside the car, I got out the silver disc and held it in my palm. A few minutes later, I watched as Jason left the house and locked the door. Oblivious to my presence on the other side of the street, he threw his work bag in the back of his car and drove away.

I watched him go, trying to imagine what life would be like if

Barney were to be returned to Jason and Vicky. After last night's revelation, that reunion now felt within touching distance. Vicky had kept his room in such pristine condition – the freshly made bed, the recently hoovered carpet – an act of defiance as much as hope. Now it seemed that hope was going to be rewarded.

Lauren's room had always been such a mess. It didn't matter how much I tidied it. Within hours it would be maelstrom of abandoned plastic ponies, scattered felt-tips and Lego. I'd pick her dirty clothes up off the floor and find myself showered with Moshi Monsters, their tiny plastic bodies hail-stoning off my hips and onto the carpet. I'd go in to wake her up for school and find myself waylaid by an assault course of loom bands, Mr Men books and tennis racquets. After one particularly nasty ankle-twist involving a forgotten game of Hungry Hungry Hippos left by her bedroom door, I'd tried to have a serious chat with her about the importance of putting things away once she'd finished with them. She'd been eating breakfast at the time, her face screwed up in concentration as she used her spoon to hunt down the bowl's three remaining Cheerios. It was early summer and she was wearing her school uniform, a blue-and-white-checked gingham dress. I'd yet to braid her hair and it hung in loose curls around her shoulders, the brown lightening to downy blonde around her temples.

'I'm sorry, Mummy,' she'd said after dispensing with the Cheerios. She put down her spoon and used both hands to lift the bowl to her mouth. She drained the milk in two gulps and set the bowl back on the table. 'I'll try to remember.' A white moustache now decorated her top lip. 'It's just so boring.'

At this I'd tried to remain stern, to expound on how some things in life were boring but necessary, but her honesty had disarmed me. She was right: tidying up was boring. I'd held it together for all of two seconds before I burst out laughing. And then she was laughing, too. Our giggles continuing all the way through the school run, right up until she kissed me and dashed in through the gates for registration.

I thought of Vicky going up to Barney's room every week with her dusters and polish. The way Jason spent his time scouring the internet forums for potential sightings. I envied their defiance, their right to keep everything ready, just in case. I envied their right to hope.

44

I parked in the shopping mall's multi-storey and made my way over to the lift. Three floors later the doors pinged open, and I headed right, towards the ground level concourse and the large Boots.

I crossed the shop's brightly lit threshold and felt another menstrual cramp slice at the side of my belly. Trying not to wince, I asked a member of staff to point me in the right direction and made my way over to the aisle nearest the pharmacy counter. It didn't take long to find what I was looking for. Nestled between the blood-glucose meters and allergy-testing kits was a row of large white boxes, each one decorated with a green double helix and the words Cellmark Labs. I picked up the box nearest the front and was surprised to discover something so important could weigh so little. I remembered the furore when they'd first announced they were going to start selling such things. The newspapers had claimed this new, easy access to paternity testing could tear certain families apart. It was strange, when you thought about it. This slavish obsession we had with DNA. Memories and experience seemed to me to shape our identity so much more than a series of cells and chromosomes.

Giving it a shake, I heard a paper-plastic rustle and, reassured, placed it in the basket. On the way to the till I felt another twinge, stronger this time, and decided to pick up some paracetamol and tampons while I was here, just in case.

Purchases made, I beelined for a nearby coffee shop. Ordering a black coffee, I settled myself at a secluded table and got out the Cellmark Labs box. Studying the instructions, I soon discovered that, although the kit itself had cost £15, there would be an additional lab processing fee of £129. I winced. I couldn't have afforded this even when I had a job to speak of. I'd have to put it on my credit card.

I looked further down the page. Boxed off from the rest of the text in bold black capitals was a warning. Asking anyone considering a paternity test, or any type of DNA test, to think carefully about the potential repercussions, it urged me to properly consider and assess the impact the results would have on the child or children involved. Skimming over the subsequent list of counselling helplines and websites, I found the bit I needed: step-by-step directions for paternal sample collection.

I'd taken Jason's hairbrush from the dressing table before I left the house. Removing it from its sealed plastic bag, I selected four strands with the white root plug still intact and placed them in the long blue envelope provided. Once it was labelled, I was ready to repeat the process.

I got Lauren's compass out of my bag and held the silver disc flat in my palm. Careful not to disturb the treasure inside, I gently popped the pull-fit catch. There, curled round the cover's inside diameter were three strands of blond hair. Only one of the strands had a viable root plug still attached. Hopefully it would be enough. Placing all three hairs in the long yellow envelope, I forged Jason's signature on the consent form, filled out the credit-card details and sealed them both into the pre-addressed Jiffy bag. A couple of first-class stamps and I was good to go.

I knew I had some in my purse but, after mooching through it for a few minutes, I lost patience and tipped the entire contents onto the table. Bingo. There amidst the jumble of old till receipts and loyalty cards was a book of twelve. Attaching three to the envelope, I was putting everything back in my purse when I came across Mark's business card. The journalist. The name of the newspaper he worked for was in its upper-right corner, garish and red. He hadn't bothered us since that day I'd caught him hanging around outside the college. Still, who knew when he might decide to show his face again? I decided that, for the time being, it would do to keep hold of his details, just in case.

While I'd been sitting down, my tummy cramps had seemed to subside but now I felt my belly spasm: a short, sharp pain that left me fighting for breath. Searching for the paracetamol I'd bought, I washed down the tablets with the last of my coffee and hoped it wouldn't be too long before they took effect.

Leaving the café, I put the Jiffy envelope into my bag. I'd pop it into the first postbox I saw. I checked the time. It was barely 10 a.m. I still had an entire day to kill. I decided to try and find an internet café. I could start trawling for a new job. If I got a couple of applications in today, then maybe by this time next week I'd be going for interviews.

I hadn't gone far when the cramps at the side of my abdomen took a turn for the worse. I took a seat on one of the benches in the middle of the concourse. A few minutes later and a couple wheeling a pram sat down next to me. Lifting the baby out, the woman cradled the child in her arms and offered it a bottle. The baby was hungry and, before long, the formula was gone. The woman took the bottle away and the baby's mouth went slack. As its eyes flickered towards sleep, she placed her hand on its chest and reaching down, gave it a kiss on the forehead. I remembered how it used to feel when I held Lauren like that. Her tiny ribcage and her heartbeat inside, fast and frantic, like a bee caught in a glass.

That had been at the beginning of her life. The end had been quite different.

Lauren had spent her last few hours in the boot of a Ford Mondeo. While she was in there she had wet herself, soaking the pink summer shorts she was wearing. The police knew this – that she had wet herself in there and not at one of the other locations she had been taken to – because the amount of urine that had seeped into the fabric lining underneath her was 'too much to suggest simple transfer'.

She'd been found wearing a white sandal on her right foot. When questioned in court, her murderer had explained that the other shoe had fallen off in his struggle to get the boot closed without trapping her fingers. This had confused me. Still did. I couldn't understand why, when he was about to do to her what he did, he had worried himself about that.

The throbbing in my stomach was getting stronger. I felt like I was going to be sick. Gingerly, I got to my feet. Hit by another jolt of pain, I doubled over. Breathing through the nausea, I staggered back towards the automatic doors, clutching my side. Outside, I made it as far as the grassy picnic area. I cried out and a few people looked in my direction, concerned. I gave them a wave, trying to let them know I was OK but then the pain ripped through me again and I slumped to my knees. I felt the thick, telltale wet

between my legs that usually signified the start of my period and
then someone was at my side, lifting me up.

'Are you OK? Are you hurt?' they asked, taking my hand.

But I couldn't speak. I was falling, everything going dark.

45

One week later and Mum had put me up in my old bedroom for the duration of my convalescence.

Turns out I was pregnant. Only five or six weeks along, but still, pregnant all the same. Problem was, the baby hadn't taken root in the right place. The surgeon had had to remove one of my fallopian tubes, although the other remained intact.

When I came round the doctor explained what had happened. I hadn't taken the news well. After that it had been decided it was probably better for me not to be left alone, at least until I'd recovered. At first, Jason had stayed home, but we couldn't afford for him to miss too many classes, and so, after a few days, he drove me to Kent to be looked after by Mum and Dad.

My room was painted pink and grey and one wall was entirely taken up by mirrored wardrobes. I got out of bed and went over to the wardrobe nearest the window. In the week since I'd been out of hospital, pale blue, almost purple, shadows had appeared under my eyes. I moved closer. There was now such a thick, uniform line of grey rooting out from the top of my fringe it looked like I'd had it dip-dyed that way on purpose.

I turned away from the mirror, towards the window. White plastic pots filled with geraniums dotted the patio. The tiny flecks of mica in the patio concrete were winking in the sun. I'd been cooped up for days. I wanted to go for a walk.

Opening the bedroom door a touch, I heard Mum and Dad in the kitchen down the hall, preparing lunch. A thick fug of carrot, potato, cabbage and roast pork filled the air and I could hear the clinking of cutlery being set on the table. It would be easier if I left without telling them.

Closing the front gate behind me, I decided to do a lap round the lane that connected our row of houses with the main road. It should take about half an hour.

Glad to be outside, I set off at a pace. To my right were the houses of Mum and Dad's neighbours. Identical seventies bungalows, each of their front gardens was perfectly manicured and littered with tasteful stone birdbaths. Before long, these began to peter out and the land opened up, revealing the fields and orchards beyond. A mile or so later I reached the stables where I used to go riding as a little girl. The horses were out in the pasture, tartan coats tied around their steaming bodies. I walked up to the fence and, after a short while, a brown mare came over to where I stood. She nodded her head and whinnied, wanting to be stroked. While I obliged, my palm smoothing down the soft white hair on her forehead, I watched one of the other horses eating apples that had fallen from a tree, his munching like that thuddy, dense sound boots make in fresh snow.

Still stroking the mare, I reached my other hand down towards my stomach and traced a finger across the new constellation of scars on my abdomen. Three small red dots. If you were to join them together with a pen they would form a kind of obtuse triangle.

I'd been out of surgery a few hours when Jason called Bullingdon's to tell them I wouldn't be in work for a while. During the course of the conversation it came to light I'd been fired. He waited till we got home from hospital to ask me about it. I'd apologised for keeping it from him. Told him I was embarrassed, that I'd planned on telling him once I had another job to go to and offered stories of unrealistic sales targets in explanation for my termination. My invalidity allowed me to hide behind a vague set of reasons and excuses I might not otherwise have got away with. It was clear Jason suspected there was more to it, but he didn't push – for now, anyway.

It was dark when I headed back up the drive, to the bungalow.

'There you are,' said Mum before I was even through the door. 'You've been gone ages. Are you sure you should be up and about?'

Her mouth dropped open.

'Did you go out like that? In your nightie and dressing-gown? You must be freezing.' Her gaze found its way to my feet. 'But you haven't got any shoes on either.' I also looked down. She was right. My toes were covered in dirt.

'I needed some fresh air.'

'You must be starving,' she said, hustling me into the kitchen. 'I'll warm up some leftovers.'

As I sat down, Dad looked up from his paper, his half-moon glasses low on his nose.

'Hello darling.' He looked at my muddy feet. 'Go out for a little stroll, did we?'

My dad. Lauren had adored him. She loved nothing more than climbing up onto the round of his belly and tickling him under the arms with her tiny hands. When she was kidnapped he went for three days without sleep – mobilising local search parties, liaising with the police and going door to door with her photo – before finally collapsing with exhaustion. He'd been a civil engineer at a good firm in town. But, after the court case, he'd taken early retirement and now he spent his days pernicketing with his lawn, in constant battle with the slugs that plagued his vegetable patch.

The man who murdered my daughter, my father's granddaughter, was called Gavin Nunn. The day he took Lauren he already had three previous sex offences to his name. Lauren was his fourth. We don't know how he persuaded her to leave the front of our caravan. He might have promised her something; he might have grabbed her against her will. We do know that he took her to his car and that he then drove her to a number of different places where he raped her and then strangled her to death.

Ten days later a couple walking their dog discovered her corpse in a wood.

Mum put some reheated roast dinner on the table but I wasn't hungry and, after a few mouthfuls, I couldn't eat any more. While Dad cleared my plate, Mum came and sat next to me. I realised that she was balancing something on the flat of her hand.

'I was having a clear-out earlier. You'll never guess what I found.'

'What?'

She proffered it up near my face.

'Your cradle cap.'

I looked down at her palm but all I could see was a white envelope.

'Cradle cap?'

She tutted at my ignorance and began to shuffle whatever was inside the envelope onto the table.

'I kept it all these years. It came off in one piece, perfectly intact. It's meant to be lucky when it does that and so we kept it.'

Finally, a round patch of thin skin with a smattering of fine blonde hairs still attached emerged from the envelope.

I thought of the package at the bottom of my handbag. The hair samples still inside. Sending it off had seemed important. Critical. Now, I wasn't so sure.

'Do you want it?' she asked, picking the edge of it up between her forefinger and thumb. I moved back in my chair.

'Why would I want that thing?'

'I just thought . . .'

'Throw it away.'

'It's meant to be lucky, that's the only reason I kept it,' she said, putting it back in its envelope. 'It's meant to be lucky.'

We were sitting watching the *Six O'Clock News* when I decided to go home. Jason was due to come and collect me at the weekend, but there was no way I could last till then. I brought up the train times on my phone. If I was quick, I could make the express. Slipping out unnoticed to my bedroom, I used one hand to start throwing clothes into my suitcase and the other to dial for a taxi.

46

I watched the landscape go from plucked fields to ridged furrows, frosted solid by the night. Resting my head against the train window, I'd just closed my eyes when my phone rang. I answered expecting to hear Mum and Dad, calling to check on me again. Instead, I was greeted by a soft Glaswegian burr.

'Hello Heidi.'

Tommy.

Despite a number of increasingly irate voicemails, since that night at the fireworks display, I had neither seen nor spoken to him. Still, I'd thought that if I ignored enough of his calls, he'd give up. I was wrong. If anything, it seemed to make him more persistent.

'I've been thinking about you.'

I cut into his words. 'I don't want you to think about me.'

He paused and I imagined him on the other end of the line, his sleeves pushed up over his tattooed forearms.

'I'm not sure you get to decide that, Heidi,' he said eventually, a new bite to his tone.

'I took your call just now out of common courtesy.' I kept my voice low. 'I could have continued to ignore you, but I thought this was the right thing to do. Seems I was wrong.'

'I think you'll find things have gone too far for common courtesy,' he said. 'That *you've* gone too far.'

I'd expected him to be difficult – I'd led him on a merry dance and now I was telling him things were over – but the way he was talking unnerved me.

'I'm sorry,' I said, sick of his constant, confusing allusions to something I wasn't party to. 'Please don't contact me again.'

47

It was after midnight when the taxi pulled up outside our house. I paid, grabbed my suitcase and got out. I hadn't told Jason I was coming home early and so it was no surprise to see all the curtains closed. He must have already gone to bed.

Closing the front door quietly so as not to wake him, I was about to creep upstairs when I heard voices coming from the living room. He was still awake and, from the sound of it, he had company. The door was open a crack and so I peered through before going in. The TV was the only source of light in the room and it was showing an old video, recorded on a mobile phone.

One of Jason's favourites (I'd seen it countless times), it featured a two-year-old Barney and a younger, less tired-looking Jason, both wearing aprons and silly white chef's hats, baking cookies together. Their hair and faces were covered with flour and the video had just reached the point where Jason had made a moustache out of dough and stuck it to his face. Barney couldn't stop giggling. From behind the camera came Vicky's voice.

'Make sure to give the mixture a good stir.' Barney struggled to move his wooden spoon through the thick batter and so she offered more words of encouragement. 'Look how strong you are. Just like Daddy. My two big strong boys.'

It was because of this, because of Vicky's voice coming out of the TV, that I didn't immediately realise she was also there talking in person.

I froze.

What was she doing in my house?

The video came to an end and automatically reverted back to the main menu. The door wasn't open wide enough for me to see round to where Vicky was sitting but, now that the TV was dark, I realised I could see her reflection in its screen. Sitting on the sofa next to Jason, she was wearing a hoodie, the zipper pulled all the way up to the top so that it covered her mouth and nose.

'I miss him every day,' said Vicky, opening her zipper a little to speak.

'I know,' said Jason. 'So do I.' They spoke without looking at each other, their voices low. I got the impression they'd been having this same conversation over and over for quite some time.

The faces of our children stared out from the mantelpiece. Lauren with her first three baby teeth, grinning widely at my dad, who was behind the camera making the raspberry noises she loved. Barney playing with his fire truck in the bath, his hair dark with soapy water. And then, there on the windowsill was our wedding photo, taken in the gardens of the registry office. My bouquet of yellow calla lilies was stark against the white of my dress; Jason's shoes had been polished till the leather shone.

'Sorry about the baby,' said Vicky, quietly. 'I didn't know you two were trying.'

'We weren't.'

I went to retreat back out into the night. I didn't want to hear them talk about me, about what had happened. But then Jason said something that made me want to stick around.

'I paid Tesh a visit on-site the other day.' He waited a beat, as though he was reluctant to release the next piece of information into the room. 'Danny was there.'

Vicky pulled the hoodie tight around her skull. The opening ruched against her face.

'I didn't talk to him,' said Jason. 'I thought I'd be able to, but I couldn't. Even now.'

I remembered the man I'd seen pacing up and down outside the Portakabin in the rain. The way he'd kept looking up to the top of the power station, as though he'd wanted to make sure Jason was still there.

'What if we came clean?' This was Vicky.

'It wouldn't make any difference. It didn't then and it certainly won't now.'

'But Jason –'

'No,' he said, cutting her off. 'What you did is irrelevant.'

'You mean what you made me do.'

Her response was switchblade fast, but Jason didn't flinch.

'I didn't make you do anything and you know it.' It seemed this was an accusation he'd had levelled at him before. 'It was your choice. Don't lay it on me.'

'Don't lay it on you!' Vicky dropped the hood's drawstring and it fell away from her head, releasing her long black hair.

She seemed like she might be about to get to her feet. I tensed, torn between the urge to hear more of their exchange and the fear of being caught eavesdropping.

'You gave me an ultimatum. Get rid of it you said, get rid of it or I'll leave. Then you went and left anyway.'

'Can we not go through this again?'

'It's getting harder to live with, not easier.'

'What do you want? Do you need me to say that I forgive you? Is that it? Is that what you need me to say?' He dipped his head as though he was shy, and looked up at her through his eyelashes. A mannerism that, until now, I'd thought was reserved for me. 'Well, I do, OK? I forgive you.'

The exchange seemed to have exhausted them and they slumped back together into the cushions. Vicky leant her head on Jason's shoulder.

'And I forgive you.'

Vicky reached for Jason's hand. He let her take it.

I felt like I was unravelling from the inside out. My thoughts spun and swerved, struggling to process everything I'd just heard.

What had Vicky done? Who was Danny? Were they talking about something that happened before Barney went missing or after?

I'd been leaning further and further forward to hear what they were saying and now I felt the strap of my handbag start to slide off my shoulder. I managed to push it back into place before it fell off and hit the floor with a thump but, as I did, the friction of the strap against the fabric of my coat made a squeaking noise.

Vicky started and sat up straight.

'What was that?' She looked over to the door, but I'd already moved back into the shadows.

'I didn't hear anything.' They both sat there, listening to the silence.

'Just the wind,' said Jason. 'Nothing to worry about.'

Not wanting to risk standing in the hall for very much longer I tried to work out what to do next. As I saw it, I had two options. One, I could go and slam the front door and pretend like I'd just come in. I'd fiddle with my bag in the hallway, take my coat off, give them time to compose themselves and then have to have a very awkward conversation with them both. Or, two, I could leave without them knowing I was ever here and come back in the morning when Vicky would, hopefully, be long gone.

I decided it would be best if I left them none the wiser. After everything I'd just heard, my head was a mess. I'd spend the night at Carla's. She wouldn't mind.

I didn't leave until they'd restarted the video. Using the noise to disguise the opening and shutting of the front door, as I slipped back out into the night, I tried to forget the easy chemistry of Vicky's head on Jason's shoulder, the way he'd seemed to lean into her touch, the way their hands had managed to find each other in the dark.

48

Carla's living room was warm, the only source of a light a single standard lamp covered with a blue silk scarf.

'Sorry to impose,' I said, putting down my suitcase. 'Did I wake you?'

'Not at all.' She gestured to her open laptop on the table in the corner. 'I was working late when you called. I've got to give a paper at a conference in a couple of days and I'm nowhere near ready.'

I collapsed back onto her battered red leather Chesterfield and kicked off my heels. Jasper was on my lap and purring in an instant. During the journey over I'd replayed the conversation I'd witnessed between Jason and Vicky so many times that I'd started to mix up who'd said what to whom. They shared a secret, that much was clear, but what?

'I thought you were staying at your mum and dad's?' said Carla, taking a seat beside me. She was wearing purple harem pants, cable-knit bed socks and an Amnesty International hoodie; her black curls were arranged on top of her head with what seemed to be a combination of clips and chopsticks.

'I was. I just got back.' I placed my finger on the bottom of my jumper and traced out the laparoscopic triangle of dots on the skin underneath. 'Thought I'd surprise Jason. But then when I got home, Vicky was there.'

'Was she visiting?' asked Carla carefully.

I smoothed my hand down Jasper's spine.

'The doctors said I have to wait a few months, but they said that what happened shouldn't stop me from being able to have another baby. Did I tell you that?'

'You did. I came to see you in the hospital, remember?'

I looked at the screensaver on Carla's laptop. A slideshow of photos, the current picture showed Carla atop a hill in the rain, her cagoule cinched around her face.

'This conference. Who's going to feed Jasper while you're away?'

'I was going to ask the neighbours.'

'I'll do it.'

'Not necessary. Not with everything you've got going on at the moment . . .'

'I'll do it,' I said again before she could continue. 'No arguments.'

She conceded with a sigh.

'It's almost two.' She stretched her arms in the air and yawned. 'I'll get you a blanket and some pillows.'

Later, tucked under Carla's blanket, I watched the changing sequence of pictures on her laptop and tried to let their slow slides and dissolves lull me to sleep. But every time I closed my eyes I would be confronted with the image of Jason and Vicky in my living room.

Was she still there with him now? What were they doing? Would she end up staying the night?

I reached my hand out of the blanket and down to my bag on the floor. Finding Lauren's compass, I brought it up to my mouth and pressed it to my lips, my breath condensing on the smooth silver.

I thought of Vicky and Jason on the sofa. The way Jason had sat in close and held her hand. She was no longer his to have. But the fact I knew Vicky was with Martin offered no reassurance. What was to stop her from ditching the detective and trying to put everything back to how it used to be? I could imagine all too easily how a reconciliation with Jason might take shape. At first it would be strange, their movements awkward. They might bash teeth when they first tried to kiss. But then, tracing his fingers along her stretch marks, Jason would press his mouth up against her skin, up against this proof that Barney had left behind, this evidence that he'd lived and, before long, he'd realise how good it felt, how familiar.

I saw another photo slide into position on Carla's screensaver. A selfie. It showed Carla prone on a pillow, sporting her electric-blue hair-streaks from a few months back. Her cheeks flushed, she was leaning in to kiss the person lying next to her. Mark. The journalist.

Popping open the compass, I watched as the needle pivoted beneath the glass, the earth's field exerting a torque it was powerless to resist. Not thinking, I used my index finger to flick the metal ring loop at the top of the disc and it spun round on its axis, letting out a loud, high-pitched clicking sound. The noise was brutal against the silence. I grabbed it quickly and listened for any sign that I might have woken Carla. After a few seconds had passed without incident, I relaxed. I looked at the noise culprit. That bloody ring loop. Lauren had been obsessed with it. I used to hear its clicking in her room at night, long after lights out, and then I'd have to go in and take the compass away for safekeeping until the morning.

Pushing the blanket to one side, I exchanged Lauren's compass for my purse. It didn't take long to find Mark's business card. The one he'd given me the night of the barbecue. Going over to the computer, I rubbed my finger against the mouse and, once the screen had woken up, I opened the search page. A few minutes later and I'd set up a Hotmail account under a random name. Balancing Mark's card against the keyboard, after typing in his email address I set about composing my message. His pre-existing interest in the story should mean he'd start digging immediately.

Moving the mouse over the *send* icon, I let it hover. It was strictly forbidden for a police officer to get involved with someone on an active case, especially a family liaison officer. I could ruin Martin's career. I hesitated. He didn't deserve to be thrown into the shit-storm that would inevitably ensue. I thought of Jason and Vicky on the sofa. Jason needed to know that she belonged to someone else and he needed to learn about it from someone other than me.

I looked at the journalist's email address.

Closing my eyes, I pressed down hard and with a single click, the message was sent.

49

The next morning, I arrived at the house unannounced. Slamming the door and dumping my keys on the table, this time I was certain to make my presence felt. Worried I was some kind of intruder, Jason appeared in an instant.

'Heidi?' Seeing me he relaxed. 'You're back?'

'You know my mum and dad,' I said. 'Their mollycoddling was starting to get on my nerves and so I decided to come home early.'

'Here, let me get that.' He took my suitcase and dashed it upstairs, into our bedroom. Alone in the hall, I had visions of him using this opportunity to hide any evidence of Vicky having spent the night. Thumping back down to where I stood, he gave me a quick, breathless kiss.

'How are you feeling? I mean, how have things been?' he asked, unable to mention the pregnancy directly.

I took off my coat.

'Get up to much while I was away?' I wanted to give him every chance to come clean of his own accord. To have him tell me to my face that Vicky had been here, in my house.

'Not much. Work, stuff, you know.'

'Off out for a run?' I nodded at his shorts and T-shirt.

'I was. Needed to clear my head. But now you're home . . .'

'Go,' I said, before he could say any more. 'I want to have a shower.

I'll be done by the time you get back and then we can catch up.'

He hesitated.

'Sure?'

'I am. Go.'

Left to my own devices, and still without a satisfactory answer as to whether or not Vicky had stayed over, I began unpacking. I'd just finished when I heard someone knocking. Making my way downstairs, through the door's half-moon, frosted glass I could see the outline of a man's head. Something about the way he ran his hands through his hair made me stop. Tommy. Tommy was here.

Hit with a mixture of panic and confusion, I was about to run back up to the bedroom and stay there until he (hopefully) went away, when he got down on his knees and started shouting through the letter box.

'I know you're in there,' he said. 'Open the door or I'll cause a scene. Your neighbours have already started twitching their curtains.'

Putting the chain in the bolt, I peeked out through the gap.

'What are you doing here? How do you even know where I live?'

'I followed you.'

'You did what?'

'After the fireworks display.'

'You have to go. My husband will be back.'

Moving forward, he squashed his face up against the space between the door and the frame.

'Because you really care about that husband of yours?' he said, his eyes flashing. 'You've really got his best interests at heart?'

I tried to think straight, to come up with something that would get rid of him before Jason came home and caught him here.

'I'm sorry, but this thing between us, whatever it was, it's over.' I had to resist the urge to shut the door in his face. 'I want you to go.'

At this he retreated onto the pavement. He squinted at the town at the bottom of the hill, thinking.

'OK,' he said, turning back to me. I knew it was too easy, but still my hopes leapt. He was going to do as I'd asked. It was all going to be fine. But then he crinkled up his face, his mouth twisted into a cruel smirk. 'I'll go. Once you've agreed to see me again.'

'I've told you, it's over. Don't you get it?' I screamed. He dusted an imaginary speck of lint off his arm.

'If you don't, I'll wait here until your husband comes home and then, when he does, I'm going to tell him everything.' He winked.

I studied his face, trying to work out whether or not he was serious. 'You wouldn't.'

'But I would,' he laughed. 'I would.'

I looked at my watch. I hadn't noticed the time when Jason left, and I wasn't sure how far he had been intending to run. Five miles? Ten? He could be back any second. Whatever it took. I had to get rid of Tommy.

'When?'

'This Friday. At a hotel.'

'What about your flat?'

He reached his hand through the gap in the door and, as he spoke, he used his finger to pat out the syllables on my nose.

'I don't think,' – pat, pat, pat – 'you're in any position,' – pat, pat, pat – 'to question me right now.'

'OK, a hotel,' I said, searching the street for signs of Jason. 'Text me the details and I'll be there.'

'You promise?'

'Yes. Now will you please go?'

'I want you to kiss me first.' I hesitated. 'Kiss me now. Here. Or the deal's off,' he challenged.

Realising I had no choice, I shut the door, slipped the chain out of the bolt and reopened it wide. As soon as I stepped forward, Tommy grabbed my face and put his lips to mine. I kept my eyes open. He'd just pushed his tongue deep into my mouth when I saw Jason appear over the incline of the hill. I cried out and tried to push him off but he had me held tight.

Less than a hundred yards away, his earphones still plugged in, Jason was focused on fiddling with the timer on his watch. He had only to look up and he would see us. With a surge of effort I freed myself.

'You have to go,' I said.

'I'll be in touch.' He leant in for one last kiss.

As Tommy got back into his Jeep on the other side of the street, Jason wiped his face on the sleeve of his T-shirt and gave me a wave. Tommy started up the car and soon he and Jason were passing each other – Jason on the pavement, Tommy on the road – Jason's shadow sliding across the Jeep's blue metalwork like a blurry ghost.

50

Friday morning, two days after Tommy had shown up on my doorstep, and I was strung out, my temper tinder dry.

I was upstairs, getting dressed, when Jason shouted up the stairs.

'Have you done something with my keys?'

'Sorry, no,' I yelled back. I was running late and I didn't want any distractions. If I failed to show up at the hotel on time then Tommy might come looking for me here.

There was a pause, and then I heard the banging and swearing that meant Jason was searching the kitchen drawers. This went on for about thirty seconds and then I heard him stomping back into the hall.

'They're not in the bowl where I always leave them.'

I tensed, ready for the line I knew was coming next.

'Have you moved them?'

'No.' I kept my voice neutral. 'Have you checked your jeans pocket?'

'You must have,' he shouted, and then, a little bit quieter, as though he didn't want me to hear. 'You're always tidying my things.'

Fortified for the day ahead in my black suede stilettos with the polished metal heels, I came down to find him in the living room, busy upending every drawer in the sideboard. Bottle-openers, packs of cards and bits of string littered the carpet.

'You'd better put all that away when you're done.'

He thrust his hands down the back of the sofa.

'I'm sick of never being able to find things when I need them.' When the sofa proved fruitless, he moved on to the armchair, flinging the cushions onto the floor.

'Maybe I didn't move your bloody keys. Maybe you put them somewhere. Maybe you hid them.' Once I got started, the words rushed out of their own accord. 'Because, let's face it, when it comes to hiding things you've got a bit of a track record.' I wanted to stop, but still, I kept going. 'Where in the house is your Vicky folder stashed now Jason? Under the floorboards? In the loft? A metal safe only you can access using the secret combination?'

'Careful,' warned Jason. He came in close to where I stood and pushed his face into mine. 'There are some things that, once you say them, you can't take back.'

Heeding his threat, I stopped. I was already ten minutes late for my meet-up with Tommy. Every extra minute I stayed was an extra minute in which he might bang on the door and make good on his threat to tell Jason everything. I wanted to go, but this exchange, this argument, seemed to have levered open a tiny chink in the dam. A gap through which, given half a chance, all things unsaid could escape. It felt like an opportunity.

'Who is Danny?'

'What?' The change in topic threw him. His anger collapsed into confusion. But then half a second later I saw his eye twitch. Fear. His brain had yet to catch up with what his body already knew. 'What are you talking about?'

'I heard you. The other night. You and Vicky. You were watching old videos together.'

He floundered, reaching for what he and Vicky might have said. 'There's nothing to tell.'

'It didn't sound like nothing.'

'You're poking your nose into things you don't understand,' he said, shaking his head. 'It's none of your business.'

'What is it she wants you two to come clean about? And to whom?'

He went to leave the room. Sick of his evasion tactics, I pushed in alongside him, making sure to get to the door first.

'Stop bullshitting.' I blocked his way. 'Tell me – tell me right now.' I pulled out the only threat in my arsenal. 'Or I'll go and ask Vicky myself.'

He took a step back, shocked.

'You really want to do this? Then let's do this.' He looked to the floor, his bravado gone. 'Vicky had an affair.'

'She what?' This I hadn't expected.

'A bloke I worked with. Danny.' He said the man's name through gritted teeth.

I was so lost for words I couldn't even formulate a question, but he continued.

'She realised she was pregnant the day Barney went missing.' He shook his head, a reluctant surrender. 'She drove over to Danny's house that morning. She went to tell him it was over.'

I thought of all the times he'd recounted the events of that day. The idyllic scene with the dippy egg and soldiers in the kitchen. The way Barney had bounced on their bed, blowing raspberries.

'Danny didn't take it well.' He laughed bitterly. 'After she'd gone he kept calling her on this pay-as-you-go he'd given her. Flashy shit.

Thought he was the bee's knees. Still does. He has this ridiculous tattoo on his back. A tree. The branches go all the way up to his neck.'

'Did you know about this right from the beginning?'

He paused and looked me in the eye. He seemed to be deciding which answer to give.

'Vicky was scared to tell me about it at first, about the baby.'

'And then?'

'A week or so after Barney had gone, she broke down. By that point the press had turned their crosshairs on us. The police didn't have a suspect, there was no body and so they were trying to make Vicky the story.' He rubbed at the short undercut on the back of his head. 'She wanted to go to the police but I knew that, if we did, it would be a disaster. Right from the start Martin had told us it was important to keep the press on side. You of all people know what it's like. If people start thinking the parents did it then they're much less likely to call in anything suspicious. If we'd come clean, it would have added nothing to the investigation and the story would have changed. They would have made it all about the affair, not finding Barney. Lose, lose.'

'And you got her to agree?'

'For a time, but she's a good person. She's still worried there might be some detail about that morning, that day . . .' He faltered. Again, he seemed to be locked into some internal decision-making process about what he was or wasn't going to tell me.

'So that's why you jacked in the steel?'

'Welding is a small world.' He shrugged. 'You come across the same crowd of lads again and again. I couldn't face the thought of bumping into him. Danny.'

He came forward and took my hands in his. He seemed to be telling the truth.

'I'm sorry I never told you. I couldn't.' He brought his face in close to mine. When I refused to meet his eye, he reached for something else to assuage me. 'Besides, it wouldn't have been fair. If you knew any of this then you'd be implicated.'

I thought about the night I'd overheard them talking on the sofa. Vicky had mentioned something about an ultimatum.

'What about the baby?'

At this he dropped my hands and moved away, towards the bay window.

'She decided to terminate the pregnancy.'

He adjusted a framed picture of Barney on the windowsill so that it faced head-on, into the room.

'Does Martin know?'

I was pretty sure I already knew the answer to this question, but I wanted to know if Jason had any inkling.

'Martin? Of course not.'

I thought of Vicky and the detective that day outside the police station. The text-message exchange I'd read on her phone. Her distress. He knew. But Jason believed the secret he and Vicky shared was one between them and them alone. Secrets like that can keep you bound to a person. Connected. Until, I thought, the day you learn they shared your secret with someone else.

'So that was why you split? Not because of Barney – because of her infidelity, her pregnancy?'

'Yes and no.' He rubbed again at the hair at the back of his scalp, his hand hard against the short undercut. 'Vicky always swore the thing with Danny was a one-time occurrence, a mistake. I found out later it had been going on for months.'

I had a sudden and horrible realisation.

'That's what your file on Vicky was about?' I didn't know whether to feel stupid or jealous. 'You were trying to work out whether or not she'd had an affair, or just a one-night stand?'

His subsequent silence told me everything I needed to know.

I realised I felt embarrassed – for him not me.

'She didn't want to get rid of the baby, did she?'

'Enough.' He threw his hands up in the air and collapsed back onto the sofa in defeat. 'You wanted to know and now you know.'

It could have been the other guy's child she was carrying. On the other hand, there was always a possibility . . .

I might not have said the words out loud but we'd both heard them. I'd already stayed longer than I should. Tommy was waiting for me. Grabbing my bag and coat, I headed for the front door.

51

The hotel was a grubby sixties block. Situated next to a dual carriageway, it had a pale, concrete exterior and tiny metal windows. Beneath each window were dark, damp stains from where rain had collected on the sill and drained out onto the concrete. The dripping was so consistent it looked deliberate; an eccentric pattern decided upon by the architect.

Sliding doors led into a maroon-coloured lobby. It was empty except for a plastic spider plant in the corner and a vending machine, chained and bolted to the floor. Light jazz muzakked from invisible speakers in the ceiling.

Tommy had said he would be in room 323 and so, after checking the wall signs, I headed for the tiny lift.

I'd spent the drive here replaying Jason's revelations in my head. Now, as the lift climbed to the third floor, I continued to pick over the debris. He'd said that he'd lied to protect me, to ensure I wasn't implicated. But the more I thought about it, the more I doubted whether this was actually the case. His priority had been to protect Vicky, to protect himself.

The doors dinged open and I tried to focus on the task at hand. Right now I had to deal with Tommy, to find a way of despatching him quickly and cleanly from my life.

Out of the lift, I counted my way down the corridor to his room, knocked and stood back to wait. The air smelt of mould and stale cigarette smoke.

There were footsteps. I heard the sound of the metal spy-hole cover on the other side of the door being slid open and made sure to stare, unsmiling, into the glass fish-eye. I wasn't entirely sure why he'd asked me to meet him at a hotel and not his flat, but I suspected it was because he thought it more likely that it would lead to some kind of tryst. I crossed my arms. From the outset I needed him to know how things stood. Nothing was going to happen.

A minute or so passed and then finally the door opened a sliver and Tommy peered out. Without saying a word, he leant his head forward and scanned the corridor, like he was looking for somebody. Satisfied I was alone, he ushered me inside.

We stood facing each other in the long passage that led into what seemed to be the bedroom. To my left was a door, presumably the bathroom, and to my right was a fitted wardrobe. The wardrobe wasn't shut properly and as I followed the line of the middle door to the floor, I saw that there were two large holdalls stashed in there, one on top of the other. Resting on top of the holdalls were two picture frames. I'd seen one of them before, in Tommy's flat. A small bleached-out snap framed in silver, it showed Tommy and his brother and sister as kids, their arms wrapped around each other. The second picture was in shadow and more difficult to make out.

I realised Tommy was smiling shyly.

'What's so amusing?'

He shrugged, his smile goofing into a wide grin.

I needed to stay calm, but I felt like he was goading me.

'OK, funny man,' I said. 'How about this for a joke? What the fuck were you thinking, coming to my house? Why did you think it was OK to follow me?'

'Heidi.' He shook his head as though I'd disappointed him. 'You don't mean that.'

This exchange felt like the one we'd had the other day. It was as though we were having a conversation about two very different things, as though he was alluding to something he thought I should know all about but didn't.

'I don't like being blackmailed,' I said, determined not to let his weirdness throw me off course. 'Don't come to my house again.'

'Or what? You'll tell your husband?' He nudged me gently with his elbow. He seemed to think we were enjoying some shared joke. 'You won't tell him, same way he won't tell you.'

'What do you mean?' I asked, sick of these insinuations that made no sense.

Silence.

'Look,' I said, softening my tone. 'You're a nice guy, but what happened between us, it didn't mean anything. I'm sorry if I led you on.'

For a brief moment his grin disappeared. I'd hurt his feelings. He stopped to consider the veracity of my words. A beat, and then he shook his head, my protest dismissed, and the smile returned, wider than before.

'What is it you want?' I asked, unable to stop myself from escalating into a shout. 'Why have you brought me here?'

Tired of his games, I took a step back and was about to leave when something in the wardrobe caught my eye. It was the light, catching on the silver framed snap of Tommy and his siblings. I stopped. From this spot I was granted a full view of the second frame lying next to it.

The air seemed to tighten and flex.

I had seen it once before: in the room at the back of the off-licence. Looking down through the tiny window, that day I'd only been able to make out that it was a shot of a larger man, the boy and another adult on some kind of a fishing boat. Now, up close, I saw that the larger man was indeed Keith. But I was also able to identify the third person. There, holding a fish aloft, his forearm tattoos brazen in the sunshine, was Tommy.

I looked back to where he stood now, in front of me. He offered a tentative smile. He seemed hopeful. Like he had just presented me with a surprise gift.

What was going on?

I heard the bathroom door handle push down. Someone had been in there the whole time. Keith? I felt a stab of fear. Had they brought me here to hurt me?

But then the door opened and the person in the bathroom stepped forward.

Wearing jeans and a hooded top, he looked from me to Tommy, his eyes wide.

'Tommy, please can I come out now?' he asked in a small voice.

I felt my knees go.

The boy.

52

I looked from the boy to Tommy, unable to process what was happening.

Tommy ruffled the boy's hair and pointed at me.

'You remember Heidi?'

The boy nodded.

I watched as he padded over to the far corner of the bedroom, grabbed the remote and turned on the TV.

'What is he doing here?' I pointed at the photograph. 'Why are you in that picture?'

'Shush,' said Tommy, scooping me away from the door and putting his hand over my mouth.

I struggled to get free but his grip was too strong. Pulling my head back into his shoulders, he marched me into the bedroom.

'If I take my hand away do you promise to remain calm?' he asked. His tone was gentle, benevolent almost.

I nodded as best I could, his hold making it difficult to move my head even slightly. A few seconds later and he released me.

'What's going on?' I asked between gulps of air. 'What the fuck . . .'

'Come, now,' he said, pushing me onto the sofa. 'We've done this dance long enough. Time to stop pretending.'

He sat down, put his arm around my shoulders and crushed me towards him. I tried to wriggle away, but he had me held firm. He leant in and kissed my ear and neck. His breath had a whisky tang. I looked at the boy. Absorbed in a cartoon, he seemed unaware of the drama going on behind him.

'I asked you here because I thought it was time for us both to come clean. About him.' He nodded at the boy. 'And about us.' He ran his hand up and down my leg.

Us? What was going on?

'That first day, I knew you were there to snoop.' His hand came to a stop at my knee. 'We should have run.' He lazed his finger back, along my inner thigh and zigzagged it up towards my knickers. 'But I had this feeling. About you,' he paused and looked me in the eye, his finger touching my crotch. 'And later, about you and me.' Panic leached its way into my lungs. 'Turns out I was right.'

I looked at the boy, mortified this was happening in front of him. Thankfully, he hadn't seen. Sitting cross-legged in front of the television, all his attention was focused on a brightly coloured superhero.

'You'd been knocked over in the street. You were hurt and yet all you were worried about was that someone might call an ambulance. That was the first thing to give me pause. You didn't want anyone to know you were there. Why? It didn't make sense. I decided to take a gamble. When we got through the first twenty-four hours without incident, I knew. You hadn't raised the alarm and you were never going to. You didn't want him found.'

'What?' My fear temporarily replaced with pique, I turned to face him. 'Jason took one look and said it wasn't him,' I explained. 'No one would listen.'

My outburst surprised him. I remembered he was oblivious to the first time I'd laid eyes on the child, the day I'd insisted Jason come to look.

'Then there was other stuff. Like say you appearing on my doorstep.' He mimed the way my jersey dress had slipped from my shoulders. 'That night at the fireworks I took a big risk letting you go off with Mikey. I needed to know we could trust you.' He beamed with pride. 'You brought him back.'

He presumed I knew all about his and Keith's secret. Not only that, he believed I condoned it. But if that was the case, then why had he asked me here today, to this hotel? I ran through events in my head, and then it hit me. I had tried to break things off with him. Blocked his calls. Did he think I'd had second thoughts, that I was getting ready to report them to the police? Was I here now because he needed to make sure of my silence?

Dread corseted my ribcage. I hadn't told anyone where I was going and it wasn't like work were expecting me. Anything could happen and the only point at which Jason might clock something was up would be tonight, when he got home from work and noticed I wasn't there. But then again . . . After the argument we'd had before I left the house this morning – after his confession – if I didn't show up for dinner he'd no doubt put my absence down to nothing more than my anger at him and his lies.

My hands started to shake. Was Tommy going to hurt me? But no, he would never do that, not with the child here.

'So,' I said, trying to disguise the tremor in my voice, 'you took Barney?'

Tommy recoiled, offended.

'He's called Mikey,' he whispered, checking to make sure the boy hadn't heard, 'and no, I didn't "take" him.'

'Who did? Keith?'

'No.' He pinched the bridge of his nose between his finger and thumb as though he had a headache.

'He should be with his dad,' I ventured. 'He should be with Jason.'

The mention of Jason's name seemed to irritate him. He got up, went to the window and pulled the long net curtain to the side.

'You say that,' he said, looking down at the car park below. 'You want everyone to think that.'

I thought about the strands of hair I'd taken. The Jiffy envelope was still somewhere at the bottom of my bag, ready to be sent off to the lab.

He turned to look at me, his face full of mischief. 'If Jason were to get his kid back, how long do you think it would be until he realises you and he no longer have anything in common? One month? Two?'

'He should be with his family,' I persevered. 'He has a mum and dad.'

Tommy laughed.

'I didn't think you were that naive.'

'Naive?'

'You don't seriously think that if he comes home everything is going to be OK?'

'There'll be a period of readjustment, that's only natural.'

'Come on,' he said. 'He's not the same kid. He's him but he's not him,' he tried to explain. 'Don't you understand? Five years is a long time. Especially at his age. It doesn't matter how much you try, he's never going to be able to think of those people as his parents. They're strangers. It would be cruel.' He'd been working up to a rant but he'd overreached and now his voice started to thicken. 'We're the ones he loves now. Me, Keith and Jenny. We raised him. We're his family.'

'Jenny,' I said. The face from the photofit. 'Keith's sister?'

Tommy nodded.

I was right. I'd always been right. The one thing I'd been wrong about was Tommy. What was his involvement?

I looked at Barney, a new and horrible thought beginning to form in my head. I had assumed the child's presence guaranteed my safety. But what if I'd got it wrong? What if Tommy had blackmailed me into coming because he intended to hurt both of us? To solve both problems at once. Was that what the two holdalls I'd seen in the wardrobe were for? Were they to transport my and Barney's bodies out of here?

I assessed the layout of the hotel room. I was probably no more than six paces from the door. Tommy was strong, but if I was quick, I could probably make a run for it. The only thing was, I didn't want to risk leaving him alone with Barney.

I gave him a minute or so to calm down, and when I next spoke, I made sure to do it in a low, soothing register.

'Tell me what happened. Tell me why. Why did she take him?' I said, trying to buy myself some time. I got up from the bed and moved close to where he stood. I needed to figure out a way to get myself and Barney out of there unhurt. 'Please.'

After turning on a lamp, he poured himself a generous measure from an already half-empty bottle of Bell's whisky. Then he grabbed a curtain in each hand and pulled them together with a swoosh, casting the room into darkness.

53

He sat next to me on the sofa and before he relaxed against the cushions, he reached across to tuck a stray hair behind my ear. As he withdrew his hand, his finger brushed against the delicate skin there and I shivered. I pushed the corners of my mouth into an encouraging smile. I wasn't sure of his plan, but I needed to make him trust me and if that involved him believing his feelings were reciprocated, then so be it. I figured that if I could get him to drop his guard even a little, I might be able to take my chance and steal the boy away.

'Jenny kept him hidden for a good few weeks before Keith found out.' He gulped at his whisky and rested his glass on his thigh. 'He hadn't seen or heard from her in a while and she wasn't returning his calls, so he went to the house. There was no answer at the front door, so he went round the back. There they were, her and the kid, painting collages at the kitchen table. There'd been so much news coverage. Keith recognised him immediately.' He shifted on his haunches, trying to get comfortable. 'Keith's first instinct was to give him back, no matter what the consequences for Jenny. It was the right thing to do. Jenny agreed but begged for a last night alone with the kid, so she could say goodbye. Keith went home. But then something happened.'

He traced his finger around the rim of his glass and I sensed we were coming to a part of the story he would rather forget.

'The next day Jenny's social worker called. Her case had been reviewed and, after years in foster care, Kimberley and Jake were going to be returned.'

He waved his glass in my face and nodded at the bottle of whisky on the cabinet. I did as he asked, making sure to pour him an extra-large measure. I had no idea how well he could or couldn't hold his booze but, at the very least, I hoped it would compromise his reaction times.

I was about to return to the sofa when I noticed my handbag on the floor. I must have dropped it when he dragged me into the room. Most of the contents, including my mobile, had spilled out onto the carpet, not far from where I stood. I looked at my phone. It was inches away from my left foot. Jason was the last person I'd called. All I needed to do was reach down, press a button and it would start ringing. Once the line was open Jason would be able to listen in on everything Tommy said. If I could find a way to mention our location and make him realise what was going on, he could raise the alarm.

It was a bit of a hit-and-miss plan but, right now, it was all I had. The only problem was how to get near the phone without Tommy realising what I was up to.

On the wall in front of me was a framed watercolour. In its glass I could see Tommy's outline on the sofa. I looked to my far right, to where Barney was sitting on the other side of the room. If Tommy caught me in the act, who knew what he might do to me or the child? But then, what was the alternative? Do nothing and wait for him to hurt us anyway? I had no choice. I had to try.

My heart thudding, I moved forward, as though I was about to lift his glass off the cabinet. At the same time, I used the back of my hand to flick the top of the whisky bottle onto the floor. Tutting at my own clumsiness, I got down on my knees. While I retrieved the bottle top, I used my other hand to reach for my phone.

Tommy was on his feet in an instant.

'What are you doing?'

My phone was underneath me. As long as I stayed like this it would be shielded from his view. I had to find a way to hide it, but where? I had no long sleeves to slip it into and its rectangular shape was too large to hide in my fist. My only option was to secrete it under the cabinet to my right. But there was only a thin gap between it and the carpet. Would it fit in such a small space? Inching my knee forward, I gave it a sharp shove towards the gap and, to disguise the movement, simultaneously lifted my hand in the air.

'I dropped the bottle top.' I trembled as I gave Tommy the metal lid. 'I was just bending down to get it.'

He checked the carpet, suspicious. I tensed, not sure how far under the cabinet I'd managed to get the phone. Closing my eyes, I braced myself. If Tommy saw even so much as a corner of it peeking out, I was done for. But I must have wedged the phone further in than I'd thought, because the next thing I knew he was guiding me back to the sofa.

This time, as he retook his seat I noticed he made sure not to slouch.

Curious as to the source of all the commotion, the boy turned away from the TV and looked in our direction. I tried to give him a reassuring smile but as I widened my lips I realised my teeth were chattering. I didn't want him or Tommy to see my fear and so I squeezed my jaws together. My mobile phone lost somewhere underneath the cabinet, I decided to abandon any hope of outside help or rescue. The only person who was going to get the two of us out of here was me.

'Unsurprisingly,' he said, returning to his story, 'that call changed things. Keith didn't want to do anything that might put Jenny's reunion with Kim and Jake in jeopardy. They needed a plan that would allow them to give the child back without implicating Jenny.'

He sighed and I realised he was retreating into himself again. Not wanting to waste any more time, I tried releasing my jaw a little and was relieved to find that the chattering had subsided.

'What did he decide?' I coaxed, getting him to focus.

He lit a cigarette and took a drag.

'He had some notion of leaving him in the street with a name tag or outside a police station, somewhere he'd be found safely and quickly.' He scratched at his beard. 'Meanwhile, Jenny was becoming more and more attached to the child.'

Tommy cleared his throat, readying himself for the next part of his story.

'Keith is all set to go through with it. It's getting harder and harder to keep the child a secret.' Tommy's voice had changed. It was becoming more confident. He seemed to be coming to the part of the story he was the most comfortable with. 'That morning he goes round to Jenny's house. She's watching something on TV, some drama, and one of the parents smacks the kid. Mikey turns to Jenny and says, "My Daddy does that to me. He makes me cry."'

'What?' I was incredulous.

Tommy shrugged, not caring to get into it.

'Mikey made it sound like a regular thing. After that Jenny was adamant. She would not give him back. She made all kinds of threats.'

'Threats?'

'She told Keith that if he tried to return the child anonymously she'd report him. She said that now he was involved and she'd make sure everyone knew it.'

'And he agreed?'

He nodded at Barney. 'What do you think?'

I thought of Kimberley, behind the counter in the caff.

'Jenny kept him even after she got her kids back?'

'She told Kimberley and Jake that while they were gone she'd had another baby. They still don't know any different.'

He smiled at the boy.

'I remember the first time I met him. He was such a funny little thing. He kept whistling the tune to this advert he liked, except he couldn't really whistle properly. It made me laugh.'

I followed his gaze. Wearing trainers with flashing red lights in the soles and totally absorbed in watching his cartoon, the child was oblivious to us and the things we talked about. Things that had decided the course of his life so far. In his features I could see the curve of Vicky's lips and the line of Jason's nose. I tried to imagine what it would be like to have him in front of the TV in our living room at home. His toys scattered all over the floor, a third place at the dinner table. Would Jason and Vicky share custody or would they have to see him together for a period of time, until he could readjust?

Tommy had emptied his glass and so he got up for another. While he helped himself to the last of the whisky, I took the opportunity to scan the length of the room from right to left. The boy was sitting watching TV by the window, the farthest spot from the exit door. Not only that, but I realised the whole time I'd been here

Tommy had made sure to keep himself positioned between me and the child. I took in his bull-like back, arms and shoulders. If I tried to get past him, he'd easily overpower me. I wouldn't stand a chance. No, I needed to find a way to get Barney nearer to the door, somewhere that Tommy could no longer act as a human barrier. That way, if and when the time came, I'd have half a chance of being able to grab Barney's hand and making a run for it.

'What about you?' I asked, struggling to understand his place in it all. 'How did you get involved?'

He laughed and returned to the sofa.

'Hard not to. You know what they say about family affairs.'

'Family?'

'Keith and Jenny are my brother and sister. Half-brother and sister if you want to get technical.'

I thought about the difference in accent between him and Keith.

'We grew up in different parts of the country,' he explained, acknowledging the puzzled look on my face. 'Every holiday Dad would bring me to stay with them.' He smiled. 'We've always been close.'

I thought of the bleached-out snap in its silver frame. Tommy had said it was of him and his brother and sister: Keith and Jenny.

'So you took care of Barney, the three of you?'

'I was in the Navy from the age of eighteen.' He rubbed the tattoo on his right forearm. 'By the time I came out, Keith and Jenny had been taking care of him for a couple of years. At first, they'd made sure to move around every few months or whenever people started asking questions. But then they started to relax.'

He was starting to slur. Good. The whisky was taking its toll.

'Mikey adores Jenny. As far as he's concerned, she's his mother. And he loves his brother and sister. He's happy.'

I wanted to scream at him. To rail and shout about how much unnecessary heartache they'd caused. To make him understand that their selfishness had ruined Jason's and Vicky's lives. It galled me, but I had to keep my mouth shut. I gave him the sweetest smile I could.

He reached out to stroke my cheek.

'We raised him and loved him like our own blood, Heidi, you have to know that.'

But, I thought, he wasn't your son to raise.

'So you haven't hurt him,' I asked, working hard to keep the bite out of my tone. 'Keith and Jenny haven't hurt him?'

He recoiled, shocked at the suggestion.

'We would never do that. We wanted to protect him.' His voice dipped an octave. 'We'd do anything to keep on protecting him.'

My veins felt like they were slowly being lined with concrete. Concrete that would harden and expand, busting me up from the inside out. I nodded and took his hand in mine. I'd worked it out. I'd realised the only way I might be able to get the boy closer to the door.

'Why come back to the North-East after all this time, to where he was first taken? Surely that was asking for trouble?'

'We had no choice. Keith and Jenny are from round here. Their mum was diagnosed last year. Liver cancer. Stage four. They were desperate to come and be with her for the final months. I knew it would be risky, but what can you do, it was their mum.'

'Was?'

'She died last week.'

'And Keith and Jenny?' I asked. If my plan was going to work then I needed to make sure they weren't due to turn up here at any moment or that they were waiting downstairs in the car park. 'Do they know you're here with me? Do they know that I know?'

'Jenny knows nothing about any of this and Keith never recognised you. He has no idea who you are. He doesn't read as many papers as I do.'

'But where are they now?' I asked, anxious for specifics.

'They're staying here tonight, in the hotel. Jenny's at work. Late shift. Keith's got some mates over to watch the football.'

'Look,' he said, misreading the expression on my face. 'You don't need to worry. I'm going to talk to Keith and Jenny, explain your connection, assure them you can be trusted. I know you've had the odd wobble. Totally understandable. But you've more than proved yourself.'

The reason I thought I was here kept shifting. Tommy wanted to introduce me to Keith and Jenny. That meant he thought I was still on side. He hadn't brought me here to hurt me. But what would happen if I did something to make him doubt that? What then?

'I know you find it hard to admit.' He took my hand and placed it on my sternum. Then, gently, his hand on top of mine, he began guiding it down, inside my blouse. 'How much you like me, how much you like what I do.' His hand still on top of mine, he pushed my fingers in underneath the edge of my bra. 'But that's all part of it, isn't it Heidi?'

I wanted to contradict him but I didn't, I couldn't. I needed him to keep believing everything he'd just said was true.

'You're obviously not getting what you need from your husband, otherwise why do you keep coming back for more?'

He nudged my fingers forward, onto my nipple, and withdrew his hand. Then he sat there for a few seconds, watching. When I held the pose he'd created, he smiled, vindicated.

'We're leaving in the morning. Come with us if you like.' He nodded at my hand, still inside my bra. 'We could have fun. Real fun. Where do you fancy? Spain? France?'

'You want me to run away? With *you*?'

I failed to hide my displeasure and he moved back, away from me.

'I mean, it's just – leaving the country,' I said, trying to backtrack. I adjusted my bra and withdrew my hand. 'Seems a bit extreme.' But it was too late. I'd messed up. His lips were puckered, his eyes narrowed. I was losing him.

'What?' His voice was thick with contempt. 'You want to stay here with your husband? With those stories he peddles to the police and the press. You want to stay with a liar?'

Liar? I thought about the argument I'd had with Jason this morning.

'He never told you?' He shook his head. 'You really don't know?'

I didn't rise to the bait.

'Everything he and his missus said happened that day is a fairy tale. I don't know why they lied, but they did.'

There was no way he could know the secrets Jason had shared with me. It wasn't possible.

'Jenny thought it was because she felt guilty, the wife. If she hadn't left him alone like she did, then it would never have happened.'

'What are you talking about?'

'The kid didn't just randomly go wandering out of that flat. He left the flat because he went looking for his mother.'

'That's not possible.' This must be some kind of cruel prank or trick.

'Jenny saw it all. She was there that day because she'd heard a place might be coming up for rent. She'd gone to have a scout around, but she approached the building the wrong way, through the back entrance. She's on her way in and she passes a woman, arguing with some bloke. It was a hot day and he didn't have his shirt on. She said he had a tattoo. A tree. Covered his whole back.'

Danny. Jason said Vicky had broken things off with him that morning. That afterwards he'd kept calling her all day, that he wouldn't take no for an answer.

'Jenny carries on into the building. She climbs the stairs for a bit of a look around and then this little boy appears. He's crying. He wants his mummy.'

The room seemed to reel and turn. No wonder Vicky wanted to come clean, no wonder she was so racked with guilt.

Why would Jason know any of this? He wasn't there. What's to say Vicky didn't lie to him, what's to say he doesn't know any better? But even as I defended him, a part of me knew this wasn't true. I thought of Jason's earlier hesitancy, the way he seemed to weigh up what he was or wasn't willing to share. The things he'd finally agreed to relinquish didn't marry up with Vicky's level of distress, with her desire to confess.

Somehow forcing all of this down, I turned to Tommy with a smile. Whatever Jason did or didn't know about what actually happened that day, his son was alive and well and sitting here, only a few feet away. He was my priority now, this child. I had to get him away to safety.

Leaning forward, I kissed Tommy, pressing my face so hard against his that his beard chafed and scraped against my chin and cheeks. He'd invited me here because he believed his feelings for me were reciprocated. For this to work I had to maintain that illusion. His lips were dry, his tongue furred with alcohol. Still I opened my mouth wide, bringing him into me. Then, breaking away briefly to check the boy was still glued to the television, I reached for his crotch. He was hard. I began stroking him through his jeans. He moaned and so I kept going, bringing him on, judging his breathing, and as soon as I could tell he was close, I withdrew.

His eyes snapped open.

'Don't tease,' he said, this voice thick with drink and desire.

'What about Mikey?' I said nodding at the boy.

Tommy's eyes roamed and blinked as he struggled to locate him in the room.

'I want you,' I whispered, massaging his thigh, 'but not with him here.' I moved away, back against the cushions. 'We'll wait till later, when he's gone to sleep.'

My trap set, I studied my nails, praying for him take the bait. He said nothing and as the seconds ticked, I started to panic. If this didn't work then I was out of ideas. But then, just when I'd given up all hope, he cleared his throat and looked towards the TV.

'Mikey!' he shouted.

Reluctantly, the boy turned away from the cartoon.

'I need to have a private conversation with Heidi. Can you do what you did before and wait in the bathroom? You were so good last time, so quiet,' said Tommy. 'Like a little mouse.'

Mikey smiled, unable to resist the praise, but then his gaze was drawn back to the screen.

'But I'm watching *Power Rangers*.'

'You can take your iPod Touch with you.'

'Okaaayyy,' he relented.

As soon as I heard the bathroom door click shut, I went over to the bed and lay down. I'd managed to get the boy as close to the exit as possible and now it was time for the next part of my plan: making Tommy drop his guard. I beckoned him towards me and he did as I asked, a little unsteady on his feet.

I tried not to think about the line I was about to cross. To go through with this I had to remain numb. If I were to let myself consider the consequences of what I was about to do for even one second, I would falter and to falter would be to fail.

He was too drunk to unbutton my blouse and so, after groping at my breasts, he turned me onto my front. I got up on all fours and, before long, I heard my tights rip and felt him pushing my skirt up around my waist.

There was the jangle of his belt buckle as he undid his jeans and then a slight dip in the mattress as he knelt behind me. Leaving my knickers in place, he placed a single finger against my gusset. Applying the tiniest pressure, he waited until he felt the cotton blot and then, very slowly, he inched it to the right. Finding the gap between the fabric and my skin he slipped his finger inside and held it there. Testing, teasing. Making me ask for it.

I held out for as long as I could and then, closing my eyes, I stretched my arms out towards the headboard and pushed back towards him, like a drowning woman reaching for shore.

54

Once he was done, he collapsed and we both lay there, panting. Unable to move from underneath the weight of his body, my face stayed pressed into the duvet, my ribcage crushed into the mattress. He took a few seconds to recover himself and then, after kissing the back of my neck, he rolled off onto the bed next to me.

I turned my head towards the exit, trying to plan an escape. If I could move to the edge of the bed, I might be able to get up under the pretence of wanting to put my clothes straight. Then, if that worked, I could run the three steps to the bathroom, open the door, grab the boy's hand and pull him out to the hotel corridor.

I flattened my palms onto the quilt and tensed my shoulders. I'd yet to hear his belt buckle clink, which meant his boxer shorts and jeans were still tangled somewhere round his ankles. Hopefully, when he tried to make chase, this would slow him down considerably.

I was about to push myself upright when I felt Tommy's arm snaking across my back. Hooking his hand around my hip, he spooned me towards him and nuzzled his face into my shoulder. I froze. But then he began making a peculiar, high-pitched whistling noise. I turned to look at him. He was snoring, his face slack with sleep. This was my chance. I waited for a few minutes and then, desperate not to wake him, I slid out from under his arm and eased myself off the bed. Pulling up my tights and pushing down my skirt, I was about to go to the bathroom when I remembered my phone. It would be useful.

Stretching my hand underneath the cabinet, I patted the carpet until my fingers brushed up against its smooth, rounded corners. Sliding it and the rest of my things into my handbag, after one last look at Tommy I crept over to the bathroom and opened the door.

Barney was sitting on the floor. I put my finger to my lips and came inside.

'Tommy is tired and so he's decided to have a nap,' I whispered, bolting the lock behind me. 'He said that while he's asleep he wants me to take you to the shops and get you a toy. He said you deserve a special treat.'

Barney's face lit up.

'He did?'

'Yep.' I beckoned him forward. 'Come on, let's go.'

He got to his feet and was about to come towards me when he seemed to think better of it.

'I don't know. Tommy said it was important we stay in the hotel room until Mum gets here. He said I wasn't even allowed to play in the corridor.'

'He must have changed his mind,' I said, lunging for his arm. I had no time for this. Tommy could wake at any moment. But I wasn't quick enough for him. Ducking his shoulder down and away from my grasping hands, he jumped backwards, towards the loo, and crossed his arms.

'No, thank you very much,' he said, lowering his eyes. 'I'm going to stay put.'

I lunged again and again he dodged away, my fingertips skimming the edge of his sleeve. Frustrated, I raised my palm to my forehead and, thinking I was going for him, he recoiled into the farthest corner of the bathroom.

Trying to signal that I'd meant him no harm, I held up my hands in surrender. But it was too late. He appraised me warily.

I thought of Tommy, asleep on the bed. How much longer before he rattled the handle on the bathroom door and shouted curses through the wood? I knew I had to make a run for it, and soon, but there was no way I was leaving without Barney.

Cutting through the panic clogging my brain, I assessed my options. Dragging him out against his will was going to be physically impossible. That meant I needed to get him to come of his own volition. I was trying to figure out how I might go about achieving this when I felt some of Tommy's wetness seep out of me and onto my knickers.

The morning's bran flakes rose in my throat, the milk rancid on my tongue. Trying not to vomit, I took some short shallow breaths and reached in my bag for Lauren's compass. The second my fingers made contact with the solid metal disc my nausea began to subside. Rubbing my thumb over its thistle engraving, I popped the catch and, after opening the lid a fraction, I clicked it back shut. And then I did it again and again, the action helping to calm my jumbled thoughts. Feeling better, I was about to return it to my bag when I realised Barney was looking at me curiously. Moving slowly, so as not to startle him, I re-popped the pull-fit catch and this time I tilted the dial towards him. He watched the needle pivot on its axis, his eyes wide.

'Ever seen one of these before?'

Nothing.

'Would you like to hold it?' I offered it out to him.

Twitchy with indecision, he looked from me to the compass, torn between fascination and instinct: to keep safe in the corner or to come forward for a better look?

'It's very old,' I said, clicking the lid shut. 'A hundred years ago it belonged to a sea captain.' I twirled the small loop handle, demonstrating its ratchet-and-pawl burr. I used to tell this same story to Lauren. 'He used it to help escape from pirates who wanted to steal his gold and whenever he got lost it would help him to find his way home.'

Uncrossing his arms, he took a few, tentative steps over to where I stood. Again, I offered it out to him. Worried this was some kind of trick, he leant forward, taking care not to get too close, and snatched it from me. Weighing it in his hand, he ran his fingers over the smooth diameter, relishing the tiny components.

'You can have it, if you want,' I said as he waved it around, astonished at the needle's ability to keep pointing in the same direction.

The compass still held aloft, he stopped and looked at me, disbelieving.

'Do you want it?'

He tipped his head, his eyes greedy.

'OK then,' I said slowly. 'It's yours to keep.' He grasped the compass to his chest and gave his hips an excited, victory wiggle. 'There's just one condition. You have to come with me, now.'

'But Tommy –'

'Never mind that,' I said, trying to keep him focused on the prize in hand. 'Do you want it or not?'

He traced his finger around the edge of the glass dial. I held my breath. If this didn't work then I was out of ideas. Keeping his gaze fixed on the compass, he gave a single nod.

'Good,' I said, fighting the urge to snatch it back. The compass belonged to Lauren, not Barney. I told myself I'd get it from him later, once we were safe. Herding him over to the door, I dropped my voice to a murmur.

'We don't want to disturb Tommy, so we need to be quiet,' I said, bracing myself to go back into the bedroom.

Blood roaring in my ears, I curled my fingers around the handle, opened the door and peered round the corner. Tommy was still passed out on the bed where I'd left him, his penis flaccid against his thigh.

Guiding Barney out of the bathroom and over towards the main door, I pressed down on the handle and was about to usher him over the threshold when I saw him draw back his finger, ready to spin the handle on top of the compass. I tried to stop him, but I wasn't fast enough and soon the air was filled with its clicking, metallic whir. Immediately, Tommy's snore stuttered. I kept going, hoping we'd got away with it. But then he coughed. He was waking up. There was no time to waste.

Shoving Barney into the corridor, I grabbed his hand and ran.

'Help!' I shouted, hammering every hotel room door we passed. 'Please, somebody, help us!'

With an increasingly confused Barney at my side, we were halfway down the corridor when one of the first doors I'd banged on opened and a man squinted out.

'Thank God,' I said, dragging Barney back towards it.

I went to go inside, but the man put out his arm, blocking my way. I looked past him, into the hotel room. The air was hazy with cigarette smoke. I could make out a group of men sitting on chairs, a TV blaring in the corner. One of the men had his back to me. Wearing a striped black-and-white football shirt, he was leaning back against his chair, his hands interlaced behind his head. Gold sovereign rings covered his fingers. The action had made his football shirt rise up. I lowered my gaze to the flabby midriff, bulging out and over the back of the man's jeans. Keith.

Barney seemed to clock him at the same time. He smiled and went to take a step forward.

'Wrong room,' I said, grabbing Barney's arm and dragging him away before he could alert Keith to our presence.

'Wait,' he said trying to go back the way we came. 'I want to show Keith my new compass.'

I held his arm firm and continued on down the corridor, looking back to make sure we weren't being followed. The bloke who had answered the door was standing there watching us go, more bemused than concerned. Good. He hadn't recognised Barney. Still, as soon as he relayed the source of the disruption to the others in the room, Keith might smell a rat. If that happened, he might try and make pursuit.

Ahead, I saw a sign for the fire exit. Ignoring Barney's protestations, I kept guiding us forward. There was still no sign of Tommy, but as soon as he came round he'd come looking, and when that happened I didn't want us to be waiting for the lift.

The fire doors would take us down the stairs and, hopefully, out to someone I could ask for help.

We rounded the corner and were almost at the fire exit when I saw the chain. Illegally looped around the handles of the push-bar doors, it was held together with a small padlock.

I tried pushing on the doors anyway. If I could get them to open even a little then we might be able to squeeze through the gap. But it was no good. The chain held. We'd have to retrace our steps past Keith and Tommy's rooms.

Barney stood back, watching my progress with mild curiosity. He seemed to find me amusing, if not a little eccentric. But now, as I faltered, he seemed to tire of my bizarre attempts to leave the hotel. Slumping against the wall, he retrieved the compass from his pocket, opened it up and began to waggle it around in the air.

I decided to check the coast was clear and then make a run for it, but when I peered round the corner I instantly recoiled.

Tommy.

Buckling his belt, he was moving towards the lift at the opposite end of the corridor. He was alone. My lungs seemed to squeeze and twist against my ribs. I could not let him find us here. I'd tried to steal Barney back. Now he knew where my true loyalties lay, he'd need to be sure of my silence.

I put my head up close to the wall and inched forward as far as I dared. Tommy was now stood by the lift. He reached for the call button and kept his finger there, pressing it over and over while he muttered curses about my betrayal under his breath.

On the off-chance that we might find somewhere close to wait things out, I began pushing handles on the three rooms that populated this small area of the corridor. But they were all locked. I checked back on Tommy. He was still waiting for the lift and had started to scan the nearby area.

I reappraised our options. It was through this fire exit or nothing.

I looked around for something – a fire extinguisher, a removable light fitting – anything I could use to break the padlock. But the corridor was empty, the lights all grimy halogen bulbs fitted into the yellowing ceiling. There was an old metal NO SMOKING sign fixed on the wall. Flat and thin, there wasn't much to it, but right now I was willing to try anything. It was up high, just out of my reach; I jumped up and tried to dislodge it from the wall with my hand. My fingers brushed against its corner. I tried again, this time hooking my nails underneath its bottom edge, but it was stuck firm and, as I came back down to earth, I went over on my heels and fell onto my side.

Barney took a step back, uncertain but also intrigued as to what I might do next. I smiled and pulled a face, trying to make out that this was all a bizarre game. Picking myself up, I went to put my shoes back on and try again. But looking at my feet, I stopped. My stilettos. I'd worn the ones with the metal heels.

Kneeling in close to the door, I gripped the suede, upper lining part of the shoe, lifted it high in the air and bashed the heel hard onto the padlock. Moving in close to examine my handiwork, I saw I'd managed to chip some black paint away from the padlock's metal face but nothing more. Undeterred, I brought the heel down again and this time I tried to direct the spike into the keyhole. And then I hit it again and again, with as much force as I could. Stopping to check my progress, I saw that it was starting to weaken.

Emboldened, I gave it one last bash and the heel broke off the shoe, taking the lock with it. The chain slid to the floor with a clunk. Panting with the effort, I got to my feet and checked on Barney. Pressed flat against the wall, mouth agape, he couldn't decide whether to be scared or impressed. I pushed down on the door's metal bar. It opened to reveal a stairwell.

'Come on,' I said, not that much taller than him in my stockinged feet. My broken heels were now useless. 'First one to the bottom gets a Mars Bar.'

And then we were running, taking the steps two at a time, the lights in Barney's trainers flashing red the whole way.

55

The fire door at the bottom of the stairs opened onto a thin strip of grass. We seemed to have come out somewhere around the side of the hotel. My first instinct was to find my car and drive us both as far away from here as quickly as possible. But I'd parked directly in front of the hotel, in clear view of reception. That meant, in order to get anywhere near it, we'd have to go to the exact spot where Tommy was probably looking for us right now.

I considered going for it anyway. If he caught us before we could get inside and lock the doors, I could always scream to a passer-by for help. But no. There was too much at stake. Tommy wouldn't think twice about dragging Barney away from me in broad daylight, no matter who was around to see it. I needed to find us another escape route, another way to safety.

A low wall bordered the strip of grass we stood on. Next to it was a pavement and then a dual carriageway. In the distance, on the opposite side of the road, I could see the metal and glass peaks of Eldon Square, a list of the shops it contained emblazoned on the side in cursive script. A shopping mall. It would have crowds. We could lose ourselves there.

I looked at Barney. Lauren's compass in hand, he was waving it around in the air, watching the needle change direction. I realised he was shivering. Our coats were back in the hotel room.

I pointed to the dual carriageway.

'The toy shop is over the other side of that road,' I said, slipping my hand around his wrist. 'But there's a lot of traffic, so you need to be fast and you need to keep hold of me, OK?'

He screwed up his face, about to complain, but then he took in the speed of the cars zipping past and seemed to think better of it.

Checking left and right for any sign of Tommy, I tightened my grip and bolted for the pavement. The ground was rough beneath my feet, the grit shredding my tights and then my skin. As we cleared the low wall, my breathing quickened, the cold air searing my lungs.

We reached the dual carriageway and lurched to a halt. Cars, vans and trucks raced in opposite directions. We needed to wait for a break in the traffic, but standing here on the pavement would leave us too exposed. I looked back at the hotel. We had to get out of sight before Tommy thought to search the perimeter. There was no time. We had to make a run for it.

Pulling Barney close, I took a breath and launched us into the road. There was a screech of brakes. I heard Barney cry out, but still I kept running, my hand locked around his wrist.

Reaching the pavement on the other side, I continued to urge him forward, in the direction of the mall's metallic gleam. We needed to get to safety; we needed to get to where they couldn't find us. Weaving our way through the low shrubs that divided the pavement from the narrow feeder lane that guided cars into the multi-storey, before long we hit the pathway that led into the shopping centre. It was sheltered on both sides by steep grass verges. I slowed our pace to a walk.

'Let go,' said Barney, shaking me off. Nursing his wrist, he stopped and turned around, intending to go back the way we'd just come. 'I want to see Tommy and Keith. I want my mum.'

'We'll go back in a bit,' I said, blocking his progress. 'We have to get you that toy first, remember?'

'I don't care about the toy.' He looked at the dual carriageway. He seemed to be working out whether he could make it back across without me.

'You haven't even seen what they've got in the shop,' I said. 'There might be something you want.'

'Please, take me back.'

'Come on, let's go inside, out of the cold.'

'Take me back. Now.' He held Lauren's compass in the air and clicked the pull-fit catch. Its bevelled glass glinted in the sun.

'Put the compass down,' I said, slowly. 'I'll take you back later, I promise.'

'I don't believe you.' Tipping his palm, he let the disc slip forward, out of his hand. I dived towards it, my hands cupped. But I wasn't quick enough and, after landing on its clam edge, it bounced twice across the concrete before coming to a halt with a single, glass-shattering smash.

Looking at the mess of tiny screws and bolts on the floor, I crawled over to the two circles of silver and picked them up. Cradling them in my hands, I let out a sound that was part howl part scream. I clutched the broken bits of compass to my chest. Barney came closer, trying to peer at the mangled mess. I caught his eye, and, thinking I was going to admonish him, he went to retreat. Not before I could reach out and squash him to me. Letting the scraps of compass fall away, I held him tight, so very, very tight, the miniature springs and coils scattered at our feet. This boy, this beautiful, precious lost boy, found at last. After a little while he took my hand and, helping me up to standing, he guided me forward, towards the mall's sliding glass doors and the warmth within.

Inside, Christmas lights blared overhead and tinny carols blurted from the mall's sound system. We drifted with the crowds, forward, to Santa's Grotto in the central atrium. Made out of glittering white and blue fibreglass, it was designed to look like a giant sleigh chock-full of presents, and had a battalion of huge, silver reindeer out front. Taking a seat on one of the benches that lined the surrounding walls, I looked through my bag until I found my mobile and called Jason.

As his phone began to ring I looked at the queue for Santa's Grotto. It stretched almost all the way back to the other end of the shopping centre. Balloon blowers and magicians were working their way up and down the crowd, trying to pacify the waiting kids.

I watched as a clown approached a small boy in the queue. Sitting on his father's shoulders, he stared agog as the clown turned, twisted and tied a limp red balloon into a fantastic reindeer, complete with antlers. The clown presented the reindeer to the boy and he squealed with delight.

On the other end of the line I heard Jason's phone click through to voicemail. Still focused on the kid with the balloon, I wondered if I should try calling Vicky instead. It meant she would get here first, but that was OK. Jason would soon follow.

The kid gave his reindeer balloon a kiss and then reached down to touch the reindeer to his dad's cheek, miming another peck. The dad smiled and then, as though in some kind of a chain reaction, he turned round and gave his wife standing next to him a kiss on the mouth.

I looked at Barney, sitting by me on the bench, and imagined him sandwiched between Vicky and Jason. A complete family unit. I turned back to the family with the reindeer balloon. They were just strangers in the queue and there was no reason for them to acknowledge or include me in any way, but suddenly I felt left out, invisible. Absolutely, totally invisible.

56

The taxi pulled up outside Carla's flat just before six. She'd said she would be away at the conference until tomorrow night and, as Tommy knew where I lived, I'd decided this was the next best place to keep Barney safe until I could get hold of Jason.

I'd spent all afternoon trying to get in touch. While we'd wandered around the shopping centre I'd dialled his number again and again. Jason had always said that, come the day his son was found, he hoped to be able to go to him straightaway. That he didn't want their reunion to be mediated by the police or psychologists, authorities who would only give him access once they'd finished with all their tests and checks. And so it was for that reason – because I wanted him to have this time alone with Barney before everyone else got involved – that I continued to call him and not the police. But each time it kept ringing through to voicemail. I was sure he was ignoring me. That I was being punished for what I'd said, or what I'd almost said, this morning. Still, unwilling and unable to leave a message about something of such import, I kept trying. He couldn't stay angry with me for ever.

Inside, Carla's flat was cold and dark. I went through each room, turning on the lights and closing the curtains. Before long, Jasper, excited by the prospect of company, slinked his way around my legs, wanting to be fed.

Despite my best efforts to keep him distracted, Barney had

become more and more nervy and withdrawn during the journey here. Now, as Jasper brushed past him, he cried out in fear.

I picked Jasper up and showed him to Barney.

'Don't be scared. Look. It was just the cat. He's called Jasper. Say hello to Barney, Jasper,' I said, nuzzling the cat's neck.

He reached his hand forward, about to give him a stroke, but then he hesitated.

'Who's Barney? I'm called Mikey. My name is Mikey.'

'I know another little boy called Barney. I must have got confused.' I put the cat down and went over to the boiler to turn on the heating. As soon as I heard the pilot light flare, I turned back to him. 'Hungry? Shall I make you a sandwich?'

But his cheeks were flushed and his bottom lip had started to quiver. He'd finally reached the end of his tether.

'I want to go home, I want Jake and Kimberley,' he said, looking at the floor. 'I want my mum.'

'And you will go home,' I said, stroking his hair and tucking it behind his ear. 'But first, I think you'd better eat something. Tommy won't be happy if he discovers I haven't looked after you properly.'

He didn't say anything.

'Will he?'

Reluctantly, he nodded.

'Why don't you go in the living room and I'll bring you a sandwich. Do you like peanut butter and jam?'

'Yes.' He was about to go on his way but then he stopped. 'I don't like the crunchy type in my sandwich.'

'Got it.'

I put the sandwich and a glass of orange juice on a tray, walked through to the living room and set them on the coffee-table. He looked at the sandwich and then me, as though he was trying to work out whether or not it was safe to eat, and then picked it up and finished it off in four large bites. He must have been starving. Had he asked for food and I just hadn't heard? I berated myself for not thinking to get him something earlier.

He took a gulp of juice and wiped his mouth with his sleeve.

'I want to go now,' he said. 'Please can you call Tommy?'

'Not just yet.'

As I went to clear his tray he started to cry.

'Please ask him to come and get me,' he sniffed, 'please.'

Putting down the tray, I tried to give him a cuddle, but he was too upset and he struggled in my arms. I didn't give in and held him tight. After a while, I felt him go limp. I stroked his hair and face.

'Where did you get that scar?' I asked, tracing my finger over the white semicircle of raised skin on his cheek.

'I fell off a wall,' he said, his words juddery from the crying. 'Mum said it was just a scratch.' He stopped, proud. 'She said I was brave.'

I continued to smooth back his hair, giving him time to calm down.

'Have you always been called Mikey?' I asked, curious to see if he remembered anything from his life before.

'Please call Tommy,' he said. 'Sorry I broke your compass.' He started to cry again. 'Where are they? I want to see them.'

'What about your first mummy and daddy, can you remember them?' I persevered.

'I don't have a daddy. Please,' he begged, 'please call Tommy.'

I didn't respond and, eventually, his heaving sobs fizzled out to a whimper. When I looked down I saw that he'd fallen asleep, his face smeared with snot and tears. It was past midnight. Taking care not to wake him, I arranged him on the sofa and covered him with one of the patchwork ethnic blankets from Carla's bed. As soon as I'd tucked him in, Jasper jumped up and curled himself into a ball by his feet.

I looked at his sleeping face. He was peaceful for now, ignorant of the fact that the world he'd known and felt secure in for the last five years was about to be pulled from under him. What would that do to the child? How would he deal with being wrenched away from the woman he now knew and loved as his mother? It would be hard, but no doubt there would be therapists and psychologists Jason and Vicky could call on to help make Barney part of their family again. And anyway, if it meant him being back where he belonged, then all the distress and confusion would be worth it, wouldn't it?

His lashes fluttered. There was a pause and then his eyelids began to twitch. He was dreaming. I watched his forehead pucker and smooth, the soft skin rippling into a frown.

I smiled. At long, long last, after all the searching, the child in my lap was Barney. And yet.

Jason had not been able to recognise him as his son. I remembered the day I had brought Jason to the off-licence to show the boy to him. His certainty had been absolute. Unwavering.

Now I realised what it was about this that surprised me the most. Not Jason's mistake. His credulity had been stretched so often and for so long it had left him half blind. Very young children can change greatly in just a few years. Of course it was plausible for this boy to no longer resemble his three-year-old self.

No, what surprised me was Jason's inability to even consider this loss of connection between a father and son as a possibility. It seemed that, in his grief and fear he had needed a certain idea of parenthood to cling onto. An idea that, even in his darkest days, could serve to reassure him he was still a dad. This idea had been a necessary part of his survival these five years, and he had held onto it at all costs. To doubt his ability to recognise his own child was not an admission he was ever able to make. It would have undermined the one thing that was keeping him going, the thing that let him face every day.

I sat there for hours, watching the child sleep.

When I reached for my phone, the sun was coming up, the birds chirruping outside.

I dialled and, after ringing a few times, it went through to voicemail. Determined to talk to him in person, I kept trying. Redialling, over and over until, eventually, he answered.

'Please don't hang up,' I said as fast as I could.

'What's going on?' he said. 'Where are you?'

'I was out of order yesterday. I made a mistake. But I'm going to put it all right.' I paused. It felt like I was dangling from a precipice. 'What I'm about to say is going to come as a bit of a shock and so you need to listen to me very carefully. OK?'

There was a pause and, for a moment, I thought he'd gone but then I heard him cough.

'OK,' he said, 'but make it quick. I don't have time for any more of your bullshit.'

I cleared my throat and took a breath, trying to formulate a sentence from the words jumbling around my head.

When I was done, I gave him Carla's address.

'Get here soon,' I urged, 'we'll be waiting for you.'

Epilogue

I held my hands under the tap, cooling my skin for the pastry. The temperature outside was below freezing and soon the water ran so icy that my fingers burned with the cold. I forced myself to wait until they were numb and then I pulled away.

As soon as the blood began to return, hot and needling, to my fingertips, I set about flattening the shortcrust mixture with a rolling pin. Once it was the right thickness, I got a cutter and pressed it down into the soft, floured dough. I lifted the cutter back up and it brought the circle of dough with it. I let the shape fall into my hand and placed it in one of the dipped spaces in the baking tray, ready to be filled with mincemeat.

Baking mince pies from scratch hadn't been strictly necessary (I had two shop-bought boxes in the cupboard), but I'd wanted to give the boys some time alone together and this had seemed like the perfect excuse. He'd spent the morning at Vicky's house before coming over to see Jason and, although things between them were still difficult, they were definitely making progress.

I put the last of the lids on the mince pies and popped the tray in the oven. The small TV I kept on the side was showing *The Snowman* and so I settled on one of the breakfast-bar stools and sat back to watch the final ten minutes. It had just reached the point where the snowman and the boy were holding hands, flying across the fields together. As I hummed along to Aled Jones, the pies filling the house with their sweet spicy smell, I patted my stomach and smiled. I'd done a pregnancy test a few days ago and it had been positive. I'd decided to hold onto the news until tomorrow, Christmas Day.

Though I had yet to find a new job, the build up to Christmas had been busy. Jason had taken on a short welding contract and, as a consequence, he'd spent the past month trying to juggle Barney stuff with the rigour of twelve-hour shifts, six days a week. He hadn't been terribly keen on the prospect of dusting off his toe-capped boots, not least because it meant he'd had to miss his first-aid exam, but without my salary coming in, the money had been too good to turn down.

It soon came to the part in the film where the boy cries because the snowman has melted. This bit never failed to upset me and so I looked away from the screen. My eye caught on the Advent calendar pinned to the noticeboard. Like my diary before it, the neat line of numbered days seemed to mock me and the magic blue line that had appeared on the pregnancy-test stick. Jason and I had hardly been at it like rabbits and that time with Tommy aside, I'd struggled to marry up possible conception dates.

I turned off the TV and began attacking the washing up. I was halfway through when the timer on the cooker beeped. I grabbed my oven gloves, pulled out the tray and then, with the help of a palette knife, fished each of the steaming pies onto a cooling rack.

All done, I leant forward for the final touch – a sprinkle of icing sugar – and, as I pressed against the cupboard, my apron pocket rustled. This morning's post. Wanting to look over the letter one more time, I got it out as soon as I had finished with the pies. A brown envelope with a green double helix logo printed near the stamp, it was from the DNA test lab.

Since that day at the shopping centre, the two hair samples had stayed lodged in their padded envelope at the bottom of my bag. I knew the results were now nothing more than a formality. Still, I hadn't wanted to be left with any vestige of doubt and so last week I'd decided to send them off for testing. Here was the verdict.

I scanned the second page for the millionth time. It confirmed Jason as a paternal match. I rolled the letter into a tube. There was no reason to keep the thing lying around. Going over to the sink, I turned on the waste disposal and, in one simple motion, fed the letter into its roar.

I wanted the boys to be able to enjoy the mince pies while they were still warm and so I arranged a couple on a plate and took them through to the living room. The weak afternoon sun had already started to disappear and the fairy lights we'd hung on the tree gave the room a twinkly, comforting glow. *The Muppet Christmas Carol* was playing on the TV, but the volume was too low for them to be watching it properly.

'Heidi,' said Jason, not even trying to hide his relief at the fact he would no longer have to be alone in the same room as him. 'Come and put your feet up.' He patted a space on the sofa.

Once more I found myself thrown off-kilter by his new hairstyle. He'd had it shorn a few days after being back on the welding site and even now, weeks later, I found the effect surprisingly harsh. Cut so near the scalp you could see the curve of bone pressing up through the skin, it reminded me of those tiny bird skulls you see on display in natural history museum cabinets.

I placed the mince pies on the coffee-table and then did as Jason said, tucking my feet up under me so that I could snuggle all the way back into the cushions.

The three of us sat there for a few moments, watching Michael Caine and the Muppets on screen, before Jason broke the silence.

'These look amazing,' he said, reaching for the mince pie nearest to him.

'Thanks, Heidi. Very festive,' said Martin from his spot in the armchair.

I nodded vaguely in acknowledgement and then we were back to pretending to watch the movie.

It had just got to the bit where the Ghost of Christmas Future makes his entrance, when the detective cleared his throat and sat up straight. For the first time since I'd entered the room, I let myself look directly at him.

It had been a while and I saw that he'd gained some much-needed weight. It suited him. Anchored by the new girth of his waist and chest, his limbs seemed to have finally realised that they were all part of the same body. Gone was the marionette dangle of his arms and legs, and in its place was a slow, controlled, almost robotic way of moving that was calming to watch.

'I should be going soon but, before I do, I wanted to say thanks for letting me come round, especially on Christmas Eve.' He focused his gaze on Jason. 'I know that, after what happened, you're well within your rights to say you don't want anything more to do with me.'

Jason nodded, unable to make eye contact.

'I'm sorry about the way you found out,' he continued. 'I never meant for it to happen like that. I realise I should have told you as soon as I knew things between me and Vicky were getting serious.'

'Apology accepted,' said Jason, clearly wanting to bring the subject to a close.

We sat there in the silence, each of us nursing a different set of secrets. We were like safety deposit boxes, locked next to each other in the bank, oblivious to what our neighbours actually contained.

Martin shuffled himself to the edge of the armchair. It seemed he wasn't quite done.

'Also, I wanted to come by because I know that this is always a hard time of year for you both.'

At this I felt Jason tense and, as I didn't want there to be a scene, I decided to be the one to respond.

'It is,' I agreed. 'But we struggle with it together.' I took hold of Jason's hand and kissed it. 'That's what makes us strong.'

I thought back to the last image I had of Barney. Shivering in the early-morning sun, he'd pressed himself flat against the small brick wall that bordered Carla's front garden. As soon as he'd seen Tommy's jeep approach, he'd leapt forward, his face opening into a smile. Tommy had got out along with a woman. She'd changed her hair and had aged somewhat in the last five years, but it was definitely her: the woman from the photofit. Jenny.

Barney had run to her with blind abandon and Jenny had hugged him tight, her kisses lost in his hair. They'd stood like that for a while, eyes closed, taking in each other's smell. And in that moment I saw it. She loved him, truly, and he loved her. After helping him into the back seat, she gave me a quick nod of gratitude and then they were gone.

'I've obviously not been allowed any further access to the case,' said Martin, his cheeks pinking at the allusion to his ongoing suspension. 'You'll be assigned a new family liaison officer soon but, until then, I wanted to make sure you know that, despite the disappointments of this year, I've got it on good authority the team are still one hundred per cent committed to the investigation.'

I squeezed Jason's hand and kept my face fixed firm. The last three nights I'd woken at dawn to discover him on the old nursing chair next to our bedroom window, his face bathed in the blue glow from the laptop. He was scouring missing persons forums. Then, this morning, I'd found him sat cross-legged on the living room floor with Barney's fire engine. I'd watched as he repeatedly extended and retracted the ladder attached to the vehicle's roof. Each time he'd let the ladder collapse back into its metal casing, it had made a loud aluminium crash and each time I'd felt my heart catch in my throat.

But life is a series of trade-offs, of choices considered and choices made.

I have made my choice.

The detective fiddled with the cuff of his shirt, pushing his watch under and then over it.

'Actually, Jason,' he said, his voice now swollen with emotion. 'That was the main reason I wanted to come and talk to you. I wanted to promise in person that they won't stop looking.' His eyes were wide and unblinking. 'I swear to you, as long as I'm still living and breathing, Barney's case will be kept open.' He held his hand to his heart. 'I wanted to tell you, they won't ever give up searching for your boy. I wanted to promise you that.'

Acknowledgements

This book's journey to publication has been long and complicated and certain people along the way have helped and supported me immeasurably.

Nicola Barr. Finding the right agent is like finding the right husband. You need someone who gets you totally, who always tells you the truth, who is tough when they need to be and who believes in you no matter what the rest of the world may say. Nicola is in my corner. For that I am and always will be grateful.

Kate Rizzo and the team at Greene & Heaton.

Joel Richardson. I like clever people and Joel is really, really clever. He makes me a better writer. I'm lucky to have him as my editor.

Kate Parkin and the team at Twenty7.

Emily Burns and Carmen Jimenez. Publicists extraordinaire.

Detective Inspector Steve Roche. For lending me his expertise and for reality-checking my various early drafts.

Chris Sussman, who is as smart and brilliant as he is kind. Chris was one of the first people I told I wanted to be a writer. His friendship and critical feedback helped me become that writer.

Tom McDonald. I mentioned I like clever people. Tom is next-level clever. Not only does he continue to give me early gold-dust-like editorial feedback but he was also pivotal in helping me get this book out into the world. Thank you for stepping in at just the right moment and for telling me to give myself a fair fight.

Naomi Kelt and Sam Gardiner. For your first readings, friendship and unfailing support.

Team Twenty7. The most unexpected and wonderful part of being published by my imprint are the other debut writers. I now have this whole new set of friends. They make me laugh almost every day (reader, we have a secret twitter group) and whenever I have a question or a crisis they are the literary equivalent of calling 999. Team Twenty7 you are a sheer bloody delight.

Louise Doughty and The Faber Academy.

Kate Norbury, for her rigorous editorial eye and careful, intuitive notes.

CPL Productions. Barry, Charlie, Luke, Quincy, Amanda, Arabella, Danielle, Murray, Janet, Heather, Alex, Charles and Jess. Thank you for giving me such a wonderful home these last three years. I basically get to go to work every day and hang out with my friends.

Daisy Goodwin. For her generosity in everything.

My English teachers: David Litchfield, Les Robinson and Ray Honeybourne. My Director of Studies at Newnham, Jean Gooder. For fundamentally changing the course of my life.

Barbara Johnson, my mother. Who, against all odds, raised me so well. She's also a top-notch first reader and stepped in whenever I needed help brainstorming a tricky plot point or character.

Danny O'Connor, my brother. For being there with me every step of the way and for the best pep talk emails known to man.

But most of all thank you to my husband and best friend, Alan Wray. For the time, for the absolute belief.

Reading Group Questions

Heidi states that, 'What happened to my daughter now defines who I am.' Is this true? Does a single event have the power to shape and define a person?

Why is Heidi attracted to Tommy? What does he seem able to give her that Jason cannot?

When Heidi suggests that Jason may no longer be able to recognise his son, Jason tells her a story about when the midwife first handed him Barney. He describes a primal, unbreakable bond with his newborn son. What does this book have to say about the parent-child connection?

Heidi was overweight for most of her adult life, until Lauren went missing. She compares losing the weight to losing control – what do you think she means by this?

When Heidi and Jason first meet they discover they have lots in common, especially the fact that they now feel 'their dreams had the power to sustain and frighten them.' What do you think this means?

Does Heidi want Jason to be reunited with his son? How do her feelings change throughout the novel?

Heidi believes that the reason the media were so quick to blame Vicky for Barney's disappearance was because they (and the general public) can't cope with the idea that a child can be randomly stolen. How much do you think this is true of the world we live in today?

At the end of the novel, Heidi realises that Jason has survived the last five years by clinging onto an 'idea of parenthood' – which idea is she referring to?

Heidi does something extraordinary at the end of the book. Why do you think she does this? Is there ever an instance where it is right to do the 'wrong' thing?

Why do you think Heidi chooses to stay with Jason?

Join the conversation online
#MyHusbandsSon @BonnierZaffre @deboc77